Las Vegas Girl

LESLIE WOLFE

ITALICS PUBLISHING

Italics Publishing Inc.
Cover and interior design by Sam Roman
Editor: Joni Wilson
ISBN: 1-945302-16-X
ISBN-13: 978-1-945302-16-9

Acknowledgments

A special thank you to my New York legal eagle and friend, Mark Freyberg, who expertly guided this author through the intricacies of the judicial system.

A warm thank you to Jessica Berc, who brings color, style, and glamour to my characters with her unparalleled sense of fashion. None other can play dress-up with fictional characters like she does.

1

Elevator Ride

Her smile waned when the elevator doors slid open and her gaze met the scrutiny of the stranger. She hesitated before stepping in, looked left and right uneasily, hoping there'd be other hotel guests to ride in the elevator, so she wouldn't have to share it alone with that man. No one came.

Her step faltered, and her hand grabbed the doorframe, afraid to let go, still unsure of what to do. The hotel lobby sizzled with life and excitement and sparkled in a million colors, as can only be seen in Vegas. Nearby, clusters of gaming tables and slot machines were surrounded by tourists, and cheers erupted every now and then, almost covering the ringing of bells and the digital sound of tokens overflowing in silver trays, while the actual winnings printed silently on thermal paper in coupons redeemable at the cashier's desk. That was Las Vegas: alive, filled with adrenaline, forever young at heart. Her town.

The elevator had a glass wall, overlooking the sumptuous lobby. As the cage climbed higher and higher, riders could feel the whole world at their feet. She was at home here, amid scores of rowdy tourists and intoxicated hollers, among beautiful young women dressed provocatively, even if only for a weekend.

She loved riding in those elevators. Nothing bad was going to happen, not with so many people watching.

She forced some air into her lungs and stepped in, still hesitant. The doors whooshed to a close, and the elevator set in motion. She willed herself to look through the glass at the effervescent lobby, as the ruckus grew more distant with each floor. She didn't want to look at the man, but she felt his gaze burn into her flesh. She shot a brief glance in his direction, as she casually let her eyes wander toward the elevator's floor display.

The man was tall and well-built, strong, even if a bit hunchbacked. He wore a dark gray hoodie, all zipped up, and faded jeans. He'd pulled his hood up on top of a baseball cap bearing the colors of the New York Mets. A pair of reflective sunglasses completed his attire, and, despite the dim lights in the elevator cabin, he didn't remove them. The rest of his face was covered by the raised collar of his hoodie, leaving just an inch of his face visible, not more.

She registered all the details, and as she did, she desperately tried to ignore the alarm bells going off in her mind. Who was this man, and why was he staring at her? He was as anonymous as someone could be, and even if she'd studied him for a full minute instead of just shooting him a passing glance, she wouldn't be able to describe him to anyone. Just a ghost in a hoodie and a baseball cap.

Then she noticed the command panel near the doors. Only her floor number was lit, eighteen. She remembered pressing the button herself, as soon as she'd climbed inside the cabin. Where was *he* going? Maybe she should get off that elevator already. Maybe she should've listened to her gut and waited for the next ride up.

A familiar chime, and the elevator stopped on the fifth floor, and a young couple entered the cabin giggling and holding hands, oblivious to anyone else but each other. She breathed and noticed the stranger withdrew a little more toward the side wall. The young girl pressed the number eleven, and the elevator slowly set in motion.

That was fate giving her another chance, she thought, as she decided to get off the elevator with those two, on the eleventh floor. Then she'd go back downstairs, wait for the stranger to get lost somewhere, and not go back upstairs until she found Dan. She'd call him to apologize, invent something that would explain why she'd stood him up. Anything, only not to go back to her room alone, when the creepy stranger knew what floor she was on.

A chime and the elevator came to a gentle stop on the eleventh floor. The young couple, entangled in a breathless kiss, almost missed it but eventually proceeded out of the cabin, and she took one step toward the door.

"This isn't your stop, Miss," the stranger said, and the sound of his voice sent shivers down her spine.

Instead of bursting through that door, she froze in place, petrified as if she'd seen a snake, and then turned to look at him. "Do I know you?"

The stranger shook his head and pointed toward the command panel that showed the number eighteen lit up. Just then, before she could will herself to make it through those doors, they closed, and the cabin started climbing again.

Her breath caught, and she withdrew toward the side wall, putting as much distance between herself and the stranger as she possibly could. She risked throwing the man another glance and thought she saw a hint of a grin, a flicker of tension tugging at the corner of his mouth.

With an abrupt move, she reached out and pressed the lobby button, then resumed leaning against the wall, staring at the floor display.

"I forgot something," she said, trying to sound as casual as possible, "I need to go back down."

On the eighteenth floor, the doors opened with the same light chime and quiet whoosh. The stranger walked past her, then stopped in the doorway and checked the hallway with quick glances.

She was just about to breathe with ease when he turned around and grabbed her arm with a steeled grip, yanking her out of the cabin.

"No, you don't," he mumbled, "you're not going anywhere."

She screamed, a split second of a blood-curdling shrill that echoed in the vast open-ceiling lobby that extended all the way to the top floor. No one paid attention; lost in the general noise coming from downstairs, her scream didn't draw any concern. It didn't last long either. As soon as the man pulled her out of the elevator, he covered her mouth with his other hand, and her cry for help died, stifled.

He shoved her forcefully against the wall next to the elevator call buttons and let go of her arm, pinning her in place under the weight of his body. Then his hands found her throat and started squeezing. She stared at him with wide-open eyes, trying to see anything beyond the reflective lenses of his sunglasses, while her lungs screamed for another gasp of air. She kicked and writhed, desperately clawing at his hands to free herself from his deathly grip.

With each passing second, her strength faded, and her world turned darker, unable to move, to fight anymore. The man finally let go. Her lifeless body fell into a heap at his feet, and he stood there for a brief moment, panting, not taking his eyes off her.

Then he picked her up with ease and carried her to the edge of the corridor that opened to an eighteen-floor drop, all the way to the crowded lobby below. Effortlessly, he threw her body over the rail and watched it fall without a sound.

The noises downstairs continued unabated for a few seconds more, then they stopped for a split moment, when her lifeless body crashed against the luxurious, pearl marble floor. Then the crowd parted, forming a circle around her body, while screams erupted everywhere, filling the vast lobby with waves of horror.

His cue to disappear.

2

Partners

No wonder I felt like I didn't belong.

It wasn't that I'd just transferred from Henderson West, after serving a thirty-day suspension, and had no idea what to expect. It wasn't that I recognized only a few faces there, at Las Vegas Metro Police Department, because Henderson wasn't technically a part of LVMPD; most of them were still complete strangers to me. It wasn't the fact that the coffee was terrible, or that I was about to meet my new boss, and starting on the wrong foot no less, because all police chiefs are just itching to get some other precinct's disciplinary transferees, just to make things interesting in their lives.

No... it was the bloody weather.

It was cold. A bitter wind, biting to the bone, and a fine drizzle to make things worse, even slippery at times, since the temperature stubbornly hovered just a tad above freezing. It was awful for Las Vegas, and even more awful for me, because it reminded me of home.

London.

But London was ages ago, when I was a young police inspector in Sutton, barely starting to make a name for myself, only miles away from the borough I grew up in, a place called Kingston in southwest London. Yeah, ages ago. How I got from there to Las Vegas? Long story... maybe some other time.

For now, let's just say I was still amazed at myself, at how the tiniest drop of rain, rarely seen in the Nevada desert, or the short-lived winter cold could bring back memories so quickly. It wasn't something I welcomed, not really. Because if I thought of London, I thought of Andrew, and that was still unbearable.

I heard commotion near the entrance and sprung to my feet, curious and grateful to have some distraction while I waited for Deputy Chief Mark Wallace to roll in and decide my fate. Detective Jack Holt was hauling someone in, a vocal and unruly young thug, adorned in enough jewelry to start his own pawn shop.

Holt dragged him to booking, and I followed at a distance, listening in, amazed at the total lack of imagination Americans have when it comes to swearing. One word is all they know; one word is all they use. Okay, maybe two or three, but that's it.

The man kicked and struggled to free himself, but Holt handled him firmly, not impressed with his verbal and physical attack. Then he handed him over to two uniformed officers.

"This stinker's TwoCent; book him," he said, then pulled a handgun sealed in an evidence bag out of his coat pocket. "Have this tested for ballistics in the Park case."

"Cop killer, huh?" the officer growled in the thug's face. "Nice going, Detective."

"Thanks," Holt replied. "Schmuck was asleep in his car, top down, gun on the passenger seat, right there in plain view."

"You got lucky?" the other officer asked with a crooked smile that didn't reach his eyes.

"Yeah, you might say that," Holt replied, adjusting his tie. "Is the DC in yet?"

"Not yet, but he called in for you and Baxter."

"Who?"

I took a few steps forward and extended my hand, pasting a smile on my lips.

"Detective Laura Baxter, in from Henderson."

He checked me out, head to toe, letting his eyes linger over certain areas of my body. That happens a lot, and I never flinch, nor do I lower my eyes or feel embarrassed. If anything, it entertains me.

After a moment's hesitation, he shook my hand firmly.

"Welcome to Metro, Baxter. Know what this is about?"

"No idea," I replied, then turned and followed him to the two chairs in front of DC Wallace's office.

We were about to take our seats when DC Wallace stormed in, nodding quickly in response to everyone's greetings.

"You two, in my office," Wallace beckoned, then walked right in.

I'd seen him before on occasions, giving speeches at Metro PD events. A tough cop, not much older than me, with a tight-lipped grimace that never really went away and piercing eyes that read right through you. The dangerous kind, the kind most likely to catch you in a lie. The wrong kind of boss for me.

We waited for him to take his seat, but he remained standing.

"You two, I see you already met. Good."

I nodded, and so did Holt.

"I'm partnering you up for a new case, the Aquamarine murder."

I remained silent, hoping my ignorance would go unnoticed. Thankfully, Holt didn't.

"What Aquamarine murder? Is this new?"

"Yeah. Nieblas and Crocker are already on-site, but I'm pulling them out and sending you two in."

How interesting. I wondered why he was doing that, but before I could formulate a polite way to ask, Wallace clarified.

"Both of you are high up on my shit list, and this is a case where I want my detectives to impress me, to walk on eggshells, and play it by the book, as if their jobs depended on it. Because they do." He cleared his throat, then continued. "The thought that both of you are one mistake from being out gives me reassurance. You'll try harder."

He looked at me intently, and I held his gaze, even though it took some effort. By all appearances, Wallace was a much bigger arse than I remembered.

"Holt, Detective Baxter here is the last partner you're ever going to get. Make it work, or make for the door. And Baxter, you know what you've done. This is your Hail Mary pass, and you know it. One false step, one tiny blunder, and you're out. Is that clear?"

"Yes, sir," I replied, and heard Holt saying the same words.

"Nieblas and Croker are still wrapping up the Park murder, and—"

"I collared the perp today, sir," Holt said, letting a little pride show on his face in the form of a crooked grin.

Wallace froze and turned an icy glare toward Holt.

Holt's smile vanished. "Sorry for interrupting you, Deputy Chief."

Wallace pressed his thin lips together, probably in an effort to maintain his calm. After staring Holt down for a while, he checked his notes briefly, then spoke in a normal voice.

"Madeline Munroe, twenty-eight, took a fall from the eighteenth floor of the Aquamarine, in plain sight of hundreds of tourists, a little over an hour ago. No one saw anything. ME just texted me that it's a homicide."

"Munroe, how is this name familiar?" Holt interrupted again.

"That's the key point of this case. The vic's sister, Caroline, has recently announced her engagement to the governor. They're getting married at the end of the month, here in Vegas. The mayor is hosting the ceremony at the MGM. Need I say more?"

I refrained from groaning and just fidgeted a little in my seat. These days, whenever I feel like punching a hole in a wall, I do my Kegels. I can actually clench a muscle as hard as I want, and no one can tell.

What could a cop like me do for a living, other than being a cop? I might need to solve that mystery fairly soon, because I'm definitely not catching a break when it comes to my job. After a month's suspension, I'm nearly broke, and there's no way in hell I won't screw it up somehow on this case, no way. One look at Holt, and I can tell he must be doing Kegels too. Yet he managed to restrain himself and didn't say a word; he just allowed a few of lines to appear at the root of his nose.

"You're not to approach the victim's family or the governor," Wallace stated, speaking slowly and in a menacing tone. "You won't be handling next-of-kin notifications; I will, as soon as we're done here."

Well, that's better, I thought. *Let him walk on the damn eggshells.*

"Play this by the book," Wallace continued, "as if every move you make is to come under scrutiny, because it will. I'm confident, being how you both need to redeem yourselves, that you will do more than everything in your power to impress me. Am I wrong?"

Wallace propped his hands on his hips in an unspoken invitation for us to leave the room. I stood, and Holt followed, and I replied with a determined, "No, sir," managing to instill more confidence in my voice than I was actually feeling.

"No media, no leaks, no screwups. Dismissed," Wallace said, then buried himself in a case file.

I trotted out of there in a hurry to put some distance between me and my new boss. Well, technically Wallace was my new boss's boss, being that I now reported to the head of Homicide and Sex Crimes Bureau, the fierce Captain Morales, whom I haven't even met yet. Deputy Chief Wallace was Morales' boss.

Yeah, plenty of ways this could go terribly wrong, but I wear big girl pants. I'll figure it out somehow. I only have to investigate a murder without being able to talk to the victim's family. Piece of cake. I wonder what other surprises are lined up ahead.

Oh, bugger.

LESLIE WOLFE

3

Introductions

The fastest way to the Las Vegas Strip was via Interstate 15, and Holt didn't think twice. I didn't even have my car assigned yet, so I rode shotgun in his white, unmarked Ford Explorer and kept quiet, studying him discreetly. Definitely not hard on the eyes. A tall forehead under dark, almost black hair, with virtually no gray. I squinted, trying to figure out if he dyed his hair, but no, no hint of that, despite his mid-forties appearance, with tiny laugh lines at the corners of his eyes.

Unfortunately, the silence didn't last long.

"So, Baxter, 'you know what you did'?" Holt asked in an incredulous voice, quoting DC Wallace. "What *did* you do?"

"Seriously? You're going to ask me that?" I replied dryly and turned to my right, choosing to observe traffic instead of continuing to look at my new partner. "How about you? What did you do to get you so high up on his shite list?"

Holt let out a quick laugh. "It's shit, not shite. Are you British or something?"

I shook my head. I'm English, but, hey, whatever. "Or something," I replied, "and shite rolls off the tongue better."

The second I said that, we burst out laughing, both of us.

"You first, Baxter," he insisted. "I need to know if you're able to have my back."

Before saying anything, I let out a stifled sigh. Every time I talked about that day, I hoped it was going to be for the last time. It never was.

"I beat a suspect senseless. Didn't stop until I put him in the hospital. There, happy?"

Holt's lips twisted as if he tried to stifle a smile. "Did he deserve it?"

I rolled my eyes, then closed them for a moment. Not really. Not more than other scumbags like him. But that particular lowlife was to blame for everything wrong with my life.

"Um, yeah, I guess," I said, choosing to keep most of the truth to myself. "He's a street corner coke dealer whose reckless garage chemistry led to several people dying. He's not getting out any time soon."

12

He nodded, but didn't say anything else until he took the off-ramp at Flamingo.

"He probably had it coming. I'm glad to know I have a partner with street skills, Baxter, relax. How come they let you off the hook with just a transfer?"

"Plus a suspension," I clarified, "and a letter of reprimand in my file." I sighed again, almost unaware I was doing it, and tried to swallow the dry knot that nested in my throat. "There were, um, extenuating circumstances they were willing to consider. I'm on probation for the next twelve months. How about you? What did you do?"

He didn't reply immediately, apparently focused on the thick traffic around the entrance to the Aquamarine Hotel & Casino.

"I'm not seen as much of a team player," he said without any preamble. "I sometimes go off on my own, especially when things are moving too slow for my taste. Or at least that's what they say. My former partners hated that."

"Like, say, the fact that you collared some other detective's perp, all on your own? You... just happened to pass by when he was conveniently asleep with the murder weapon in plain sight?"

"Yeah, just like that."

"And that's it?" I asked, as he rolled us to the main entrance, already crammed with police cars flashing red and blue, the black-and-white coroner's van, and two Crime Scene units that drew cheers from the public.

"That's it, partner, take it or leave it."

A wry laugh came out of my constricted throat. A maverick, huh? I'd be curious to see how that was going to play out, especially since I figured I shouldn't mention right off the bat that I was one myself. I had different methods, though.

"Then I better keep up, right?" I asked, smiling widely.

"Exactly," he threw over his shoulder, as he made his way inside the hotel lobby.

I'd never been to the Aquamarine before, but I'd seen it in passing many times. Back when Andrew and I used to come to the Strip for a night out, we never caught a show there; that's just how it happened. I was accustomed to the over-the-top luxury in those high-end Vegas hotels, only I wasn't ready for the Aquamarine.

4

Crime Scene

The lobby itself covered most of the hotel's footprint, and vaulted all the way up to the top level. The floor was a masterpiece in blue marble, an intricate floral design that followed the walls and layouts effortlessly in a style that must have cost a fortune per square foot.

A large section of that breathtaking floor was cordoned off with yellow tape, keeping the gawkers at a safe distance, where most of their phone cameras failed to capture any relevant detail. Uniformed officers kept them at bay and stood in front of the yellow tape, making sure no one came too close. Packed clusters of people lined the lower level corridors above the lobby and camera flashes flickered constantly, like it was some rock concert or football game. By the time we arrived, they must've already filled the internet with countless images of "them," selfies against a real crime scene backdrop, and what had happened to "them" while vacationing in Vegas.

I caught up with Holt as we were approaching the body, which was surrounded by the coroner's team and several Crime Scene technicians. I circled around until I could see the victim's face, ghostly pale against the darkening crimson of blood pooling around her head. I crouched and looked at her eyes, still a pure, golden brown, untouched by death's cloud, and surrounded by the telltale signs of asphyxia, broken capillaries in the conjunctivae.

The coroner squatted next to me, and we acknowledged each other silently, with quick nods.

"Dr. Anne St. Clair, meet Detective Laura Baxter," Holt said, standing awkwardly behind us and shifting his weight from one leg to the other. "Dr. St. Clair is our county coroner."

Anne and I looked at each other and smiled discreetly.

"Yeah, we've met before," I replied. "Henderson is Clark County too, you know."

I could've sworn he swallowed a cussword, probably the same overused word everyone threw around all the time. I turned my attention back to the body.

"What do you see?" Anne asked.

"Petechiae," I replied. "Probably already dead when she hit the deck?"

"Probably," she acknowledged. "Her neck is broken, and her skull fractured, not unusual with a fall like this."

Anne St. Clair wasn't one for many words. Her entire demeanor spelled out efficiency. Her hair was buzz cut, a strange choice for a good-looking woman, but she'd shared at some point that hygiene was a challenging task for a coroner in a busy county like Clark, Nevada, and she'd rather have short, clean hair, than long, curly, shiny locks that reeked of cadaver and formaldehyde. Her clothes were just as simple and practical, and rarely a different color other than black.

"I'll know more once I open her up," she added, then took a gloved finger and removed a few strands of hair that covered the victim's throat. "See here? Fresh bruising. I might be able to find some trace elements we could use."

"Time of death?" Holt asked, still standing behind us with a notepad in his hand.

"Surveillance time stamp puts her fall at precisely 4:23 PM. My TOD determination concurs. She was strangled upstairs, then thrown over the railing right after that." She looked at me briefly, then redirected her attention to the victim. "The other detectives are over there, talking to hotel security. They'll probably know more about what was caught on video surveillance," she added, reading my mind as always.

"What else can you give me?" I asked, while I gloved my right hand and examined the fabric of the dead woman's clothes. High-end, expensive, designer labels. Alexander Wang loose leg pants and a tight-fitting Anne Klein top. Red Louboutin stiletto pumps, with the right heel broken.

"She definitely left a mark on her killer," Anne replied, holding the victim's hand up and showing me her broken fingernails with bloody trace underneath. "I'll get started on DNA as soon as we take her back."

She stood and beckoned her assistants, who pushed the stretcher over and unzipped a body bag on the floor, right next to Madeline. They picked her up gently and placed her inside the bag, then zipped it up and lifted it on the stretcher.

How little it took, I found myself reflecting, *for a life to be interrupted, for someone to cease existing and become a case number on the coroner's table.* I forced myself to snap out of my contemplative state; Madeline Munroe didn't need my philosophical dissertation on the ephemeral nature of life. I bet if she could still speak, she'd tell me to find her killer and make him pay.

"How well do you know the coroner?" Holt asked, looking at me intensely, keen on catching any sign of deception.

"Well enough," I replied, frowning a little and shooting him an inquisitive look. "Why do you care?"

"I like to know my assets and liabilities," he stated without blinking. "Let's go see Nieblas and Crocker," he added, then hurried toward them, not waiting for my reply.

Yeah, my partner was an arrogant arse, probably envisioning himself as the unofficial leader of our two-person team, but, other than that, I couldn't find much fault in his logic. Anne didn't seem too thrilled to see him, and the relationship between detectives and the coroner's office can be crucial to a case. It speeds up the process, and, on rare occasions, it entices the overly procedural coroner to formulate speculative theories, volunteering case scenarios that can help break a case early and catch killers before they get a chance to disappear. Nevertheless, Holt needed to work on some of his people skills, or so I thought at the time.

Speaking of people skills, Holt scored a decent point by introducing me to the other two detectives, Julio Nieblas and Josh Crocker. But that's where all pleasantries came to a stop.

Nieblas shook my hand, then turned to Holt. "Heard you collared TwoCent this morning."

"Yeah, I did. I just got lucky."

"And you couldn't call us?" There was bitterness in Detective Nieblas' voice, and Crocker nodded his support with a grim look on his face. "That's not okay, Holt. Better not happen again."

"I was at the right place, at the right time, nothing more," Holt said, with increasing irritation seeping through his words.

"And no cell phone coverage? No radios either, huh, brother?" Crocker pushed back.

"None," Holt snapped, taking a step forward and bringing his scrunched face inches away from Crocker's. "It's done. Live with it. If you got a problem with that, I'm right here."

I put a fresh glove on my hand and intervened before blood could be shed. "I heard you guys had the victim's wallet?"

The death-glare contest between the three continued for a few moments, then eventually Nieblas broke away and handed me an evidence bag with an open wallet inside, showing the victim's driver's license.

"We just got here, not even ten minutes ago. Madeline Munroe, twenty-eight, local," Nieblas recited.

"Yeah, we knew that," Holt blurted out. "The DC brought us up to speed."

"Then we're done here," Nieblas said, and turned on his heels, ready to leave, but stopped in midstep and turned to Holt. "I'm glad you're taking over this case, Holt. Maybe someone else collars your perp for you, to make you feel all warm and fuzzy inside."

Holt grinned sideways and didn't say a word.

"Anything else in here?" I asked, lifting the wallet in the air.

"Credit cards, thirty-four dollars in cash, a gas receipt," Crocker replied. "Good luck to you," he added, then scampered to catch up with Nieblas, who was halfway to the main entrance already.

"Bloody hell," I reacted, as soon as they were out of earshot. "Are you normally that popular, or is it just with these two?"

"It's nothing," Holt replied, but I wasn't going to let him get off that easily.

"I need to know if I should watch my back, and yours," I said, grabbing his sleeve with my ungloved hand. "Why the hell did you lift their collar and not call them?"

He stopped and turned to look at me, while the tongue-in-cheek grin vanished from his lips. I held his gaze steadily, honestly, waiting to hear what he had to say.

"That perp, TwoCent, is a cop killer," he eventually said, lowering his voice to a level I could barely distinguish against the background noise in the busy hotel lobby.

"I heard something about that," I replied calmly.

"I knew Detective Park, the cop who got shot. Park was a friend, a good cop and a good man." He paused for a moment, then rubbed his forehead with long, nervous fingers. "Let's just say I didn't have the patience to wait for Nieblas and Crocker to screw things up much longer."

I frowned. "Not sure I follow. Were they screwing up the investigation?"

"Maybe not," he admitted reluctantly, while his hand went briefly back to his forehead, then into his pocket. "They weren't moving fast enough for my taste, that's all. TwoCent could've vanished anytime."

"Ah, I see. You offered some help, and they couldn't stomach it?"

"No. Let's just say that the murder weapon wasn't really in plain sight, and let's leave it at that." His eyes met mine, looking for confirmation that I'd keep his secret safe.

Ah, so he must've stopped good ol' TwoCent without probable cause, based on his gut or some informant's fodder, and got lucky. Ballistics would confirm if the seized gun was indeed the murder weapon, and whose fingerprints were on it. I didn't see much of a problem with any of that. I smiled while I nodded almost imperceptibly. Sure, I would keep his secret. After all, a cop killer was in jail and that was the only thing that mattered.

5

Vantage Point

We crossed the lobby toward the reception desk, closely observed by a hotel security manager. He signaled a front desk clerk to take care of us immediately and remained at a polite distance, yet within earshot of our conversation.

I looked at the crowds for a moment. It was annoying to work under the public eye like this, as if caged inside a store window, at the focal point of countless camera lenses. As of that moment, only casual witnesses monitored us; the press had arrived but was kept at bay by the unis and thankfully hadn't learned the identity of the victim yet. When they did, that's when the real media feeding frenzy would start.

I placed Madeline's bagged wallet on the front desk counter.

"Was she a guest here?"

Professional beyond reproach, the clerk typed her name on the keyboard without showing any sign of that morbid excitement that we usually encounter at crimes scenes.

"Yes, she was," he confirmed. "Room 1819. Should I generate a key for you?"

"Yes, please," I replied, then frowned. Why was that girl staying here? She was local, and if she were on a hot date, I'd expect the room to be registered under her partner's name, not hers. Maybe I was being old-fashioned. Then an unwanted thought crossed my mind, and I reached up to Holt's ear to voice it without being heard.

"I hope she wasn't working."

"Uh-huh," he replied, not taking his eyes off the crowd gathering around the press near the entrance. People looking for seconds of fame, even if that was to come in the form of a short, televised appearance during a breaking news insert, had surrounded the TV crews already. That actually helped us some, because it delayed the media crews, kept them from reaching the front desk where the victim's identity would soon be leaked.

"Here you go, Detective," the clerk said, handing the room key in one of those colorful paper key holders with the room number written on it. "Will there be anything else?"

"Yes," Holt intervened. "Any incidentals on the room?"

"Um, just breakfast for two this morning."

"Anyone else registered?" I asked, although I already knew the answer.

"No, I'm sorry. Miss Munroe had the room until tomorrow, but we're not showing anyone else listed."

"Was she a regular?" I asked, looking at him closely, ready to catch the moment his pupils dilated. They didn't. His only reaction was a hint of a frown.

"I'm not sure what you mean," he replied calmly. "Would you like me to see if she's stayed with us before?"

I nodded, and he quickly typed something, then said, "She has, in fact, stayed with us a few times, two, maybe three times a year, for the past few years. I'm assuming that's what you mean by her being a regular?"

I almost laughed at his innocence; it had to be feigned. No one can work front desk in a Vegas hotel for more than five minutes and not be aware of what was going on right under their noses. One look at the scantily clad beauties strolling around in small groups or accompanying older men, and you get the picture. But prostitution is still illegal in Clark County, which makes any front desk clerk tight-lipped when it comes to talking to law enforcement. Maybe that's why the security manager wouldn't leave our side, or maybe he wanted to be helpful. Yeah, right.

One look at Holt, who continued to observe every detail of the lobby layout, then I thanked the clerk and said, "Shall we?"

The three of us took an elevator up to the eighteenth floor, and Mr. Avalos, per his name tag, made himself useful by utilizing a fire key and putting the elevator exclusively under his control. The elevator went all the way to the eighteenth floor without stopping, while I couldn't keep my eyes off the amazing view through the cabin's glass wall.

Once on the eighteenth, we walked past a cordoned area, toward the vic's room.

"This where it happened?" Holt asked, and Avalos nodded.

"We have the whole thing on video."

That was the first piece of good news I'd heard since that morning, well, maybe the second, if I counted the fact that DC Wallace had offered to do next-of-kin notification on his own.

I unlocked the door and stepped in, careful not to disturb anything. The bed was slept in, and there was a faint smell of heated bodies, of sex. I peeked inside the bathroom from the doorway, and saw two toothbrushes in a plastic cup and a pair of men's slippers.

"We'll need Crime Scene in here," I said, and Avalos nodded, unable to hide a beam in his eyes. All Las Vegans took personal pride in anything having to do with the Crime Scene Investigations Unit, ever since the TV show *CSI* made prime time for millions of viewers and put their city, once again, on the world's map. Cops everywhere cringed, and district attorneys downright hated the show that had built unreasonable expectations in the minds of jurors and the

LESLIE WOLFE

public. In law enforcement lingo, the phenomenon was called "the CSI effect."

Nevertheless, our own, real-life Crime Scene unit might find a few interesting things in that room. DNA for sure, based on the smells. Maybe some hair and fibers too.

Holt stepped out of the room and beckoned one of the Crime Scene techs, who was dusting the elevator call buttons for prints, and instructed him quietly. The technician nodded, then went back to work on the elevator command panel, while two unis took position next to the room.

"We're ready to look at surveillance video now," Holt said, sounding angry for some reason. I sent an inquisitive gaze his way, but he shrugged and turned his back to me.

We followed Mr. Avalos to the security office on the second floor and found the recording waiting on a laptop, reeled at the right time code, ready to be shown. Effective, that Mr. Avalos. Quiet too.

The full-color feed was from the eighteenth-floor camera installed across the hallway from the elevators and showed the perp getting out of the elevator first, checking out the area, then grabbing the victim and dragging her out of the cabin. There wasn't any sound on the recording, but I could see when she screamed, but was quickly silenced by the man's hand. Then Holt and I watched that man strangling her while she fought back, then throwing her over the railing. A few moments later, he'd vanished.

I never do well watching real crimes on video surveillance feeds. The fact that I can't intervene, that I can't do anything renders me a frustrated, irritated mess, but I watch those recordings carefully, looking for clues, trying to understand the killer's psychology, to learn who he is. That particular video was only frustrating, nothing more. During the seven minutes it took the perp to kill Madeline and throw her body over the railing, he didn't show his face. Not once.

We had nothing.

Just a man in a hoodie, baseball cap, and shades, medium height and weight, and Caucasian. His bare hands were visible for an instant as he strangled his victim. He hadn't worn gloves, and that was the only glimmer of hope I was left with after watching that video; maybe he'd deposited some trace evidence behind, in addition to the skin samples Anne was going to scrape for DNA from underneath Madeline's broken fingernails.

"What happened next?" Holt asked, and Avalos lowered his head.

"Nothing, I'm afraid. He vanished," Avalos replied. "We have him briefly on two other corridor cameras, then he disappears from view. He seems to know all the blind spots in our surveillance."

So, he was smart, and he'd done homework. He'd planned the kill.

"How about before the murder?" I asked. "Do you have Madeline boarding the elevator?"

"Here you go," Avalos replied, starting a new video recording for us to watch. This time, it came from a camera inside the elevator. "He was already in the elevator when the woman climbed in, at lobby level."

"Is there a lower level?" Holt asked. "Parking, right?"

"There's another dining and entertainment level, covering half the floor. We call that the lower main. Then we have the spa level, then two parking levels. Our structure goes four levels underground."

I turned toward Holt, letting my forehead scrunch. "This was random? Strangling is personal, passionate. It doesn't feel random."

"No, it doesn't," he replied. "We need to see when he boarded the elevator, on which floor."

One of Avalos' staff repositioned the recording to show the man in the hoodie board that elevator on the lower main level, just moments before Madeline took the same cabin up.

My frown deepened. There were four different elevators; there was no way he could be sure she'd get on that particular one. Unless...

"Mr. Avalos, is there a place on the lower main level where someone can watch the lobby elevators from a distance?"

"Um, yes, the downstairs café. The view of the elevators is an attraction for that particular café. I'm sure you've noticed; the cabins are completely exposed. Anyone can watch them operating, and people love looking at them."

"So, he could've sat there, in that café, waiting for Madeline to come to the elevators, then... what? How do these elevators work?"

"They're equipped with smart systems that optimize their usage. They will go all the way up, then back down again, and only change direction if beyond their current location there's no active call."

I thought I understood, but wanted to be sure.

"So, if the perp saw the victim press the call button, he could tell for sure which one she would take?"

"Precisely," Avalos replied. "The first elevator to respond to her 'going up' call would've been the closest one below her level on its way up, or, in the absence of that, the lowest elevator on its way down."

"We want to see that," Holt replied. "I'm sure you have video surveillance that covers that particular view of the elevators, what the perp would've seen."

Avalos turned to his technician. "Lower main cam six, please."

He displayed the video recording on the big screen mounted on the wall. The camera covered the bank of elevators, from a distance, and part of the lobby, as well as the lower main floor. From that vantage point, someone could potentially see Madeline, from a hefty distance, call an elevator. That someone could easily figure out which elevator she'd take, and, with a quick sprint and a bit of luck, could manage to press the 'going up' button just in time to board the same cabin before she did.

But it was far, across a vast expanse of crowded floor, and the angle was a little tricky too, being that the vantage point was lower, not higher. He'd need binoculars, or something.

"Same time code, café patio view, please," I asked, and the technician obliged immediately.

It didn't take me more than a split second to identify him. He was the only one holding a military grade monocular to his eye, barely visible under the brim of his baseball cap.

"There he is," I said, pointing him out. "That's a military grade, ten times magnification monocular."

"Perp's military then?" Holt asked.

"Not necessarily," I replied. "You can buy these online now. Where was he before the café?" I asked, turning to Avalos again.

This time, their search took a while and returned nothing. They couldn't find the man on any other feeds before appearing on that café patio.

My guess was he changed his clothes somewhere and looked entirely different crossing the immense lobby before taking his table at the café. I shared my conclusion with Holt, but his mind was elsewhere.

"How did you know what kind of equipment he was using? Are you ex-Army or something?"

I didn't want to go there.

In a split second, flashback images came rushing to my mind, each of them tearing at a wound that wouldn't heal. The dusty smell of Andrew's uniform when he came home on leave from deployment. His warm hand guiding mine as I adjusted his monocular to watch wild horses near Cold Creek, in the early spring snow, up on the mountain. His voice, telling me it was time to go home, because he had an early flight the next morning, a nonstop C-130 flight to Kandahar.

"Baxter?" Holt said impatiently, yanking me back to the present.

"No, I'm not ex-Army," I replied, putting a chill in my voice, and hoping he'd let it go.

"Then how?"

"Drop it, Holt."

6

Grunt Work

It was already dark when we left the Aquamarine, heading for the precinct, but I didn't even notice the bright lights of the Strip, nor the light drizzle that felt so unnervingly familiar. I pulled up my collar and shoved my frozen hands deep inside my pockets, wishing Holt would've parked closer to the main entrance.

Not a word was spoken on the way back, and an irritated, fidgety Holt barely looked at me after I'd refused to answer his question. Which brought another question to my mind, this time one to ask myself: Why in bloody hell can't I just lie in situations like that? What would've happened if I'd just said I'd seen those military grade monoculars in some Army magazine, or online somewhere? But no, I had to infuriate my new, already distrusting partner for no reason whatsoever, other than a misplaced sense of honesty.

Because, really, what honesty? Was I trying to atone for my sins or something? The subconscious mind is a powerful thing; sometimes it tricks people like me into doing completely senseless crap only to give itself the impression that it can still tell the truth for a change. Or maybe I yearned for the feeling of being honest for a minute, albeit on an irrelevant subject, because on any of the relevant ones I couldn't afford any candor. Not with Holt, not with anyone. Not ever.

Holt led the way and I followed, grateful he stopped for a minute in front of the coffee maker and poured us some. I thanked him with a nod and a tentative smile, but he didn't acknowledge in any way. Then he continued toward his computer, while I tasted the hot swill and wished it were green tea instead.

Holt powered up his computer and I pulled a chair, then decided to break the loaded silence.

"We need to find her cell phone," I said. "She didn't have one on her, but she was holding a pink phone in one of the surveillance videos."

"Saw that," Holt replied, waiting for the NCIC database screen to load. For some reason, Holt had decided to search for our victim's priors on the National Crime Information Center, going wide instead of local. He held the evidence bag with her driver's license with one hand and typed the number with the other, then waited for a quick moment.

Madeline Munroe was as clean as fresh fallen snow. No arrests, convictions, or outstanding warrants. Outside of an old, paid speeding ticket, her record was spotless.

I was itching to run a few searches of my own, but I hadn't even met my boss yet, and that would've been the first step in getting a desk and a computer assigned to me. Resigned to sit next to Holt and wait, I let my mind wander a bit.

Why was Madeline by herself, when she'd come to spend the weekend with a companion, perhaps a boyfriend? Where was that man, and why hadn't he come forward while we were at the scene? Was the boyfriend her killer? Anne would tell us soon enough, once she processed the DNA scraped from underneath Madeline's fingernails and compared it to the fluids found on the bedsheets. It was the age of low-copy DNA, and, no matter how tiny the sample, Anne St. Clair could extract a DNA profile from it.

"Okay, got it," Holt said, then shifted in his seat and ran the back of his hand against his nose in a quick, sudden move. Maybe he had allergies. "Single, no priors. Lived in an apartment in Spring Valley. Studied social sciences at UNLV. IRS records have her working for a small accounting firm, Denson Tax Services."

"Phone?" I asked, at the risk of pissing him off even worse.

He sighed and ran another search. Then he wrote a number on a yellow sticky note and scampered across the room, where a technician was typing on his keyboard faster than anyone I'd seen before.

"Hey, Fletch," Holt said, "run this for me, will you?" Then he turned and saw me standing behind him like the stalker I'd become. "This is Fletcher, our techie. He's incredible."

Fletch was barely twenty-four and didn't look like he worked for the police; more like he was running from them. A mane of unruly hair so curly it made me wonder if he'd ever been able to comb through it. A gray, stained T-shirt that was at least three sizes too large for him hung over his thin, bony frame and partly covered the lowered waistline of a pair of ripped jeans. In perfect harmony with his attire, a mischievous smirk popped briefly on his face, whenever he uncovered any bit of information.

I couldn't help but chuckle. "Glad to see there's no dress code at this precinct."

"For him, no," Holt replied, and for the first time since we'd left the Aquamarine, his voice had thawed a little. "But he's the only exception. You try this, and it's not going to fly."

"Got bad news for ya," Fletch said. "This phone's turned off. No way can we tell where it's at. It pinged the tower near Aquamarine last, before someone switched it off or it ran out of juice. Sorry, my man."

"What about call and text history?" I asked. "Can you pull?"

"That's on the carrier side, so, yes, I can dump this phone," he replied, typing some more and shifting through screens faster than I could keep track.

"There you go."

Holt and I looked at the list of recent calls, and I pointed at one number, while he pointed at another.

"This number, it's quite frequent. Let's find out who owns it, please," I asked.

"This one too," Holt added.

"Okay, the first number belongs to a Caroline Munroe, and—"

"That's the sister," I interrupted, then apologized quietly.

"The other is for Elizabeth Munroe," Fletcher continued, unfazed by my rudeness.

"Probably the mother," I ventured. "I was hoping for a boyfriend we could talk to. We need the guy she spent the night with."

"Yeah, yeah," Holt replied, irritated. "Stating the obvious won't make it appear out of the blue." He ran his hand over his face and I thought I saw his fingers trembling slightly. By the looks of it, I was making my partner angry with every word I said. "How about texts, Fletch? Anything interesting in there?"

"Nothing that I can see at first sight. Give me a few hours and I'll know more. So far, all I see is boring, irrelevant stuff. Shopping lists, lunch dates, hairdresser appointments, recipes. Based on this phone, your vic didn't have much of a life."

"I seriously doubt that," I said, thinking of her shoes for some reason. Maybe I had developed shoe envy and didn't even know it. I must confess I'm a closet fashionista and I love designer labels, just like the next girl, but I keep it private, reserved for after work. I have this annoying feeling that my law enforcement colleagues would respect me a lot less if they'd see me wearing the latest trends accessorized with the standard-issue Glock 17.

"Keep an eye on it and let me know the moment that phone is switched on," Holt said, then started toward his office, but I didn't follow.

"Let's go talk to the DC," I said. "We need to speak with the family. They must know who that boyfriend is."

Holt froze in place for a brief moment, then turned on his heels and followed me toward Wallace's office.

7

Direct Orders

Deputy Chief Wallace's door was closed, but I rapped gently on his window, and he beckoned us in.

"Deputy Chief," I offered, and Holt just nodded unceremoniously.

"One second" he replied, ignoring both our greetings and keeping his eyes riveted to the file in front of him, by the looks of it a medical examiner's report, but I couldn't tell whose, not from that distance.

He didn't invite us to take a seat, so we both remained standing, and I let my eyes wander to the family photo nested in the bookcase behind him. Enclosed in a simple, silver frame, the image showed DC Wallace together with a blonde, slightly overweight woman and a teenage girl against a background of snow-covered mountain peaks. It could've been taken right there, in our backyard, at Mount Charleston. They looked good together, happy, and DC Wallace's jaw was relaxed, making room for a candid smile, while his arm hung on the shoulders of his daughter. She must have been thirteen or fourteen years old in that image, pretty and innocent, a younger version of her still beautiful mother.

"What do you have for me?" Wallace asked, closing the file and resting his palm on top of it. His casual position shielded the file's name from me. I'm sometimes curious like that; I just want to know. If Wallace were reading a file related to our case, he'd let us know. He was probably working on something else, but still.

"We need to interview the vic's sister," Holt said, instantly causing Wallace's brow to furrow. "We need to identify the man she was with. We presume it's her boyfriend, but, so far, we don't have any confirmation or name. The sister might know, or the mother."

"No, you can't talk to Caroline Munroe," Wallace said coldly, "I will. I already delivered next-of-kin notifications today, but I'll go over there tomorrow first thing. Anything else you need to know?"

"Deputy Chief," Holt said, letting frustration undertones color and elevate his voice. "With all due respect, after twenty years on the job, I believe I can handle myself well in a politically charged case. You've never had any complaints about me, not about that kind of thing anyway."

"Detective Holt, this is not about your ability to interview a victim's family. Do you, personally, want to get your career shredded in the crossfire that will ensue between the governor, his future bride's family, and the media? Who knows what you'll uncover? Anything that goes wrong, it will be thrown at you, and, through you, at this organization. I believe I made my orders very clear last time you were here in my office. All interactions with the victim's family go strictly through me. Are we clear?"

"But—" Holt started, and was immediately cut off.

"No buts, Detective. Dismissed."

I followed Holt out of Wallace's office as he bolted out of there, his fists clenched, and his shoulders hunched forward. He didn't stop until he reached his desk and stood in front of it, unwilling to sit. He fidgeted in place and sniffled, then ran his hand across his face again, scratching his nose in passing.

Silently, I offered him the box of Kleenex tissue from his desk, and he almost swatted it from my hand.

"Don't need that crap," he muttered. "I need to be able to do my damn job, that's all. All he cares about is getting one more minute in the limelight, one more second with the governor. His name in the papers one more time."

I almost smiled. Yes, sometimes people did things that we didn't agree with, but there was no reason to be so childish about it. We couldn't bloody help it anyway; Wallace had given us a direct order, not once, but twice. I, for one, wasn't going to push my luck.

"It's late," I told him, "why don't we call it a day and meet tomorrow morning at the coroner's? Anne texted me she'll have something by then."

"What's with you and her?" Holt asked curtly.

Why couldn't he mind his damn business? Sometimes I wish he'd just bugger off and let me be, although I had to admire his keen intuition, the way he sensed there was something more going on than he'd been able to identify. And that was priceless in a cop, regardless of how bloody annoying.

"I told you," I replied, looking at him candidly, "Dr. Anne St. Clair and I worked together in the past. Henderson uses the same coroner's office. Anne and I have a good working relationship; we go back."

"Do you believe you, Baxter?" Holt snapped at me.

He was good, the arrogant bastard. I was fairly sure I hadn't shown any sign of deception. My hands were immobile, relaxed alongside my body. My face was tensionless, almost smiling, and my eyes calm and steady. He wasn't, continuing to fidget and nervously shift his weight from one foot to the other.

I shook my head and let a wry laugh escape my lips. "Are you all right, Holt? It seems to me you need a break, or maybe you had too much coffee today."

His blood drained from his face as if I'd accused him of cold-blooded murder. He looked away for a moment, then cleared his throat quietly. "Yeah, let's call it quits for today. See you tomorrow?"

"Yeah," I replied and grabbed my purse from his desk, then made for the door, resigned to neither understand nor speculate on what had just happened. Not a great first day at my new precinct. Nope, not in the slightest.

8

Secrets

"Hi," Holt said, looking just as uncomfortable as he was feeling, "my name is Jack, and I'm an addict."

He hated these mandatory introductions, but they served a purpose. He knew that purpose very well; it wasn't the first time he was attending an AA meeting, and it wouldn't be his last.

"Hi, Jack," the gathering replied in unison.

He forced himself to continue, although he didn't feel like sharing anything with anyone that evening.

"I've had a bad day today," he admitted, staring at the dirty floor. "My hands shook, and I felt angry, frustrated all the time. I—"

"Why should we listen to any crap coming from this pig?" A bulky, bearded man shouted, then stood up, propping his hands on his hips. "He's the piece of bacon who threw my ass in jail. For what? For being drunk, believe you me. Now he stands there, telling us about his bad day? Who gives a flying fuck?"

Holt stood there speechless, trying to remember the man. He had no recollection of busting him, but that didn't mean much. Over the years, he'd collared hundreds of perps, and since he'd made detective he hadn't collared any drunks and disorderlies. No wonder he couldn't remember; it must've happened years ago, when he was still on a beat.

Various comments erupted from the attendees. A couple of people seconded the remarks, saying, "Yeah, get him outta here!" Others, adhering to the essence of AA meeting principles, hushed the man into silence and threw disapproving glances his way.

"I apologize—" Holt started to say, but drew a bunch of boos.

"Why do you get to be a drunk and still have a life, huh?" the man continued to yell. "Does your boss know you're swillin'? Why don't we tell him, huh, boys?"

A tall, gray-haired woman stood and raised her hand, then spoke calmly. "We're going to have to ask you to leave."

"Yeah, run the damn Five-O outta here, we don't need him," the bearded giant hollered.

"No, sir, you," the woman replied calmly. "You've disrupted the meeting and broken the rules."

"Me?" the man replied with an angry scoff. "You're kicking *me* out? Jeez," he said, waiting for support from the attendees, but there was none. They'd all fallen silent, even his earlier supporters. He searched their eyes for a moment, then turned and left, muttering a slew of cusswords. The slamming of the door behind him was a signal they could resume their normal activities.

"Please, Jack, continue," the woman said, then took her seat and crossed her legs.

Feeling a wave of frustration sweep over him, he pressed his lips together, but then saw the attendees waiting patiently and forced himself to continue.

"I'm here today because I want tomorrow to be a better day. I can't afford not to; none of us can." He hesitated, his mind devoid of any thoughts he could share, then added, "That's it for me tonight, thank you."

The entire time it took him to drive home, the details of the meeting swirled in his mind, mixed with countless questions about his new partner. Who was Laura Baxter? Could she be trusted? What was she hiding? Because one thing was for sure, she was hiding something.

It didn't cross his mind that his new partner might have wanted to wait a while, to know him better before spilling everything there was to know about herself, or that she deserved some privacy. None of that mattered. Once in the dimly lit silence of his living room, Holt poured himself a generous glass of bourbon and fired up his laptop. Within minutes, he was going through everything he could find about his new partner.

Laura Baxter, thirty-six years old, British national, naturalized American three years ago. Emigrated young from the UK, at age twenty-four, as the fiancée of an American Marine helicopter pilot, Lieutenant Andrew Baxter from Las Vegas. That's where the information well dried up; there was nothing else he could find in the databases about Laura.

Unsatisfied, he dug some more and found she'd been a cop in the UK, a police inspector, per the details of her immigration forms. Then, upon being granted work rights in the US, she started working for the Henderson police and had a spotless record until a few months ago, when she apparently flipped without reason and beat a suspect to a pulp. She hadn't lied about that.

He took a sip of bourbon and looked at the screen, wondering where to go from there, still unsatisfied. There had to be more about Baxter. He pulled the background of her husband next, and his eyes froze over the last entry on his file. Andrew Baxter had died almost two years ago. An unfamiliar feeling crept up on him; he felt ashamed for what he was doing, for prying into his partner's life.

He'd almost slammed the laptop lid shut, when something else caught his attention. Andrew Baxter had received an honorable discharge; he didn't die in the line of duty, like Holt had initially assumed. He was double-tapped by an unknown drug dealer, here in Las Vegas, when he apparently stumbled upon a large heroin deal going down in his neighborhood. Coincidentally, almost two years later, his widow lost it and went Muhammad Ali on a piece of scum dealer during an interrogation.

He would've probably done the same, if not worse. Maybe she thought it was the same guy who offed her husband. Maybe she felt it in her gut, but couldn't prove it.

A long breath escaped his chest, loaded with a complicated oath, and he quenched the feeling of uneasiness nested in the pit of his stomach with the remainders of bourbon neat in his glass. One more thing he wanted to check, although his resolve was fading out. He opened Facebook and checked Baxter's profile. Nothing out of the ordinary in there, just photos, lots of them, in a long line of postings that ended abruptly a couple of years before, probably with the death of her husband.

Absentminded, he scrolled through them going back as far as he could, to the earliest photos she'd posted. One caught his attention, a picture showing two Marine pilots in full gear with a young, happy Laura Baxter between them. The picture was dated twelve years ago, about the time Baxter had moved, or was about to move, to the US. He squinted at the photo, trying to make out the features of the two pilots whose headgear only revealed the lower part of their faces. He recognized the late Andrew Baxter's full lips and dimpled chin in the man standing to Laura's right.

Then he studied the other face, and the shape of the mouth, the texture of the skin, the contour of the lips reminded him of someone. For a while, he couldn't pinpoint it, because he kept thinking that the second pilot was a man. Then he realized who that was, why the second pilot's features seemed so familiar, so feminine. It was Dr. Anne St. Clair, their coroner.

Another quick records check, and he was able to confirm: Dr. Anne St. Clair had served two tours in Afghanistan as a pilot and combat surgeon, and a medevac team lead. He tilted his head and a quiet whistle of admiration broke the silence of his house.

Yeah, apparently Laura Baxter and Anne St. Clair had a good relationship that went back.

Way back.

9

Findings

I waited for my new partner in front of the coroner's office, nursing a steaming cup of green tea and enjoying the colors of the crisp desert dawn. I love the smells and colors of Las Vegas, those found here, in the outdoors, not the ones inside casinos and hotel lobbies. The air's scent of brisk freshness, the intensely blue sky emphasized by the desert awakening, the morning chill that scatters sleep and renders the mind at its utmost clarity. None of that was possible in smoggy London; with each passing year, my old hometown becomes a more distant memory.

I kept thinking of Madeline and her last day alive. A young woman who'd lived, by all appearances, a relatively banal existence, had managed to make a passionate enemy out of someone. She worked an uninteresting job at an accounting firm. She had no priors. No apparent ties with Sin City's criminal underground. Yet, there was something that kept my mind's wheels spinning, going over the same details again and again. Maybe it was the fact that someone with her income level couldn't afford the clothing she was wearing, but, then again, maybe she came from money, as her sister's upcoming marriage with the state governor would suggest.

I made a note to myself: We should take a look at the family financials. Ask Wallace and hope he won't freak out? Fat chance. Still, we needed to figure out how to pull that off. When there's smoke, there's usually money. Fire too, but money for sure.

Holt appeared in his unmarked Ford, going at least forty in a twenty-five area, and entered the parking lot with screeching tires, raising desert dust.

"Sorry I'm late," he shouted even before getting out of his car. He slammed the door shut and trotted toward me, a thin cloud of vapor coming out of his mouth in the frozen morning air. "Why not wait for me inside, with your pal, the coroner?" His smile seemed genuine, despite his loaded comment.

I'd thought of that, but I didn't want him growing even more suspicious, and, yes, I must confess, I prefer fresh air, no matter how cold, over the smell of formaldehyde and decaying human bodies. I'm old-fashioned that way.

"Thought we should go in together," I replied serenely, and, fortunately, he stopped there with the third degree. He held the door for me, as I forced another breath of air into my lungs before entering the land of the dead and the ones who speak for them.

Anne sat behind her desk, making notes in a file, and the first thing I noticed was classical music, playing faintly in the background. Then my eyes stopped on the body lying on her autopsy table, covered with a white sheet. Locks of golden, wavy hair escaped from underneath, its color and shine intact, as if Madeline were asleep, soon to rise.

I felt a shiver down my spine.

That's nothing new for me; I struggle with seeing victims lying bare on cold, stainless steel tables, surrounded by strangers poking and probing and staring. Beyond my offended sensibility was the primal instinct to survive, triggered by any close encounter with death, and nothing can be closer than staring at its handiwork from inches away. Or smelling the immediate devastation that such demise brings to human flesh, and seeing how a young, beautiful face can be rendered almost unrecognizable by a change in chromatics, where hues of warm, live skin tones are replaced by cold shades of blue and purple, where life is defeated by death.

I wished I could rub some Tiger Balm or Vicks underneath my nostrils, but Anne had made any such practice illegal in her autopsy room, punishable by eternal banishment from the premises. She wanted to capture any bit of information that would help catch the killer, even if that information came in the form of a faint scent that VapoRub could obliterate. That morning the smell wasn't so bad, though; I'd lived through worse.

I approached Anne's desk and smiled, while noticing the dark circles underneath her eyes. She probably hadn't slept much since Madeline's body was laid on her examination table.

"Good morning, Doc," I said, then winked discreetly. I didn't want the perceptive, obsessive Detective Holt to notice too much closeness between the coroner and me, or there would be no end to his questioning.

Anne looked up at me but didn't smile back. She never does, not inside her office, not with a body lying on her table, nor while examining a crime scene. Few people knew why she chose to become a coroner with her Johns Hopkins medical degree and vast field trauma experience; she could've practiced anywhere. Yet she chose to fight her battles on the side of the victims, in the cold, quiet darkness of the autopsy room. Anne had a strong sense of right and wrong, and nothing makes her angrier than a perp getting away with a crime. We have that in common, but, unlike me, she plays everything by the rules.

Holt paced the tiled floor slowly, examining the walls above one of the lab tables, where Anne and her team had hung their diplomas. He kept his distance from Anne, which led me to believe there had to have been some bad blood between the two of them. I'd find out sooner or later.

My partner didn't seem as fidgety; probably he'd had a good night's sleep and the cup he was holding was only his first brew for the day. I almost asked him if he was feeling any better, but then I remembered his unusual reaction the night before and decided to shut up about it. No need to pry; the man had the right to some privacy.

He walked around the room with a confident gait and elastic, feline steps, relaxed yet ready to pounce, to react in an instant to the tiniest threat. He wore a charcoal jacket with light gray slacks, and a white shirt with a loose, red-and-blue tie. Probably he could've done better in the work attire department if he tried a little harder, but, overall, the result was pleasing to the eye. His raven-black hair enhanced his pallor; he needed to get some sun. His face seemed to fall prey to some unknown internal torment when he thought no one was looking, but that quickly went away when he felt my gaze on him, instantly replaced with a boyish, lopsided grin.

Anne pushed back her chair and stood, then beckoned us both to follow her to the autopsy table. She put on a surgical mask and invited us to follow her example, which I knew to accept, but Holt refused politely with an apologetic hand gesture.

"We might've gotten lucky with her," Anne said, looking briefly in our direction, then peeling off the white sheet from Madeline's body, enough to expose her head and shoulders. "We have a partial fingerprint, and some latent prints I'll be working on next."

"Fingerprints?" Holt asked, shooting his dark, thick eyebrows up. "On a body? I didn't think—"

"It's rare," Anne confirmed. "There was a partial fingerprint on her left thumb fingernail that I was able to recover. I'm guessing she fought to free herself from the killer's hands as he was strangling her, like this," she said, demonstrating with her gloved hands around my neck without touching me. "He must have touched her polished nail and left a few loops and swirls behind. We don't have enough minutiae points in this particular print to call it conclusive, but I have more."

I held my breath. We needed all the help that forensics could offer on a case with hundreds of witnesses who didn't see anything, and a killer who managed to disappear without a trace under countless surveillance cameras.

She circled the table and pointed her gloved finger at a bruised area on Madeline's face.

"He covered her mouth with his hand, like this," she demonstrated again, putting her hand at a safe distance above Madeline's mouth, careful not to touch her skin. "He left a fingerprint in her recently applied makeup."

"How the hell is that possible?" Holt asked, leaning forward to look at the victim's face.

"The only explanation I can think of was that she had applied her makeup recently, maybe a touchup, only moments before her death, and it had not fully dried yet," Anne explained. "Same deal here, on her neck, where you see these bruises. A few latent partials are embedded in her makeup here and here."

"I thought prints vanished from a body within minutes," Holt said, his voice riddled with disbelief. He didn't know Anne that well by the looks of it, but he knew forensics, at least the part of forensics that most good cops know.

"They do," Anne confirmed. "We've been lucky with her; I believe I said that before."

"What kind of makeup was she wearing?" Holt asked.

"That's the perfect question to ask, Detective," Anne replied. "It was latex based. That's why the fingerprints lasted."

"Cheap? Expensive? A brand, maybe?"

"Can't give you a brand just yet, it will take some time. But definitely not cheap. Latex-based makeup is professional grade, and this was top of the line. Think movie studios, professional entertainers. It's perfectly water resistant. The wearer can take a shower with it, sweat in the desert heat, walk in the rain, swim, whatever she wants, and that makeup will stay on."

"I definitely need the brand name for that makeup," I added, unable to contain a smile. Sometimes I have a selfish interest in certain bits of information, but that doesn't happen very often.

Holt flashed his signature crooked grin my way, not disapproving, only amused.

"Have you recovered the prints yet?" I asked, hoping for a miracle.

"Not yet," Anne replied, and, for a second, lifted her eyes from Madeline's pale face and looked at me. "It's not that simple. I tried cyanoacrylate fuming and got mediocre results. I'll try Ruthenium tetroxide next and let you know as soon as I'm done. It will take us a while though."

Holt took a few steps back. "Give us something we can use, Doc, anything."

"Official cause of death is asphyxia by manual strangulation. The killer is strong; he crushed her trachea and fractured her hyoid bone with his bare hands. That took a lot of rage."

"He?" I asked.

"Most likely, yes, based on the upper body strength needed to inflict this level of damage."

"You can tell from the video surveillance tapes it's a man, Baxter, what the hell," Holt remarked, irritated for no reason.

"You can't tell much from those tapes, Holt," I replied, as politely as I could. "We saw a hoodie, a baseball cap, some shades. It doesn't hurt to ask if science confirms our assumptions."

"Science confirms," Anne replied dryly. "Broken neck was definitely postmortem, when her body hit the ground. There's also significant trauma to her body, all postmortem, all consistent with her fall."

I shifted my weight from one foot to the other, somewhat uncomfortable to ask what I was about to.

"Was she a working girl?"

Anne shot me a quizzical glance.

"If she was, we're talking high-end escort service," Anne replied, "although I don't see any of the typical signs. She was in perfect health, well groomed, perfect teeth, recent mani-pedi."

I shook my head, feeling disappointed I couldn't get anything that I could use.

"Any sign of sexual assault?" I asked, looking at Madeline's frozen face. If she could only talk to me, I'd listen.

"No," Anne replied, "but there is evidence of nontraumatic sexual activity in the last twenty-four hours, probably even less. Her partner left fluids behind, and I have DNA pending for that donor."

I looked at Holt, and he met my gaze with the same poorly hidden disappointment. We had very little more than we had before coming to visit.

"I also have DNA pending for the epithelials recovered from underneath her fingernails," Anne added, "and from the heel of her shoe. She kicked her assailant forcefully, probably in the shin, considering she was facing him from a close proximity."

"The heel I thought was broken in the fall—"

"She most likely broke it by kicking him and tearing though his jeans. I found cotton fibers consistent with jean fabric, epithelials, and blood, caught between the heel and the dowel. Your killer has one heck of a shin bruise," Anne concluded.

"That's the technical term, Doc?" Holt asked, and, for some reason, Anne gave him a long, cold stare before replying.

"Precisely."

He smiled and started toward the door, and I followed, not before mouthing, "Call you later," in Anne's direction. He'd opened the door for me when Anne called after us.

"Forgot to say, your vic was three weeks pregnant. I'm not sure she even knew."

10

The Apartment

I decided to leave my car in the coroner's office parking lot and ride with Holt. He started the engine with his eyes fixed ahead, from underneath ruffled eyebrows and a tense forehead.

"We need to reconstruct her last twenty-four hours," I offered.

"Uh-huh," he acknowledged, then pulled away from the parking lot, heading back toward the interstate. "Let's pay her apartment a visit first."

Probably not a bad idea, although I would've preferred to timeline her weekend at the Aquamarine first. But the thing about murder investigations is that, if done right, even if you start from a different entry point in the maze, there's only one exit. One killer to catch.

The drive to Spring Valley, where Madeline used to live, was going to take about ten minutes, which gave me the time to find out a little more about my new partner.

"I sensed a chill in the air between you and Dr. St. Clair," I said, without any introduction. "What was that about?"

Holt threw me a quick glance, then resumed looking at the road ahead.

"Nothing important," he replied.

"I beg to differ. You two seem to have some history lingering on, and I might need to be aware of that as your new partner. Might help prevent making it worse by accident."

He glanced at me again with a deepening frown, probably debating if and how much he should share. The man didn't seem to trust me worth a damn.

"I, um, insisted she give me test results in a murder case, a year or so ago."

"Why would she mind that? It's her job."

He cleared his throat and let a smirk tug at the corner of his mouth.

"Not if the trace evidence wasn't really there to begin with."

"I see."

"There had to have been some blood on that perp's clothes; no way he stabbed someone to death and didn't get a single drop on himself," he justified in a lower, subdued tone of voice. "Without that blood evidence, we didn't have a case, or so I thought at that time. I might have insisted beyond the coroner's tolerance limit."

"You're saying you tried to press her into giving you findings where there were none?"

"Whoa, Detective, should I have my lawyer present?" he quipped.

"Nah, you're fine," I replied. "I'm sure you've learned by now that Anne St. Clair can hold her ground."

He chuckled lightly. "And then some. She crucified me."

"What happened with your case? Did the perp walk?"

"Nope, we caught him after all. Turned out he burned the clothes he wore when he killed the vic and bought identical ones. Smart mutt, that one; made me look like a fool in front of your coroner friend. He's doing twenty-five to life up in High Desert now."

I felt the same wave of frustration over his remark as I'd felt earlier, and decided to nip it in the bud. We still had a few minutes to go.

"Why do you keep calling her that?"

"What?"

"My friend, my pal… you know."

"Well, isn't she?"

"What if she is?"

He didn't reply, just looked away. I didn't feel like opening up our history to him, because that meant talking about Andrew, and I still couldn't do that. Not with him, not with anyone. But I pressed on.

"Are we going to have a problem over this, Detective?"

He smirked again and threw me one of those quick, side glances. "No problem whatsoever."

"Good," I said firmly, then I let silence engulf the car.

A few seconds into that silence and I was feeling uncomfortable, wishing we'd arrive already. I was being unreasonable again; expecting my new partner to trust me, but refusing to trust him. He wasn't an idiot, but I was treating him like one. He was considerate and smart and had good instincts, not trusting me being one of those good cop instincts. Maybe he was a bit rushed when it came to closing cases and locking perps up, but I didn't really see anything wrong with that. Maybe, given some time, we could improve our chemistry.

"We're here," he announced, as he was pulling to the curb in front of a four-story apartment building.

It was a neatly maintained property, with clean sidewalks and a tiny garden in front, freshly painted parking spots, and a skittish superintendent who appeared out of nowhere, eager to help and see us gone from his domain.

He unlocked the door to Madeline's apartment, then was quick to disappear, after being visibly uncomfortable in our presence. Maybe he had a record, or maybe he just didn't like cops.

I entered the apartment and smelled the slightly stale air. There was a faint fragrance reminding me of an expensive perfume, probably something she used to wear. What was it, Joy? Maybe.

The living room was neatly furnished with comfort and simplicity in mind. A cushy, white leather sofa in front of a 50-inch TV and a Bose 7.1 surround system. A tempered glass bookcase that must have set her back at least a couple of grand, if not more. Heavy velvet draperies that were pulled open, letting the sunshine in.

A few framed pictures lined the elegant glass bookcase, and I studied them closely. In one, Madeline laughed with her mouth open in the arms of a tall, dark man with intense eyes, probably her boyfriend. In another, she stood somberly while trying to fake a smile, next to her sister and an older woman, most likely her mother. It was helpful that I was familiar with Madeline's sister Caroline from recent media coverage, enough to recognize her in the photo; at least that worked to our advantage.

A third photo showed a playful Madeline hugging a young, African American woman, their faces cheek-to-cheek as they looked at the camera, both girls exceedingly happy and with looks of mischief in their eyes, and both wearing glitzy, sexy club attire, generously accessorized. I gave that third photo a long stare; Madeline seemed more like herself in that picture than in any of the rest. I took out my phone and quickly took shots of all three images, then resumed my walkthrough.

Holt entered one of the two bedrooms, while I stepped into the kitchen and opened a few cupboards. Well organized, neatly kept, clean. A bit unusual for a twenty-eight-year-old; somehow, the image I had about the fashionable Madeline Munroe did not jive with what I saw in that apartment. I couldn't picture her mopping those floors every other day, or keeping her dishes all clean and organized. I used to be twenty-eight not so long ago, and I remembered clearly the socks I routinely forgot on the floor, books and music scattered all over the house, specks of dust here and there, more like everywhere. Because I was too busy living to obsess over cleaning.

Madeline's apartment didn't seem lived in.

I looked at the three potted plants on her kitchen windowsill and absentmindedly touched their leaves. They were thriving, and the soil inside the pots was moist. They'd been recently watered, despite the fact that Madeline had been staying at the Aquamarine for the past two days.

"This house was cleaned up," I said, a bit louder than normal, thinking Holt was in one of the bedrooms and couldn't hear me otherwise.

"I agree," he replied softly right behind me, giving me a start. My breath caught, and I turned toward him.

I laughed, feeling embarrassed with my own reaction. "You nearly gave me a heart attack," I said. "What did you find?"

"Nothing out of order, not even a receipt or a piece of clothing out of place."

"Housekeeper?"

"And a good one," he agreed. "We need—"

"Financials," I cut in, and he nodded.

I walked inside the master bedroom and went straight for the double closet.

It was packed full of expensive clothing, all the valuable brand names generously represented. Modern evening attires, club fashions, and a collection of shoes I instantly envied. The scent of Joy perfume was stronger, and I quickly found it tucked inside one of the drawers, a tiny bottle that went for at least $500.

In the bathroom, everything was sparkling clean, and the toilet bowl had been flushed with a deodorizer that left bluish hues in the water. Probably there wasn't a single usable print anywhere in that house. Then my eyes fell on the clear glass holding two toothbrushes, and I drew closer. Same brand, but different sizes, different models. I remembered the similar glass at the hotel, also holding two toothbrushes.

When I travel, I pack my toothbrush, and I'm sure most people do. Seeing those two there, at the apartment, made me wonder, first of all, if the companion at the hotel was the same relationship she had here, at the apartment. I packed the toothbrushes in two evidence bags, planning to drop them at the lab later.

I went through the main closet again and found no trace of any male living on premises. No clothing, shoes, or otherwise trace of anyone else. The second bedroom closet told a different story. It held some male apparel, simple and practical, mostly jeans, T-shirts, denim shirts, chinos, and a single two-piece charcoal suit, with traces of dust on its shoulders. A difference in class between Madeline and her companion, one that neither partners cared much about by the looks of it.

Holt's phone rang, and he took the call, while I went back to the kitchen and checked out the fridge. It was neatly stocked with choices made by someone who wanted to eat healthy but well. Salads, fruit, frozen steaks, fish. Barely any booze anywhere. A six pack of Amstel on the lower shelf, with one bottle missing, and a bottle of Bacardi rum on the door shelf, almost full.

Then I looked at the plants again, for some reason. A white lily, a pink orchid, and a cluster of African violets. A strange assortment. The violets pot seemed a little darker than the others, as if the ceramic had been stained by something greasy.

"That was Wallace," Holt said, ending the call. "We have the boyfriend's ID. Dan Hutzel, thirty-three, priors for a couple of minor felonies. Marijuana possession seven years back, and stalking."

"Stalking?" I reacted, forgetting all about the potted plants. "That's promising. Where can we find this model citizen?"

"He's waiting tables at the Tartare," he replied, a hint of concern tinting his voice. "Let's go."

On the way out, we asked the skittish super if he'd seen anyone enter Madeline's apartment, of if he knew of anyone living with her. No, there wasn't anyone living permanently at that address, but, yes, she'd occasionally have a male guest, always the same man, staying a night or two. Yes, there was a maid who came in daily. And no, he didn't have her name or number.

11

The Boyfriend

I have a healthy appetite, and that makes places like Tartare unappealing to me. The only thing I really liked about that place was the patio, a prime-time piece of real estate right in the middle of the Strip, on the sidewalk, built in an elevated position, perfect to sit, indulge, and watch the colorful hordes of tourists passing by. But that's where the enjoyment stopped for me, because Tartare is a high-end molecular gastronomy place, in other words a place that will leave you both hungry and broke with the same meal. Exquisite tasting cuisine, yes, I must agree, based on my one-time experience a few years ago when Andrew wanted to impress me on our wedding anniversary. But that night we ended up grilling burgers in our own backyard, because what little food they gave us at Tartare didn't suffice.

I frowned as we climbed the stairs to the entrance; it was another place riddled with memories from another life.

"Detectives Holt and Baxter," my partner announced, while flashing his badge at the astonishing hostess, a girl whose beauty could've opened many other upscale doors in Sin City. "We're looking for Dan Hutzel."

Her professional smile didn't vanish when she heard Holt speak. She pointed discreetly at a young man dressed in a white jacket and black slacks.

"He's right over there. I'll get him for you."

We waited a few moments, not taking our eyes off that waiter, and I recognized the man I'd seen earlier in the photo displayed in Madeline's apartment. I watched the stunning hostess whisper something in Dan's ear, and I thought I saw a flicker of anxiety in his eyes, as he looked our way. For a moment, I was afraid he'd bolt out of there and make us chase him, but that didn't happen. He came our way without reluctance, yet ostensibly worried.

He was an attractive man, in a dark, tall, and handsome kind of way. He seemed to fit with Madeline in that photo, and seen in real life, Dan Hutzel looked even better, albeit a touch rough around the edges. But I didn't see the signs of wealth on that young man, and I would've been surprised if I did. He was, after all, a waiter, and they aren't exactly famous for making the big bucks.

His shoes were too worn, and his slacks were a bit shiny in places. If he wasn't making the big bucks, then who was paying the bills in Madeline's chic life?

"What can I do for you?" he asked in a low, polite voice.

"You know a Madeline Munroe?" Holt asked.

"Yes," he replied immediately, without a trace of hesitation. "She's my girlfriend. Although—" he started to say, but stopped himself midphrase. "What's this about?"

"We're investigating her death," I replied, looking at him keenly.

His pupils dilated in shock, and blood drained from his face. He covered his mouth with his hand and averted his eyes. He wasn't faking it; no one can feign the body's physiological response to emotional shock.

"Oh, my God… Madeline's dead? How did it happen?"

"How come you don't know?" Holt asked harshly, probably not buying it. "It was all over the news."

"I… don't watch TV that often. I was working late shift last night and day shift today. When did it happen?"

"Yesterday afternoon, at the Aquamarine," I replied.

"She was the one they were talking about? The girl who…" He stopped talking, then bent over, holding his stomach. "I think I'm going to be sick."

"Oh, so you did know about it?" Holt pressed on.

"Just heard people talking, that's all. Had no idea it was Maddie they were talking about."

"When's the last time you saw her?" I asked in a gentle voice, hoping Holt would follow my lead. If my gut was worth anything, Dan Hutzel wasn't the man who killed Madeline.

"Yesterday," he replied. "We stayed the weekend at the hotel; she insisted. I went downstairs to get a pack of smokes, and she was supposed to meet me at the Pizzeria across the street for a late lunch. She never showed."

"What time was that?"

"About three in the afternoon."

"What did you do when she didn't show up?" Holt asked, still harshly. "You just called it quits and went on your merry way?"

"No. I went back upstairs and banged on the door. I called her, left messages, nothing. I texted, still no reply. Then I got angry…" he added, but then caught himself and changed the topic. "I even went to the reception desk to ask them to open the door for me. I'd left my key card inside, on the night table."

"And?" Holt asked.

"And nothing, they wouldn't listen to me. I wasn't registered with them; they had no record of me staying in the hotel, so they sent me to hell. I called her a few times more and she didn't pick up, so eventually I got fed up and took off."

"Where to?" Holt asked.

"Back to the Pizzeria for a while, hoping she'd still show up, then I left. I had a shift scheduled here, starting at six. I arrived a little early, changed my clothes, and started work."

"You got mad, you said, but you just gave up on her?" I asked. "I seriously doubt that, given your priors for stalking."

"No, it wasn't like that. That stalking charge was a misunderstanding, some crazy neighbor I've never even spoken with. Judge thought so too, gave me community service." He shook his head and made a dismissive gesture with his hand to underline the insignificance of that issue.

"Then, what did you do? I can totally understand why you got angry," Holt asked. "Girl does that to me, there's no telling what I'd do."

"Yes, I got mad; she'd stood me up without a word. It never happened before. But I didn't give up. I kept on calling and texting her, every chance I had. Last night, even today, whenever I was on break. I had no idea she—"

"You called her today?" I asked, following a hunch.

"Yes, a few times. No one picked up, and I left messages asking her to call me back."

"But the phone rang? It didn't go straight to voicemail?"

"No, ma'am," he replied with confidence, "it rang."

Holt and I exchanged a quick glance. Fletcher had told us he couldn't track Maddie's cell phone because it was off or out of battery. Did she have two phones?

"What's her phone number, Mr. Hutzel? Can you please write it down?"

He obliged. The number he scribbled on his order pad was different from the one we had for Maddie's cell phone. Holt took the note immediately and made a quick call, probably to Fletcher.

"Tell me about Madeline," I asked. "What was she like?"

"Forever young at heart, I used to tell her. She behaved like a reckless teenager sometimes. Wild... she had a streak. Honest and happy to be alive, not like her sister, the snob full of airs."

"You know her sister?" Holt asked.

"Her mother too. What a bunch. I told Maddie many times she must've been adopted or something, because she had nothing in common with those two shrews. Her sister is going to marry the governor, right? A man more than twice her age, but who has money, status, and relationships. He's Nevada royalty, and Maddie's sister only talked about becoming Nevada's First Lady, being driven around in black limousines, maybe landing in the White House someday."

"And Maddie?" I asked.

"Maddie's best friend was Trisha, an awesome girl. She's a dancer at Kitty's Whiskers. Maddie wasn't a snob, like the rest of her family. Maddie was real, as real as they get. My girl was real," he added, his voice trailing off as he stifled a sob.

I pulled out my phone and browsed through the pictures I'd taken at Madeline's apartment.

"Is this Trisha?" I asked, holding the phone in front of him.

"Yeah, that's her," he confirmed. "Those two girls were besties since school, even if Maddie's mother threatened hell and fire. You see, Trisha's black, and she grew up poor. She didn't fit Mrs. Munroe's ideal of her daughter's best friend. But Maddie just didn't care; she loved Trisha."

"Where were you at four thirty PM yesterday, Mr. Hutzel?" Holt asked, maybe just to do his full diligence.

"That's when she died?" he asked quietly, then cleared his throat and swallowed with difficulty. "After begging the hotel reception to open the door, I went back to the Pizzeria across the street and waited for about an hour. I was still hoping she'd come. They'll remember me; us waiters who work the Strip, we know one another, and I pissed those guys off. I held that table for so long without ordering anything."

"Who would want Madeline dead, Mr. Hutzel?" I asked, gently touching his elbow.

He shrugged his hunched shoulders and shook his head.

"I... can't think of anyone, really. Her mother was always complaining about her. Everyone else loved Maddie, except her mother. She only loved 'her Caroline,' as she likes to say, because Maddie's sister is just as arrogant and selfish. But I can't picture that woman killing her daughter, I just can't."

"How about her father?" I asked.

"She never mentioned him. She once told me he left when she was little."

"One more question," Holt intervened. "How can a waiter and an accountant afford the Aquamarine for the weekend?"

He shrugged again. "No idea. She had money, but I never asked, and she never told. At first, I thought it was family money, but after meeting her mother, I'm not so sure."

"And you were comfortable like that, not being able to keep up with her, having her pay for everything?"

"No, not really, but I loved her," he replied, looking directly at Holt. "We've been together for a couple of years, and I got used to it. She dialed down her spending to make me happy, but every now and then, she wanted to live it large. I couldn't see any harm in that. After all, it was her money."

I pulled one of my business cards and handed it to Dan, who accepted it without a word. We turned to leave, but then he grabbed my arm and said, "Please, Detective, please catch the bastard who killed my Maddie. Make him pay."

A few minutes later, when Holt's speeding SUV turned the corner and drove past the Tartare patio, Dan Hutzel was still standing where we'd left him, stunned, too far away to hear me when I whispered, "I will."

12

The Mother

I waited for Holt to return to the car, wondering how he'd react when I was going to invite him to break a direct order given by a superior officer. Maybe with a fresh cup of coffee in hand, he'd be more receptive to a maneuver that could end both our careers. Sitting in the parked SUV in front of the East Flamingo Starbucks, I kept replaying DC Wallace's orders in my mind, hoping I'd find some ambiguity in his words we could use to disculpate ourselves after the fact.

Because I really wanted to interview Madeline Munroe's mother. But Wallace had said, "You're not to approach the victim's family or the governor." I seriously doubt he could've said it more clearly.

In any other case, neither Holt nor I would've had the tiniest hesitation to bang on that door and interview the victim's family until we'd draw some conclusions, maybe uncover some new leads. But going over Wallace's direct order? He'd been firm about it: One mistake and we're both out, Holt and me. No suspensions, no write-ups, just the door and a kick in the rear to land us at the curb, without benefits or pension.

Holt opened the door and climbed behind the wheel. He was quiet, preoccupied; two deep ridges marking the root of his nose. He handed me my hot herbal and took a sip from his coffee.

"You know what I'd like to do?" I asked, holding my breath.

"Interview the vic's mother?" he asked, and his lips stretched into a mischievous side grin. "I bet you would."

"You know Wallace better than me; what do you think he'll do?"

"If he finds out? Fire us both, I suppose," he replied calmly, then put his coffee in the door cup holder and fired up the laptop.

"*If* he finds out? You mean to say there is a scenario in which he could somehow miss this crucial piece of information?"

"He's a political wannabe, groveling to higher-ups and craving the media spotlight any chance there is. My gut tells me he didn't deliver the next-of-kin notification to the mother. He went to the governor's place instead. It was an opportunity to rub elbows with Nevada One."

"But the governor isn't Maddie's family. Not yet, anyway."

"The sister is, and she lives there now. That's no secret, and he used that as his way in."

"What kind of opportunity does Wallace think this is, delivering a death notification? That's terrible."

He chuckled quietly. "You don't understand men like Wallace. For them, any opportunity is a good opportunity, and they'll take it and use it to advance their careers."

He typed something on the laptop's keyboard, then sighed. "Wanna do this?"

I pressed my lips together, briefly doubting my sanity, then replied in typical American style, "Hell, yeah."

"All right," he said, and that crooked grin of his expanded into a sly smile. "Let's do some homework first." He typed a new search into the computer, then started reading from the screen. "Elizabeth Munroe, sixty-two-years-old, no priors. Retired, formerly a pianist for the Las Vegas Philharmonic. Divorced fourteen years ago, never remarried. The ex-husband, Mitch Munroe, owns a construction company. Caroline, the eldest daughter, is thirty-two, and we know about Madeline. All right, that's all I got. Ready?"

"As I'll ever be," I replied, still determined to do my job despite a direct order, but feeling reasonably anxious about it.

Elizabeth Munroe lived in one of the smaller properties that back into the Spanish Trail Country Club. Some of the properties on the southern and eastern side of the exclusive gated community range in the millions. Mrs. Munroe lived on the northern side, where properties rarely reached half a million dollars in price.

We rang a bell and didn't expect a butler to open the door, given the house's lower value. But there he was, in black uniform, and behaving as if he were serving English royalty, and believe me, I know what that looks like; I've seen it firsthand.

He was tall, about six-four, with a severely receding hairline and a distinguished appearance, enhanced by a stiff gait that was probably more age than job related. He was pushing sixty with dignity; he was aging well. I wondered briefly where someone like Mrs. Munroe would find a butler in our day and age, and how much a butler made in salary. What was the going rate for having someone wait at her beck and call?

He held the door with a white-gloved hand, while keeping his other hand neatly tucked behind his back, in perfect ceremony. I was impressed, and one can't impress me that easily; I've seen too much. Then he said he needed to announce us to the mistress of the house, and see if she'll see us.

Holt wanted to say something, and judging by the tension buildup in his jaws, not something very nice, but I grabbed his sleeve to hold him back while I said, "Thank you, we'll wait here."

I studied the living room without touching anything. It was elegantly furnished in a classic, yet over-the-top manner. On a mahogany table, right next to the entrance, a sealed catalog from Rent the Runway had been delivered in Elizabeth's name.

A minute later, we were escorted to the backyard, by the pool, where Mrs. Munroe was lying on a foam bed covered in white sheets, under a white canopy with sheers undulating in the soft breeze. It was cold, barely above freezing, but she didn't seem to care. A patio heater burned by her bed, and she was covered in soft blankets and propped against a mountain of pillows. Under those blankets, she must have worn a fur coat, because a stretch of genuine, silver fox fur surrounded her neck in a generous, raised collar. Bloody hell, the woman was something else.

Holt snickered when he saw her, but quickly feigned a cough and got away with it, unnoticed. I approached the bed and introduced us both in a soft, polite voice, and she smiled hearing me speak. My perfect English always scores points with American snobs; I've seen it happen many times.

"Mrs. Munroe, thank you for making the time to see us today," I said, amazed I could keep a straight face. "These are trying times for you and your family; please accept our sympathies."

She nodded, but didn't say a word, so I continued.

"By now, you must be aware of the suspicious circumstances surrounding your daughter's death—"

"Ah, yes," she said, smiling with innate elegance. "The governor was here last night. He informed me of everything. Such a considerate young man… he spent his entire evening taking care of me."

I shot Holt a quick glance. The governor, a young man? He was sixty-three, or about there, at least a year or two older than Mrs. Munroe. Maybe she called him that because he was about to marry her daughter, but still… I pushed the confusing thought aside and continued, treading carefully.

"What can you tell us about Madeline's life?"

The elegant smile quickly vanished from her lips, replaced by a grimace of contempt that brought countless wrinkles to her parchment skin. Her lips, stained a dark red, were pressed together tightly for a moment before she spoke.

"Ah, Madeline," she said, with a dismissive wave of a gloved hand. "I'm not surprised by the way she went, you know."

Holt's eyebrows shot up, and my jaw almost dropped. Mrs. Munroe wasn't exactly heartbroken. Dan Hutzel's words came to mind; he'd been right about her.

"You see, Madeline chose to embarrass the family," she continued, taking our stunned silence as an invitation to share more. "I loved her to death, but she was an ignorant, irresponsible, promiscuous little slut. Do you realize her actions could've jeopardized her sister's alliance with the governor? This family's future?"

Wow… the woman was unbelievable. She spoke in a low, conceited tone, and lied through her teeth. There's a trick I learned many years ago, in my early days as a London cop, and it's a simple one: The word "but" negates the first part of the phrase. When I hear suspects say things like, "I loved her to death, but…" that three-letter conjunction is the key to revealing the true thoughts that are hidden behind polite words. It works every time. Not that we needed any more confirmation for the obvious.

I exchanged a quick look with Holt, while Mrs. Munroe continued unabated, her smile slowly returning.

"Thank goodness, the governor is such a generous, intelligent man. He rose above Madeline's crap and didn't let her immorality, or the company she liked to keep, taint his true love for my Caroline."

"What was the company she liked to keep, if I may ask?"

"The… people she called friends," she said, putting so much aversion in her words she sounded as if she spat them out. "The terrible men she dated. Unlike my Caroline, she didn't know what was good for her and nearly ruined us all. She was friends with a stripper; can you believe it? Who knows what terrible people she met at night, when she prowled the city like a cheap whore?"

I was getting angry, and I shot Holt a glance. His jaws were clenched tight, probably struggling not to share a piece of his mind, just like I was. I suddenly felt sorry for Madeline, having to grow up with that harpy of a mother. Now I understood better Maddie's grimace in the family photo I'd seen at her place; in retrospect, I was surprised she even had that photo on display.

"But my Caroline, she makes her mother proud," Mrs. Munroe said.

"How so?" Holt asked curtly.

"She's a musician. Not the kind you think, no. She plays violin at the Philharmonic, following in her mother's footsteps. Only classical music, nothing else."

She paused for a while, as I gathered my thoughts and wondered what valuable information we could still gather from the visit that might easily cost us our jobs. So far, we had nothing new.

"You mentioned Madeline was friends with a stripper," I asked. "Do you know her name?"

She dismissed my question with a gesture of her gloved hand. "I don't bother to remember such things."

"How about Madeline's father?" Holt asked.

"He's been out of our lives for many years now. He's… not important, just a construction worker, a mistake I made when I was young," she replied. Then, without any transition, she remembered she had to feign grief and produced a sniffle. "Please excuse me… I hope you understand, I just lost my daughter. I'm heartbroken."

A gesture of her hand beckoned the butler, who came promptly after having endured the cold with his back against the French doors and his hands clutched behind his back. He showed us out and, as he closed the door behind us, I thought I'd seen a friendly hint of a smile touch his lips.

13

Altitude

"Do you know what that was?" Holt asked me, as soon as he set the car in motion.

"What? A viper, coiled comfortably in her nest?"

"No, Baxter, motive. The old shrew would kill anyone who dares to stand in her way. What do you think she'd do to the person who jeopardizes Caroline's chances to marry the governor? I believe she'd kill that person herself, with her bare hands, even if that were her own flesh and blood. What if Madeline was that person?"

"The killer was a man, Holt, you know that."

"She could've hired someone to do the job for her. I'm willing to bet a month's worth of whatever fancy herbal tea you want to drink that if we look at Mrs. Munroe's financials, we'll find money changing hands."

"That's already an avenue we know we want to pursue. However, I didn't get the killer vibe from her. I got a lot of nasty vibes, and I believe she's the most awful parent I've ever questioned, but I don't believe she's a killer."

"There was no grief—"

"No, there wasn't," I cut him off impatiently, "but the absence of grief doesn't constitute evidence. Yes, she was relieved that her daughter was gone, not at all heartbroken; you saw her barely remembering to fake it. It's sad, but it's not a crime; it doesn't make her a killer."

"What are you saying?"

"There was no guilt, no fear. We're cops, Holt. Criminals are anxious in our presence. They fidget, they sweat, their pupils dilate. They show signs of emotional angst, of distress. She didn't show any of that."

I didn't insist any further; I shut up and allowed Holt time to process what I said, but there was something I didn't disclose. I have a gift for spotting microexpressions on people's faces; I was born with it, and growing up I honed it and learned how useful it could be. Then, in my first year as a London constable, when I was beating the pavements of my precinct, I had the privilege to work a few shifts with a superintendent who wanted to get a feel for street crime in Sutton. He noticed my skill in reading facial expressions and put my name in for specialized training at Scotland Yard. A year later, I was promoted to detective sergeant, and after two more, I made inspector, the youngest in London's recent history.

It also helped that I had a college degree in psychology from King's College. After fifteen years of experience in law enforcement, when I interact with someone, a perp, a suspect, or anyone for that matter, I can tell what they think, when they lie, and, in some cases, what they're going to do, and I'm almost never wrong. In England, my rather unique talent didn't make me popular or appreciated by my colleagues; it made people shun me, fear me, sometimes despise me, as if I were able to learn everyone's secrets just by looking at them. People don't know it doesn't really work that way; I'm not a mind reader.

Nevertheless, I learned my lesson and kept my talent a secret since I moved to the States. I figured if I was offered a fresh start, I might as well use it and play my cards closer to my vest. That's why I couldn't tell Holt more than I already did. Last thing I needed was my new partner thinking he must be hypervigilant in my presence.

Speaking of my partner, about that time I started to like what I saw in Holt, although we'd only worked together for two days. He had courage, and a strong, vertical spine. Great cop instincts, and a mix of determination and stubbornness that could, at some point, drive me completely bonkers, but it made him a relentless hunter. I saw kindness in his eyes, empathy for the victim, genuine interest unaltered by ulterior motives or laziness. I saw intelligence paired up with curiosity, and a keen sense for right and wrong.

No one's perfect, though, and neither was Holt. He didn't know when to trust or when to give up, and, at least by hearsay, he sometimes was a reckless, even condescending, maverick. Other times, just a kid who never really grew up. That smirk of his irritated me, and sometimes I could see he was a total arse.

"Maybe she's a psychopath," Holt said, catching me immersed in my thoughts.

"Huh?"

"You said she showed no signs of fear. Psychopaths aren't afraid. That could explain it."

"It could, but they usually lie better. Psychopaths are keenly aware of the mask they have to wear on a daily basis, and their deceit is smoother, not as obvious as hers. They're experienced liars."

He threw me a long glance, and at that moment, I knew he was going to dig into my background in detail. I'd already said too much and piqued his curiosity. I could tell he must've been thinking: Who the hell made you an expert in psychopaths and their lies, Baxter? Well, King's College, to start with, then Scotland Yard. Damn his curiosity; I guess that was a small price to pay for having someone with good cop instincts for a partner.

"Let's talk about that motive you're seeing," I said, hoping I'd deflect him away from wondering about my background. "Mrs. Munroe has an obvious interest in her daughter's marriage, I'll give you that. I wonder if that interest doesn't go beyond hubris. What if she *needs* her daughter to marry well? What if she's broke, living above her means?"

Instead of replying, he pulled over rather abruptly and turned his attention to the laptop.

"I'm tired of saying we need to look at her financials," he muttered. "Might as well get started on that subpoena."

"Without going through Wallace?" I asked, almost entertained, despite my concern for the following month's mortgage payment in case we didn't survive the deputy chief's wrath. "That will go extremely well with him."

"Did he say we couldn't get subpoenas or conduct background checks?"

I started to nod, but then smiled and shook my head slightly. "He said no contact. I don't remember anything about background checks. Not that we obeyed the 'no contact' order either."

"See? We're golden. I know this young assistant district attorney, he's a buddy of mine. His name is Andy Gulewicz. Have you worked with him before?"

"Uh-uh," I replied. I'd never heard of him.

"Great dude, ambitious, and smart as a whip. Let's make the call."

He initiated the call through the car's media system. The ADA picked up almost immediately.

"Gulewicz speaking," the ADA said in a youthful, energetic voice.

"Hey, Gully, it's Holt and my new partner, Laura Baxter."

"What can I do for you?"

"We need a subpoena to access the financial records for Elizabeth Munroe. I'll text you her address."

"Uh-huh," he muttered, as he was probably jotting down her name. "Is this for the Aquamarine murder case?"

"Yup," Holt replied, nervously rapping his fingers against the steering wheel.

A moment of silence, while all we heard was light tapping on a keyboard at the other end of the line.

"But that's the victim's mother, not the vic, based on what I see here. What's your probable cause?"

Holt and I briefly looked at each other. Andy Gulewicz might have been Holt's buddy, but he wasn't cutting any procedural corners for him.

"The victim lived a life well above her means, and we can't find any viable explanation."

"Have you seen the vic's financials yet?"

"Not yet; we need you to get those for us too."

"Why not start there, and seek this subpoena only if you need to? That's what the judge will ask. Everyone's bound to tiptoe around this case, afraid of political backlash. Judges aren't immune, you know."

Holt frowned and swallowed a curse.

"Because we have a high risk of flight with this perp. He was able to vanish from a hotel filled with hundreds of witnesses and countless surveillance cameras. We need to move quickly; we can't waste time jumping through all these procedural hoops in the right order."

"Your immense respect for due process is noted, Detective Holt," the ADA said, with humor in his voice. "I'll see what I can do and how fast I can do it."

"You rock, Gully. Next one's on me."

Holt ended the call and gave me a long stare. "Now let's hope DC Wallace hasn't flagged the case. If he has, he'll be notified about the subpoena request before it gets in front of a judge."

Oh, crap… yeah, I could easily imagine how that conversation would go. Bloody awesome, no less. A ballbuster.

"Why don't we visit the father next?" Holt asked. "I doubt that Wallace's restrictions apply to him. He's distanced himself from the family in recent years. In Mrs. Munroe's own words, he's not important."

I had to laugh at his slick rationalization. "Okay. I'd like to start with Trisha though. She might have more to say than an estranged father no one's seen in ages."

He was about to start arguing with me, based on the long breath of air he inhaled and the sudden change in upper body posture, but the phone rang, and the car's display showed a name I recognized: Fletch. He touched the screen, and the young tech's voice filled the air.

"Hey, guys, I've got good news for you. I found Madeline Munroe's second phone. It's still on, somewhere in the Aquamarine Hotel."

"And how the hell are we supposed to locate it inside a twenty-five-story hotel? Any ideas?"

"Don't freak out, my man, I got you covered. This phone is not a burner, like we assumed. Well, the SIM card is a burner, but the phone itself is an unregistered smartphone, latest generation, with GPS built in."

"And? That will give us coordinates. But who's to say on which floor it is?"

"GPS location is three-dimensional; it can give you altitude, like it does for aircraft pilots. I was able to crack that phone remotely and push an altitude app onto it. I'll push the same app to your phone."

"Why?"

"I need to calibrate the app on-site. Otherwise, we're looking at about a fifty-foot margin of error, and that translates into about four or five hotel floors."

"I didn't know you could do that," Holt said. "You're unreal, Fletch."

He chortled. "One more thing: That phone could run out of juice any moment now. Step on it."

"Okay, got it. We're on our way."

He ended the call, then turned toward me. "Let's light it up," he said cheerfully, then pressed the two buttons that turned on the siren and lights. He peeled off from the curb with screaming tires and pulled a U-turn, then floored it all the way. He was enjoying the fast drive, grinning widely as he swerved through the midafternoon traffic. His excitement was contagious and I, although not thrilled by the rough maneuvering, was eager to get my hands on that phone. If Madeline saw fit to have two phones, that could only mean she had secrets to hide, secrets locked inside that device, something that could take us closer to finding her killer.

It took us less than ten minutes to get to the Aquamarine, and Mr. Avalos, helpful as always, was waiting for us at the main entrance, ready to unlock whatever doors we needed to access.

Holt called Fletcher and gave him the altitude reading on the GPS app. It read 2,190 feet above sea level. I had no idea that the asphalt of the Las Vegas Strip was 2,000 feet above sea level.

"Okay," Fletcher replied, "that's a little weird. The vic's phone is showing an altitude of 2,168 feet. That puts it twenty-two feet below ground level. Does the hotel have a basement?"

"A few levels," I replied.

Mr. Avalos nodded vigorously, then added, "Four basement levels."

"I'd start with the second level down," Fletch said, "somewhere in the northeast corner of the structure. I'll send you a screenshot of my locator app; it's really accurate."

Holt showed Mr. Avalos the screen with a simplified map showing the contour of the hotel, and a blue dot where Madeline's phone was located. "Do you know what this is, two stories down?"

"It's our laundry room," he replied. "Follow me, please."

We rushed toward a service elevator and, after riding it two stories down, we took an endless, busy corridor toward the massive hotel laundry. Large spring doors opened and closed incessantly, letting carts of linens and towels travel in and out of the facility, pushed by uniformed staff. The scent of softener filled the humid air, but it wasn't the usual, retail grade stuff. It was something stronger, more aggressive, with a tinge of disinfectant, yet pleasant.

"You're getting close," Fletcher said. "Continue straight forward about thirty feet, then turn slightly left."

We followed his instructions and moved quickly past two rows of industrial size washers, then past a line of automated ironing presses, where workers fed the clean, wrinkled sheets into machines that steamed, pressed, and folded them neatly.

Behind a separation wall, a few large bins caught the dirty laundry as it came from the upper floors via chutes. We stopped for a moment, unsure where to go next. Fletch had told us to take left, but where? There was nothing but laundry bins and a wall.

"You should see it now," Fletch said. "You're less than three feet away from it, and it's roughly two feet below your phone's level, Detective. I'd venture a guess that if you're holding your phone in your hand right now, the one we're looking for is on the floor somewhere."

"Maybe inside a laundry bin?" Avalos offered.

Holt kneeled on the floor and turned on his flashlight, looking underneath the bins.

"Over there," he said, pointing toward the wall, beyond two large bins. Avalos beckoned a worker who pulled the large bins away from the wall.

Holt put on a glove, leaned over, and picked up the phone carefully, then packed it in an evidence bag. It was pink and encrusted with rhinestones, the phone we'd seen Maddie carry in the surveillance videos that captured the final moments before her death. It was badly cracked; probably the killer had thrown it down the laundry chute, hoping it would disappear forever. Hopefully, that meant it could still have his fingerprints on it.

I couldn't help but smile. We were getting close to catching that son of a bitch.

14

Text Messages

I rushed Maddie's second phone to the forensic lab, eager to get a technician working on it. We waited next to the lab tech's table for a few minutes, while she applied fingerprint powder on the phone's cracked housing. I held my breath, until she confirmed she could lift numerous latent prints, most of them with enough detail to be run in AFIS, the Integrated Automated Fingerprint Identification System maintained by the FBI. Although its complete acronym is IAFIS, most people know it and pronounce it as AFIS, and we were no exception.

The tech reassured us that we'd hear from her the moment either print returned a match in AFIS, then stood quietly, as if waiting for us to be gone from there. We quickly obliged; no one works at their best when someone else is breathing down their neck.

Then I stopped by the coroner's office to check on Anne and what new information she might have. Several tests were still pending, including tox screens and DNA profiles. She normally texted me the moment she had something, but I was irrationally impatient this time. Whenever I closed my eyes, I saw Maddie's body lying in a pool of blood at my feet, crimson red contrasting sharply against the marble. I remembered her genuine laugh in that photo of her and Trisha; so full of life, so young. Until someone took that life without hesitation, in vengeful cold blood. That made me angry on a deeply personal, almost primal level.

Anne was still working to finalize the complex lifting of the latent fingerprints found on Maddie's face and throat. She'd enclosed her entire body inside a clear Plexiglas case, and was exposing the skin to yellowish Ruthenium tetroxide fumes. The door to her lab was closed, but it had a small window, and I pressed my forehead against the cold glass. I observed from a distance, curious, but unwilling to disturb Anne while she worked her magic. She'd shown me the method once before, a few years ago. The fumes react with organic compounds and fatty residues found in latent fingerprints, even if deposited on difficult surfaces, lending the fingerprint enough definition to allow it to be photographed or scanned, and ultimately captured as a searchable image.

When she saw me, Anne waved me away unceremoniously and I left. There was nothing for me to do there. I picked up my car from where I'd left it that morning and followed Holt back to the precinct, where Fletcher had some news. While driving, I constantly checked the time, anxious, aware of each passing minute, and not only because the first forty-eight hours are critical for any murder investigation. There was somewhere I needed to be at 6:00PM, and I couldn't be late.

Our next stop was Fletcher's desk, where he was sorting through the data dump from Maddie's second phone, already displayed on a large monitor.

"There you are," he said with a big grin, "just in time, 'cause I got to bounce. Got Raiders tickets tonight."

I looked at the screen, where a few frequently called numbers were highlighted in two different colors.

Holt patted Fletcher on his shoulder, then crossed his arms at his chest. "Talk to me."

"Your vic mostly interacted with these two numbers. One belongs to a Dan Hutzel; I understand you already spoke with him."

"Yes, we did," I replied. "Is the second one Trisha's number, by any chance?" I asked, hoping we'd find Maddie's best friend the easy way.

"How did you know?" he asked, just a hint of sarcasm seeping in his voice. He tapped his fingernail against the monitor, where her name was written in a screenshot of her cell phone account. "Trisha Downs, fully registered user. I have home address, credit card information, and I can find out anything else you need."

"Can you find out where she works?" I asked.

"Sure, only not from the phone company," he replied, visibly entertained. He switched screens and typed a quick search in the system. "Didn't you say she's a dancer or something?"

"Yeah," Holt replied.

"Well, she works at Kitty's Whiskers," he announced, and I could've sworn he blushed a little, while averting his eyes for a brief moment.

"Do you know the place?" I asked serenely.

"Just in passing," he replied, shooting me a quick glance, then looking away again. "It's a strip joint on Tropicana. The sign's in pink and blue neon, a cat's nose and whiskers. Can't miss it."

I bit my lip to contain my amusement. He'd lied to us and thought he got away with it. He must have visited the place at least once, but he was probably too embarrassed to admit it in front of his coworkers. How I knew? That's easy. The way he averted his eyes, the brief moment he touched his nose; all signs of deception and manipulation. The way he offered unnecessary detail, and the way he breathed with ease when he finished talking.

"Anything interesting in Madeline's texts?" I asked, moving on gracefully.

"The boyfriend started calling her and leaving messages soon after 3:00 PM yesterday. There were several texts she didn't respond to, and you can tell the man was getting angrier by the minute, but he didn't stop trying to reach her until today."

"That supports his story," Holt said.

"It doesn't explain why she didn't respond to his texts between 3:00 PM and the time of her death, almost an hour and a half later. Did they argue? Was she angry with Dan when he left that hotel room?"

"Read this," Fletch said, shifting the image on the screen to a new text conversation, this one with Trisha. It started at 3:21PM the day before, about an hour before she died.

Madeline: *BF turned into a lousy lay. Got me all worked up, then went to get smokes. Left me alone here, all hot and bothered. Need to get me some.*

Trisha: *Girl, you're crazy.*

Madeline: *Sure am, horny too. Might drop by later, raise some hell.*

Trisha had replied with a smiley face and a martini glass.

Then the messages stopped for a while, until many hours later, at 2:24AM.

Trisha: *Still here, but getting ready to leave. R U coming?*

Then Trisha sent several other increasingly concerned texts, because Maddie never responded. At that time, she was already dead. She'd died about an hour after their first text exchange.

Holt scratched his stubbly jaw, staring at the screen with an undecided frown across his forehead, probably just as intrigued as I was. It was an interesting exchange, shedding more light into Maddie's life than everything else we'd uncovered the entire day. Madeline had two phones because she was apparently living two lives. Her job, her family, her boyfriend, even her apartment told nothing about who she really was, the "hot and bothered" young woman about to hit the Strip looking for an opportunistic sex partner. Had she found an opportunistic killer instead?

I wondered what Trisha would have to add, but that had to wait for a couple of hours, no matter how much I wanted to get to the bottom of Madeline's story.

I touched Holt's elbow gently.

"Hey, do you mind if you grab some dinner without me? It's almost six. I got a quick errand to run, then I'll meet you in front of Trisha's work address at seven thirty."

"Sure," he replied. He'd been increasingly quiet in recent hours; I wondered what that was all about. I had no time to worry about that though. Instead, I offered Holt my car keys with an irresistible smile.

"Mind if we swap wheels 'til then? I'm in a really big hurry."

He nodded, shooting me an inquisitive glance that I pretended I didn't notice. He handed me the keys to his Ford, and I stormed out the door as fast as I could. I needed to make it across town in less than fifteen minutes if I wanted to keep my own arse out of jail.

15

Monday Blues

The moment I cleared the LVMPD parking lot with screeching tires, I let it rip—sirens, lights, and strobes—and floored it. I had less than twelve minutes to make it to Henderson, and I cringed every time I visualized myself standing in the wanker's office, apologizing, trying to look humble and earn his forgiveness, when I could've easily wrung his neck. Well, maybe not literally, just metaphorically speaking.

I took Martin Luther King Boulevard south and wove my way through rush hour traffic, pedal to the metal all the way to the interstate. By the time I took the East Horizon Drive exit in Henderson, it was already five past. *Bollocks... bloody, hairy, pear-shaped bollocks, the size of apartment buildings.*

I just wished the arse would sign off on my paperwork already and let me be. He must be the worst shrink to ever hold a valid license, if he didn't see those sessions were doing me more harm than good. Every time I met with him, I relived everything, and I wasn't ready for it. It sank me into an abyss of despair, where I was reminded that Andrew was never coming home again, and the bastard who took my husband's life was still alive.

I was panting as I knocked on the door labeled simply, "Dr. Beville, MD." Some MD he was... a totally clueless wanker who should've buggered off from my life at least a month ago.

He buzzed me in, and I scampered inside the lush office, willing myself to look apologetic instead of how angry I was.

"Dr. Beville, I'm terribly sorry. I'm working the Aquamarine murder, and it's a high-profile case, as you might have heard. I couldn't leave on time; it was beyond my control. I hope you can believe me when I say it will never happen again."

It wasn't beyond me to use any card in my deck to save my hide, and I played the part convincingly, with zest and the right emotion. I entered the character's persona in a split second and brought it to life: The dedicated detective who wouldn't miss her anger management sessions for any other reason than fighting crime and protecting the community. I had an innate talent for acting, but I had also acquired some skills back in the day.

When I was young and still believed in fairy tales, I wanted to be an actor just as much as I wanted to be a cop. Well, people normally say actress in the case of a female actor, but I resent that. It sounds sexist to me. An actor is an actor, regardless of gender, just like a doctor is a doctor, regardless of how bloody annoying he or she is. I studied acting, took classes, and landed a few minor parts in London's second-tier theatres, but never on the big screen like I'd dreamed and hoped. Then I woke up one day, when I was about twenty years old, with the realization that Hollywood wasn't in the cards for me, and I pursued my other passion: being a copper, as they called it back home.

"Please, take a seat," the credentialed wanker said, then he removed his rimless glasses and closed his eyes. I obliged, and he took his time rubbing the root of his nose with his fingertips, then sighed. He was trying to make me sweat, the bastard, and it was working. Having your entire existence hanging by the thread of a stranger's whim is awful in how powerless it makes you feel. Knowing you managed to piss off that stranger is terrifying.

For a fleeting moment, I wondered why I took the chance to piss him off. Why was I risking it? In all fairness, I could've made the appointment on time. I could've not missed the last one.

"Detective Baxter," he eventually said, "I've already started your paperwork."

My chest swelled. I was about to be free of him, of the dreadful Monday nights.

"To sign off on my FFD?" I asked, referring to the fitness for duty report.

"No, unfortunately. To put you back into the system. You broke the terms of the agreement."

"What? No, please don't do that!" The terror in my voice, the tears that threatened to burst were no act. My job was all I had left; I couldn't lose that too.

I stood abruptly and leaned over his desk, as if a closer proximity could make the man more willing to cave. Unfortunately, he flinched and pulled away, probably feeling threatened by my outburst. I was, after all, carrying a Glock, and I was, at least in his professional opinion, quite unstable.

"Please sit, Detective," he said calmly, but his pupils were dilated, and his jaws clenched underneath his beard.

I let myself drop into the chair, deafened by the sound of my own thumping heart. I covered my mouth with my hand to keep the rage and sorrow locked in there, where he couldn't see nor hear them.

"I haven't finalized the papers though, and I have some doubts about that."

I dared to breathe a little, letting a tiny bit of air quench the thirst in my lungs.

He scratched his salt-and-pepper beard, then rested his hands on top of the papers scattered on his desk.

"It's relatively easy to file such paperwork; I have done it many times when court-mandated anger management patients don't show up. However, before rushing into filling out a rather strenuous form, I'd like to understand the circumstances better."

"I can explain," I started speaking in a high-pitched voice, but he raised his palm, and I clammed up promptly.

"I was hoping you could explain, but as you were late today, I had no reason to assume you'd actually show up, so I made some inquiries."

I let my head hang until my chin rested against my chest. My hair covered my face like a long, wavy curtain, hiding the tears that were stinging my eyes.

"System inquiries, not people inquiries," he clarified, and I raised my head a little. He continued, "I wouldn't violate the ethics governing our professional relationship by breaching the confidentiality of everything said and done here."

I nodded once and dared to look at him through a blur of tears. His glance showed kindness and understanding, not the indifferent frustration I expected to find.

"I had already filled out two pages of this form," he said, tapping on the paperwork lying on his desk, "when I noticed that last Monday, the day you skipped our session, was your late husband's birthday."

There it was, the knife through the core of my being. Why the hell did he keep on doing that? *Please, God, make it stop.*

"How did you spend last Monday, Detective?" he asked in a low, understanding voice.

I shook my head, while my entire being was screaming. No! No more!

He waited for me to say something, but I couldn't. After a few moments of silence, he continued.

"I took the liberty of reviewing both your husband's murder case file, and the incident report that brought you here, the assault of Pedro 'El Maricon' Reyes while in police custody. While in *your* custody. There are intriguing coincidences in the facts."

I tucked a strand of hair behind my ear and stared at him directly from underneath ruffled eyebrows.

"You have access?" I asked, while my frown deepened.

"I consult for the FBI. I probably have more access than you do, Detective."

Fantastic… just bloody fantastic.

He wasn't just any shrink; he was a well-connected, powerful, dangerous one who had some serious pull.

He could read me like an open book, based on his understanding smile. I looked for condescension in his eyes but saw nothing of the kind. I hated his kindness more than I hated his power over me. It stirred me up, it made me feel weak, a victim.

"For instance," he continued calmly, "Pedro Reyes sold drugs on the same street corner for years. Coincidentally, that happened to be the same street where your husband was shot. But the murder weapon used in your husband's shooting was never recovered, and no witnesses stepped forward to place El Maricon at the scene."

I nodded quietly, keeping my eyes riveted to the floor. What was he gaining by doing this? He didn't need to recite the bloody case files back to me; all he needed to do was say he reviewed them. I had no reason to doubt that fact.

"I read the report about what your husband said to you, in the emergency room, right before he died. In his words, 'eyes like grandma,' a statement that you later explained to mean that his killer had heterochromia iridis, irises of different colors. And what do you know? Reyes is odd-eyed. That's the second coincidence," he added, raising two fingers in the air.

I sighed, a long, pained breath of air that burned my chest. There was nothing I could say.

"They weren't able to close the case on your husband's murder, but one day, fate brought Reyes into your interrogation room, and you connected the dots. That part I already know; I read it in the file. But then, what happened?"

I swallowed with difficulty, feeling my throat parched, sore. What was the bloody point?

"The DA said we couldn't risk an acquittal," I said quietly, after clearing my throat. "Most of the evidence was circumstantial. No forensics, no murder weapon, and heterochromia is apparently not that uncommon."

"Walk me through what happened, Detective. The DA refused to prosecute, took Easy Avenue, and decided to charge him for the repeated drug offenses instead, knowing they could get a guilty verdict with a lengthy sentence. But what did you do, after the DA's office told you they couldn't charge him with murder? You went back in there and pummeled him?"

"No, it wasn't like that," I replied, feeling I was suffocating. Something heavy pressed on my chest, not allowing me to draw air.

"Then what?"

"I almost believed the DA's office when they said we couldn't really be sure it was him who killed my husband. I was willing to believe that against all reason, against what my gut was telling me. But then, there was something the slime bag said when I went back in the interrogation room. He said, 'Your nights lonely these days, *chota chica*? Me homies can keep you warm.' That's when I knew it was him; I knew he'd pulled that trigger. I saw it in his mismatched eyes."

I forced some air into my lungs and wiped a tear from the corner of my eye.

"I… just lost it. I wanted him to pay for what he'd done, for the innocent life he took. I wanted him to bleed." I struggled to breathe, gasping, choked, desperately trying to hold back my tears and failing. "Andrew served two tours in Afghanistan and came back home to die at the hands of a lowlife drug dealer. Yes, I wanted Reyes to feel my pain. I still do."

Dr. Beville gathered the papers from his desk and arranged them in a neat pile, then opened a drawer and let them fall inside a folder.

"Thank you for your trust, Detective. I know it wasn't easy for you to share the details of what happened. I'm afraid we have a long way to go before I can clear you."

I let myself fall against the chair's backrest, feeling betrayed and exhausted and disappointed, all at the same time.

"Detective, you nearly killed a man while he was handcuffed and chained to a table. Before I can wholeheartedly sign off on your FFD, I need to be sure it won't happen again."

I nodded, surprised at how grateful I felt toward the man who had been at the center of my rage for the past six weeks. I hated to admit it, but he was right. I wasn't okay… not yet.

16

Credit Card

I left Dr. Beville's office in a haze and welcomed the frozen air invading my lungs the moment I stepped out of his building. It felt good to get out of there, out of that office where all bets were off and all my defenses threatened.

He'd sent me on my way with a letter-sized notepad and a pen imprinted with his name and phone number. Whenever I felt angry, I was supposed to jot down the circumstances, keep a log of the things that he'd called "personal anger triggers." What kind of events ticked me off, what time of day, around which people, what circumstances. *Seriously?* But at least I walked out of his office still having a job, even if that meant I had to humor him with some scribbles and show up on time. As a psychology graduate, I understood his methodology; I still resented it though.

I lingered for a minute before getting in Holt's car. I loved the chill in the air, the clarity it brought to my mind, the peace and quiet of the neighborhood, too far away from the Strip to be touched by the rampant craziness of Sin City's tourists.

When I finally drove out of there, I didn't rush; I relished the drive without the haste, just enjoying the moment, living it, finding myself after the difficult session. Sometimes it felt like I didn't know who I was anymore, and this was one of those times. Almost two years had passed since Andrew was killed, and I was stuck in a denying rage, going nowhere fast. *Damn…*

I pushed myself to turn on the radio and picked a channel that played dance music. Happiness was a decision, Beville had said. Maybe he wasn't such a wanker after all, and maybe I could at least give it a try. Then a thought invaded my mind, the memory of Maddie's body in a pool of blood at my feet. Her killer was still out there, free, and that ticked me off badly. *I will catch that son of a bitch, no matter what it takes; and that's a promise*, I thought to myself, then I floored it the rest of the way.

I pulled over in front of Kitty's Whiskers, behind my own car. Holt leaned casually against the side of my white Toyota, looking miserable with his collar raised and his hands shoved deeply into his pockets. He wasn't wearing a heavy coat, only his suit jacket, and it was near freezing. A bitter wind rolled in from the mountains, making it worse.

"Hey," he greeted me with a bit of an uneven smile, but I noticed the tension in his jaw.

"Thanks for lending me your ride," I said, tossing him back his keys and taking mine from his frozen hand.

"You're welcome." He looked around for a moment. "We can't leave these cars here. They'll tow you in no time. Maybe even me, if they don't pay attention to the government plates," he chuckled.

"Okay," I replied, ready to get behind the wheel.

"Why don't you get us some coffee?" he suggested, pointing at the coffee shop still open next door, "and I'll move both cars. I'm buying," he added, then offered his credit card and took back my keys. "Tall and black for me, please."

I hesitated for a split second, then decided to accept and took his card. He'd been quiet all day, and I was curious to find out what that was about. There was something lurking below the surface with my new partner.

I scampered toward the coffee shop, eagerly anticipating the warmth I was going to find in there. I opened the door and stepped inside, then waited for a minute or so for the barista to finish preparing a complicated beverage for the customer ahead of me. Judging by the layers of foam, chocolate syrup, and caramel that she topped the drink with, it contained more calories than my lunch and dinner combined.

Absentminded, I played with Holt's credit card, while looking at the menu options handwritten in digital chalk on an LED display, a perfect illustration of what happens when people aren't really that clear on what they want to do. Stick with traditions? Hold on to the old blackboard and chalk. Go modern? Use legible type font on wide LED displays, and deal away with the cursive in digital chalk imitation. I laughed quietly and looked away.

My eyes fell on Holt's card. It was a dark, matte finish, but it had traces of a white powder on it. I froze. In a split second, it all came back to me… his jittery behavior, his sniffling, the way he'd turned pale when I asked if he was feeling all right the night before. Okay, it all made sense in this cop's mind, but I still couldn't bring myself to believe it. Drugs? Seriously? He had to know better than that.

Thankful I wasn't a germaphobe, I ran my index finger across the card where the white residue was more visible, then touched it with the tip of my tongue. It was bitter; I didn't feel it immediately, but it was. Then my tongue turned numb where it came in contact with the white powder.

Cocaine.

Jeez, Holt… why?

17

Leverage

A wave of rage rushed through my brain, and I forced myself to stay calm while the young barista filled our cups. There's one thing I hate almost as much as drug dealers, and that's addicts, the people who are unwilling to clean themselves up and get rid of the plague. The people who keep drug dealers in business, plush with bloodstained cash.

I paid for the coffee with my money, unwilling to compromise the evidence on the credit card any further. As soon as I stepped out of the coffee shop, I spat on the asphalt, not giving a damn if anyone saw me. I needed that horrible cocaine taste out of my mouth. Then I sealed the credit card in an evidence bag and sunk it in my pocket.

Holt met me on the sidewalk, halfway between the coffee place and the club entrance. He smiled as he took his coffee from me, and wrapped both his hands against the hot paper cup. Then he took a long swig with his eyes half-closed.

"Thank you, partner," he said in a low voice.

"Why is there cocaine on your damn credit card, partner?" I asked, cutting straight to the point as I always do.

He instantly turned pale, or maybe it was the neon sign changing colors from red to blue above our heads.

"I have no idea," he replied, sounding convincing. I could've been fooled if it weren't for the tension in his chin and jaw, the flicker of fear in his eyes, and the slight trembling in his fingers. Okay, that might have been the cold weather, but I was willing to bet serious cash against fortune cookies it was fear, the adrenaline that runs through our bodies when we're faced with sudden danger. If Holt was an addict, I was the danger. I could end his existence as he knew it, and that was reason enough for an adrenaline surge.

But I didn't care about any of that. I only cared about the truth.

I sat on the curb and hugged my knees, trying to ignore the coldness of the asphalt under my butt.

"I will sit here until you stop lying to me, or until I finish my coffee, whichever comes first. If I take the last sip of java and I still don't have the truth from you, I will turn you in."

"That simple, huh?" he asked. His brow was furrowed, and his uneven smile gone.

"That simple, yes."

He turned and walked away, angry, kicking pebbles from the sidewalk far into the street, muttering oaths under his breath.

"I have a personal issue with drugs," I said, raising my voice a little so he could hear me over the traffic. "And I know you can't have my back if you're tripping on something."

He took a few steps toward me, about to challenge my statement. Before he could open his mouth, I took a sip of coffee, then held the cup against the light coming from a streetlamp, to gauge the liquid's level inside the cup.

"Running low here," I said impassively, maybe with a hint of regret.

"Damn you, Baxter," he muttered, while his shoulders hunched forward.

"Yeah, damn me," I replied laughing bitterly, and the sadness I felt was real and unexpected. I liked Holt. I thought we could've made a great team together, but not like that. Not if he was a junkie.

I took another sip of coffee, and this time it wasn't even necessary for me to demonstrate I was running out of reasons to delay the only logical thing I could do. I played with my car keys impassively, staring at the asphalt, trying to see if there was a pattern in its gritty texture.

"It's nothing, really," he said, sounding unconvincing. "It only happened once, and I didn't even notice the residue on the card, or I wouldn't've given it to you, right? You know there's cocaine residue on almost all money in circulation. Why wouldn't there be on credit cards too?"

Nice try. I almost told him credit cards don't change hands like money does, but judging by the way he clenched his jaws and looked away as soon as he'd said that, I realized I didn't need to explain anything. He already knew what a bad liar he was.

He took another sip of coffee, the last one apparently, because he then crushed the paper cup in his hand and sent it flying in the general direction of a trash can.

"Okay," I said, and I let a quick sigh escape my lips before continuing. "Keep on lying, I don't really care. Until yesterday, you were a complete stranger. I won't miss you when you land your arse in Lovelock, to make the day of countless oversexed cons that you put in there."

He scoffed and propped his hands on his thighs. "Un-fucking-believable! You're working me like a perp in the sweatbox."

"Well, aren't you one?" I replied coldly. "Cocaine possession is a felony in the state of Nevada."

He let his arms fall along his body and lowered his head, defeated. There was a look of despair in his eyes where denial and defiance had been. He ran his hand through his raven-black hair, then clasped his hands together nervously.

"I did an undercover stint a few years back, before I moved to Homicide.

I joined a distribution network to get to their source. We suspected ties with the Sinaloa Cartel, but we had no idea how they managed to bring the drugs from Mexico directly to the Strip." He stopped talking and searched my eyes.

"Go ahead, I'm listening," I replied calmly, my voice devoid of any emotion.

"I found out eventually and arrested Sinaloa's key people in the States. They were ingenious. The stuff came in meat, frozen packs hidden inside carcasses. The K9s would get agitated, but it was meat, and no one trusted the dogs next to the meat. Hundreds of loads of meat cross that border every day."

I shrugged and looked at him, already knowing where that was heading. "Get to the point. I'm running out of coffee."

He clasped and unclasped his hands a few times more, anxiously. "Do you know what an addictive personality is? I snorted once, only once, and just a little bit, to make my way into the dealer ring, to establish credibility. Once. Then I stopped thinking of anything else. I was hooked," he added with a wry laugh, "Even with coffee, I can't stop at just one or two. No... I have to drink them one after another, all day long."

"That's no excuse—" I started to say, but he cut me off.

"A few months later, I was in the twelve-step program. Look," he said, then fished a three-year coin out of his pocket.

"You're telling me the residue on your card is three years old? How stupid do you think I am?"

"No," he reacted, "that's not what I meant. I'm telling you how far I'd gone before failing again. And again," he added, in a somber, subdued voice.

"Are you clean now?" I asked, willing to believe him and looking for a reason.

He averted his eyes and turned sideways, ashamed.

"Damn it to bloody hell, Holt," I snapped, then stood up from the curb. I went to him and grabbed his sleeve, forcing him to face me. "When?"

He hesitated before speaking, and I tugged at his sleeve angrily.

"A few days ago. I—"

"Shush," I said, raising my voice. "I don't want to hear it. I'm better off not knowing."

I let go of his sleeve and paced the parking lot. An SUV filled with hollering youngsters pulled in, and a few moments later, they scurried through the entrance, shooting sideway glances our way.

"How did you manage the random drug tests?" I asked.

"I just got lucky," he replied. "I was never asked to take one. No one knows about this; no one found out. Except you."

Damn him to bloody hell, for putting me in that position. I knew what the right thing to do was, but that meant taking away his badge, maybe even putting him in the same jail where his collars were locked up, and that seemed wrong. He was a good cop; I knew that, I believed it with every fiber of my being, although I'd barely met the man. It doesn't take much for a cop to figure out the fabric of their partner, the quality of his judgment and his willingness to do the right thing.

Then I chuckled, thinking of the day's irony. Only two hours after Dr. Beville bent the rules and gave me one more chance to put my life back together, I was faced with the same choice. Go by the book and end Holt's career? Or take the immense responsibility of giving him another shot? I couldn't think of too many scenarios where that wouldn't end in disaster. Cocaine addiction is a bitch to beat.

He took a deep breath, then asked, "What are you going to do?"

I bit my lower lip for a moment, searching my soul, ascertaining if I was making the right decision, for the right reasons.

"You'll attend AA meetings every day, weekends included," I said firmly.

"That's going to be tough with the hours we work," he said, deepening his frown.

"Beats jail. Take it or leave it."

He nodded, then held my scrutinizing gaze honestly, without hesitation or deception.

"Every few months, I will test you myself. You walk the line, this never happened," I said, holding up the evidence bag with his credit card inside. "Feel free to cancel this; I'm holding on to it for now. It's leverage."

He nodded quietly, keeping his eyes riveted on mine.

"Thank you," he eventually said, as I was taking the last sip of coffee, now cold and tasteless.

I watched him standing a few feet away, waiting patiently. There wasn't a single sign of relief or deception in his body posture, only shame and determination. It's been a while since I cared about someone enough to take a chance, enough to complicate my own existence. I only hoped I wasn't making the biggest mistake of my career.

As I walked toward the entrance with Holt by my side, an interesting thought came to my mind. Maybe it wasn't all that bad that I'd learned Holt's secret, in case he ever found out mine.

18

Dancing Dozen

The bouncer came to greet us the moment we stepped inside the Kitty's Whiskers foyer. The lobby was tastefully decorated in black, engineered stone, the kind that sparkles, and barely lit in blacklight. The club's logo, a pink, inverted triangle representing a cat's nose, flanked by three pairs of blue whiskers, hung above the glass doors leading to the club, innocent, yet ingeniously suggestive. The place aimed to be classy, because the muscle was wearing a jacket instead of a sleeveless T-shirt and smiled politely when we showed him our badges and asked to speak with Trisha.

"One moment," he said, then dialed a three-digit internal extension on his desk phone. "Need you at the front door," he said, then hung up. "Please take a seat," he invited us with a gesture of his hand. Two cushy, black leather sofas lined the walls, but we remained standing.

The bouncer was big and strong, at least 6 foot 5 and over 240 pounds, all muscle. His polite demeanor seemed at odds with the taut fabric of his sleeves, stretched over his biceps and deltoids whenever he flexed his arms, or with the partly visible ink jobs on his wrist and neck. Through the thick, frosted glass doors behind him, we could barely see the inside of the club, engulfed in semi-darkness, but we could hear the music, upbeat and modern, yet provocative in both lyrics and tune.

The door opened and a middle-aged, elegantly dressed African American woman came to greet us. That wasn't Trisha; the woman must have been at least twenty years too old, and, by the attire she was wearing, belonged to a different class than Maddie's best friend. She wore a beige pantsuit with a matching silk blouse and a string of pearls around her neck. Definitely not a dancer; most likely the club owner.

"Melodie Davis," she said simply, extending her hand. Her handshake was firm and her eyes direct and intelligent. "What can I do for you, Detectives?"

"We'd like to speak with Trisha Downs," I replied. "Is she working tonight?"

"She is," Melodie confirmed. "She's on the stage right now. As soon as she's done, she'll join us." She gestured quickly to the bouncer and he disappeared for a moment, probably to let Trisha know. "This is about what happened to poor Maddie, I assume?"

"You knew Madeline Munroe?" Holt asked.

"Yes," she replied, with a tinge of sadness in her voice. "She used to come and dance here sometimes."

I exchanged a quick glance with Holt. I didn't expect to hear that, and based on Holt's expression, neither did he. Maddie had a college degree and a good job. Why would she dance in a strip joint, no matter how classy? Was dancing the source of her unexplained financial status? After all, we still hadn't seen her bank records; we weren't expecting them until the following morning. These things take time... too much damn time.

"She worked for you?" I asked, unwillingly frowning.

"Technically, no," Melodie replied, appearing uncomfortable. She crossed her arms at her chest and took a small step back, putting some distance between her and us. "She had a passion for pole dancing, just like I did when I was her age," she added with a tiny smile. "She wanted to dance sometimes; she showed up here, ready to go up on the stage, and she was good."

"Why would someone do that?" Holt asked.

"Dancing is fascinating, Detective. You must think only women who can't earn a living otherwise will lower themselves to stripping on a stage, and that's partly true, for some. There are others who feel elated when they see men's reactions to their beauty. It's a powerful drug, and Maddie liked that buzz. She might've had a day job, but she was a fantastic dancer."

"Did you pay her?" Holt asked.

"I let her keep her tips," Melodie replied, her smile now gone. "She wasn't on my payroll, Detective. Like I said, she wasn't my employee."

"You let her keep her tips... How generous of you. Nice racket you had going here," Holt said, and I heard contempt in his voice. "People working for you without pay."

Melodie straightened her back and thrust her chin forward before she spoke.

"It wasn't like that, Detective. She came when she wanted, wore what she wanted, stripped how much she wanted, even brought her own music. I just let her use my club as the stage where she liked to perform, on occasions."

"How often did that happen?" I asked.

"She came and danced a night or two, then disappeared for a few weeks, then came back again without so much as a phone call."

"And you let her? You were okay with it?" I asked.

"She was that good, Detective. Intense, passionate, truly exotic. She will be missed."

I nodded but something didn't agree with me. Melodie seemed a little too slick to be all kindness and charm. She was, after all, a strip club owner, and that's serious business here, in Vegas. Cutthroat.

"I still can't believe you were okay with her coming and going as she pleased. What was in it for you?"

She laughed quietly. "Except free labor, which any half-smart club owner would grab with both hands?"

"Yeah, except that," Holt intervened.

"She kept the other girls in check," Melodie replied hesitantly, and her eyes veered away from mine.

"How so?" I asked, although I believed I knew the answer.

"Just by coming in here every now and then. By showing them that they aren't irreplaceable, and that real dancers love the job. That shut them up, kept them from bickering about rude customers and high heels and what not."

Holt and I exchanged another quick glance.

"That must've made her quite popular with your crew," I said. "I bet she made some enemies here."

"Not that I know of," Melodie replied firmly. "These girls, they're good girls, Detective. Just because a woman chooses to dance on a stage, that doesn't make her a bad person. That makes her a professional entertainer, nothing more."

"How many dancers work for you, Ms. Davis?" Holt asked grimly.

"Twelve," she replied.

The music stopped and a roar of cheers and clapping erupted in the club. Then the opening notes of another song started, and the cheering subsided.

"Trisha must be done with her number by now," Melodie said. "I'll go get her for you."

"One more thing, Ms. Davis," Holt asked. "Any overly enthusiastic fans, stalkers, or men who couldn't take no for an answer?"

She thought for a moment before replying. "None come to mind, but I'll ask the bouncers if they've seen anything out of the ordinary."

"Thank you," I said, thinking there was still something I was missing from the big picture.

She shook our hands and took the business card we offered, in case she remembered anything else useful.

"If I may say, Detective," Melodie added, looking straight at me with an intriguing smile, "You would be fabulous out there, on the stage."

Holt swallowed a chuckle, while my jaw dropped. "Whoa, Baxter, she's right, you know," he said quietly, and I wanted to strangle him. Now my partner was picturing me naked and wrapped around a pole. Bloody fabulous.

"Your long, wavy hair, the shape of your body, you're exquisite," Melodie added, while I only managed to shake my head, at a loss for words. She was openly checking me out from head to toe, and, to my complete surprise, I felt my cheeks burning.

"Oh, no, I couldn't," I managed to say eventually. "That's not for me." I was unsure whether to feel insulted or flattered by Melodie's comments.

"Well, if you ever change your mind…" she added, then left the room without waiting for my reply.

The moment the door closed behind her, Holt turned to me and said,

"Great. Now we have twelve potential suspects on our hands."

19

Trisha

"You have got to be kidding me!" Holt snapped, his eyes riveted to his phone's screen, while we both waited for Trisha to make her appearance. He paced the lobby furiously, like a caged animal, and for a second I thought he was going to hurl that phone through the club's front window. The bouncer looked at him, then at me, but his expression remained neutral, unimpressed. He'd probably seen much worse.

"Remember TwoCent, the lowlife I dragged in yesterday morning?" Holt asked, as soon as he stopped swearing.

"The thug who killed Detective Park?"

"The same one," Holt replied, then muttered another string of oaths.

"What happened?" I asked, intrigued by his reaction. I'd never seen Holt so angry in the little time we'd worked together. "Was it a bad bust?"

"No, it was a good bust," he snapped, turning toward me as if I were the enemy. "Ballistics confirmed it last night, the gun was a match to the bullet that killed Park, and TwoCent's fingerprints were all over it. All peachy, perfect for indictment. Only someone broke into the evidence locker and stole the damn piece!"

"They took the gun?" I reacted. "How the hell was that possible? The evidence locker is well guarded, under video surveillance, with key card access. Bloody Fort Knox."

"Well, it happened, and they caught the doer on video, leaving in a rush after he'd zapped the officer on duty with a taser and used his card. In and out, in under a minute. The BOLO has been released, you have his mug in your inbox. Can't fucking believe it."

"Do you have any other evidence against TwoCent? Witnesses, physical evidence, blood stains, anything?"

"We have absolutely bupkis, and the DA had Wallace already sign off on TwoCent's release this afternoon. That cop killer's out on the streets again. I bet he's laughing his ass off, thinking how smart he is and how lame we are. Damn right, we are!"

Now that's something for Dr. Beville's notepad. I felt my blood boil as I pictured TwoCent's smug face flipping the cops on his way out of lockup and giving everyone a lot of lip in barely intelligible street speak. I envisioned him driving off in a black Cadillac Escalade, going to party somewhere to celebrate his release and reward his faithful lieutenant, the bold son of a bitch who'd had the audacity to break into the evidence locker, in a building buzzing with hundreds of cops.

I couldn't take it. I needed to do something about it.

I have this issue with the arrogance of thriving evil, of jubilant wrongdoers. It pisses me off to no end and drives me to take action, even if that action is not mine to take. Even if TwoCent wasn't my collar, and even if I'd never met the now late Detective Park. None of that mattered; to me, it's about right against wrong, the ages-long battle that has defined the history of our species. Sometimes, when at risk of being defeated, the good guys need a little bit of help.

I breathed, trying to calm my rage and willing myself to stay put. It wasn't the right time to burst out of the club, no matter how much I was itching to go out there and erase the smugness from that punk's face. Whatever I did, I now had Holt to worry about, and he couldn't know about it. Not now, not ever.

And then there was Maddie... I wasn't forgetting her. She felt more and more like a friend to me, not just a random victim, some stranger's face pasted in a case file or a name on a coroner's report, someone I never met. It felt as if I knew her, as if she was my neighbor, my cousin, someone I liked, and I was friends with. Someone I would miss, now that she was gone. A dangerous thing to let happen, because it can cloud this cop's judgment. It becomes personal, and once that happens, I can't rest until her killer is chained in a cage. Whatever it takes.

The frosted glass doors opened, and Trisha stepped out into the lobby. I recognized her immediately, having seen her photo in Maddie's apartment. She was stunningly beautiful. She wore her stage outfit, minimalistic yet classy, attractive and well accessorized with metallic flash tattoos on her hands and forehead. Her transparent stiletto sandals clacked with every step she took, and, for a moment, I wondered how she could dance and be on her feet the whole night wearing those. Must be a bitch.

"Trisha, Detectives Baxter and Holt," I said, and took the hand she offered. "Thanks for speaking with us."

"It's about Maddie, isn't it?" she asked, discernible sorrow undertones coloring her voice.

"Yes, it is," I confirmed. "We know you texted with her right before she died. What did she mean by, um," I checked my notes, "'Might drop by later, raise some hell'? Was she coming here?"

"Yes, that's what she meant by that message. I waited for her, but she never showed," Trisha said, not taking her eyes off the floor.

"She liked to dance here at times," Holt intervened. "Ms. Davis told us. But she couldn't tell us why."

Trisha pressed her lips together and hesitated for a moment before replying.

"She liked to dance, yes, that's true. She was amazing, sexy, and a strong, daring athlete. Pole dancing takes strength, coordination, and grace at the same time. She had it all. And she did raise hell whenever she danced."

"What do you mean?"

"She was bolder than the rest of us, because for her, this wasn't a job. It was the way she was getting back at the world, defying everyone, defying her past."

I frowned, intrigued with Trisha's comment.

"Please, tell us what you mean by that," I asked, then invited Trisha to sit on one of the sofas. She accepted, and I sat sideways on my folded leg, turned to face her.

"Maddie and I have known each other since freshman year in high school. We became best friends immediately. She was full of life; she had this energy inside her, as if the whole world belonged to her and was waiting for her to explore, to enjoy. She was unstoppable, but in a kind, decent, and innocent way. She didn't drink, she wasn't into drugs, she was just a good girl. Until the end of high school, when she took a summer job at the Royal Hall Hotel and Casino, and I went to work in my uncle's store."

Trisha stopped talking and let her eyes veer to my right, watching the street for a while. I respected her silence, waiting for her to gather her thoughts.

"She was a minor and couldn't wait tables," Trisha said with a sad chuckle. "She worked as a lifeguard at the hotel's pool, and she loved it. She enjoyed the sun and the water, and the pay was good for someone who was only seventeen. Until one day, when everything changed."

"What happened?" I asked quietly, and squeezed her hand gently.

Trisha shook her lowered head, and a tear rolled down her cheek.

"She never told me, but whatever happened to her that summer changed her, made her become who she was. Angry, defiant, hurting, self-loathing. After that summer, we parted ways for college. I went community, she went state, but we stayed friends. We still saw each other on weekends."

"And she never told you what happened that summer?" I insisted, thinking I was finally getting close to finding some relevant information.

"Not directly, no. She talked about it without specifics."

"What do you mean by that?" Holt asked.

"She kept saying that no one would listen, no one would believe her, and so on. That was then, that summer when we'd just turned seventeen. Whatever it was, it screwed her up badly."

"Trisha," I said, "if you were to guess, what do you think happened to Maddie that year?"

"I thought about it many times," she said, keeping her eyes lowered. I heard tears in her voice, choking her a little, making her sound frail, almost afraid. "I think she was roughed up by someone, maybe even raped. I don't think she'd... ever been with a man until then."

"Then what happened?" Holt asked, a bit too impatient for my taste. I shot him a quick glance to slow him down.

"Then her mother happened," Trisha replied, looking at me with a flash of something fierce in her tearful eyes. "The pompous bitch shut her up, didn't let her speak a word about what happened. She couldn't handle having the family reputation dragged through courtrooms and newspapers." Trisha let out a bitter, wry laugh. "What reputation? They were nobodies. Maybe less nobodies than my family was, but still. She didn't care, Maddie's mother. She forced her daughter to shut up about what happened and never seek justice. She wouldn't let Maddie speak with the cops."

While I listened, I tried to put the pieces of the puzzle together in my mind, but they didn't fit. That incident must have taken place eleven years ago. It was unfortunate, but most likely unrelated. Who would care now about what had happened to Maddie way back when? It wasn't a real lead... it was thinner than spider silk.

"That's all I know," Trisha said. "I'm sorry. I knew how painful it was for Maddie to talk about it, so I let her be and never asked. Her mother might know more, but my guess is she'd rather die than tell you anything."

"Then what happened?" I asked, "with Maddie? How was she after that?"

Trisha lowered her head again. "She turned dark... She started referring to herself as a piece of meat, ripe for Las Vegas prime time. It broke my heart." She sniffled quietly and looked at me briefly before lowering her gaze again. "She started picking guys up, sleeping around, then she'd stop and cry for a week or so, then start again. About that time, she started dancing; it was her relief, I guess. She'd take it further than everyone else here, because she hated herself. She felt tainted, damaged, and she wanted everyone to know it, to see it, to despise her too." She looked at me again and grabbed my arm with both her hands. "I loved her, Detective. She was a good person."

I nodded, thanking her for her help. She didn't let go of my arm, telling me she wasn't finished talking yet.

"There's something else," Trisha said hesitantly. "It might be nothing, but... She kept saying something, since her sister got engaged to the governor. She said, 'Now they're going to listen to me. Now I can get someone to listen to me.' She kept saying that, over and over these past few weeks."

Holt and I locked eyes for a split second. Spider silk might have been stronger than I thought; after all, it's one of the most resistant materials known, regardless of how delicate it seems. One phrase, and the pieces of the puzzle started fitting together nicely. Everyone knew about Caroline's engagement to the governor, including Maddie's attacker from eleven years ago. Maybe whatever happened that summer was a secret worth killing for. That meant her attacker knew who Maddie was; she wasn't just some random stranger to him. Her attacker had kept tabs on Maddie this entire time.

And maybe I was getting way ahead of myself. I didn't know any of that for sure; it was just a supposition, but one that made sense.

"Thank you, Trisha," I said, and offered her my card. "Please don't hesitate to call me. This is my cell number. Anything you remember could help."

She shook my hand, with an unspoken request in her eyes, and I nodded in response. I didn't need words to understand her.

"Do you think anyone here, at the club, might have wanted to harm her?" Holt asked. I had forgotten all about the other dancers. For some reason, that scenario didn't seem to fit in my mind, but Holt was right to ask. We couldn't ignore any lead, no matter how improbable.

"I don't think anyone here could've killed Maddie," Trisha said, a little hesitant. "Some of the girls liked her a lot. You can ask them," she added, then apologized that she had to go and disappeared through the frosted glass doors.

20

The Dancers

We huddled next to the main entrance and turned our backs to the bouncer, trying to keep our conversation out of his earshot.

"I think we have our first solid lead," I said. "Someone could've freaked out, learning the woman he'd once raped will soon be related to the governor. I like this; it makes perfect sense."

"The statute of limitations is long expired," Holt said, rubbing his stubbly chin. "I don't see why a smart perp who managed to stay hidden for eleven years would take the risk of killing someone in the middle of a crowded hotel, to do what? Make sure his secret is safe? Well, it has been safe, for years."

I had to agree he was right. My theory made sense, but only up to a point.

"Then, what do you think happened?"

"I don't know. I'm holding out hope that the fingerprints they found on the body and on Maddie's cell phone are in AFIS, and we'll scoop up the killer, case closed." He stopped talking, and rubbed the nape of his neck vigorously, then continued. "But we don't know if that will happen. Maybe one of these girls hated Maddie enough to kill her."

"Didn't we establish that her killer was a man? I don't see how someone making a living out of one-dollar bill tips can afford to contract out a murder."

"No, but these girls have men in their lives. Boyfriends, pimps, even obsessive fans who'd kill for them."

I shrugged, unconvinced. I still liked the idea of the mysterious rapist better, despite the statute of limitations. Statute or not, some people don't like to have their criminal pasts exposed; there are many things one can lose outside of their freedom: money, careers, alliances, political futures, who knows what else.

However, we were still in the Kitty's Whiskers' lobby, and it made sense to speak with a few more of those dancers. I extended my arm in an invitation. "After you, partner."

The bouncer didn't react when we approached the frosted glass doors and went inside. He stayed behind in the lobby, impassible.

The club was large, lavishly decorated with circular, elevated stages where the girls performed, surrounded by small tables for the customers. Almost no one sat at those tables though; most men leaned against the stages holding cash in their hands, hollering, wolf-whistling, pushing one another out of the way, and stretching out to try to touch the dancers. The stages, cleverly elevated about 5 feet above ground, made that impossible, and the dancers had their safe area where they could perform without being hassled. Projector lights from the ceiling moved with the rhythm of the music, rendering the entire show the look and feel of a carefully choreographed dance performance. Way classier than I'd imagined.

Holt's eyes were fixed on a hot brunette with incredible curves. The way that dancer's moves grabbed Holt's attention made me laugh, but he didn't seem to notice. Typical male in a strip joint… forgot everything he came there to do.

I touched his arm, drawing his attention to a slim redhead dressed in a strappy lingerie set with a garter belt attached to her over-the-knee stiletto boots. She wore some of her hair in a fishtail braid with extensions, and nervously ran her henna-adorned hand through her loose curls when she saw me approach her.

I pulled out my badge, and she seemed relieved. That was a first. She probably feared jealous wives more than cops.

"Detectives Baxter and Holt. Your name?"

"Diamond," she replied with a well-rehearsed smile. "Um, I mean, Audrey Preston," she added, seemingly embarrassed.

"Did you know Madeline Munroe?"

"Yes, I knew her, we all did," she replied, lowering her eyes for a moment. "What a horrible thing happened to her… I couldn't believe it when I heard."

"Did you resent her?" Holt asked, in his overly direct, almost rash manner. "Because she danced for free, for the heck of it, taking business away from you? Totally understandable if you did, you know," he added, "nothing to be ashamed of."

"No, I didn't hate her," Diamond replied, shaking her head vigorously. "Mostly, I just felt sorry for her."

"Sorry? Why?" I asked.

"Most of us, we do this to survive," she said, clutching her hands together and shifting her weight from one foot to the other. "We become numb; we force ourselves to not see or hear them anymore," she added, gesturing toward the customers clustered around the nearest stage. "Otherwise, I couldn't take it. It's… horrible," she said, lowering her voice and shooting glances all around, probably afraid someone might hear her. "I can't worry about what I'll do when I'm too old for the stage. I can't let any of their libidinous comments reach me, or the touch of their hands when they shove those dollar bills in my panties."

"And Maddie?"

"Maddie wasn't like me, like most of us. She wasn't numb. She enjoyed it, and that made me feel sorry for her."

"Can you think of anyone who hated Maddie?" Holt asked, while a deep frown had started to ridge his forehead. I wondered what was on his mind.

Diamond looked around quickly, then pointed toward a stage farther back. "Pink Fuzz over there. She despised Maddie. She and Maddie got into it a couple of times, but Maddie could hold her own and wasn't fazed by her attitude."

The girl she'd pointed out was dancing lasciviously in a bikini covered in long, pink feathers that undulated with the movements of her body, holding on to the pole as she threw her legs in the air, seeming almost weightless.

I thanked Diamond and she was quick to disappear; a moment later, Diamond was dancing on a purple shaded stage, a few feet to our left.

"Let's grab Pink Fuzz," I said, and I sensed Holt following me through the crowds. He stopped me when we were a few feet away from her stage.

"Let's wait until she finishes her number," he offered, and I laughed out loud, turning a few heads.

"You'd really like that, wouldn't you?" I asked, and I thought I saw a bit of color rushing into Holt's cheeks.

"That's not what I meant, Baxter," he said, raising his voice to cover the music.

"Uh-huh," I replied, then flashed my badge until the customers scattered and I could reach the stage. I waited for a moment until Pink Fuzz caught a glimpse of my badge, then she reluctantly approached us with a grimace of contempt on her face and her hands propped on her hips.

"What do you want?" she asked, still panting from the physical effort of her performance.

"We want to talk to you about Madeline Munroe," I said.

"What about her? The bitch is dead. End of story."

"I see you're all heartbroken about it," Holt said.

"Yeah, right," she replied with a glimmer of pure hatred in her eyes. "Wannabes like her ruin the business, drop the pay, only harm those like us who have to live from the money we make dancing."

"Why was she doing it?" I asked, wondering if we knew all there was to know about Maddie's motivations.

"Hell if I know," she replied. "Bitch was rich, college educated, didn't know what to do with herself and came here whenever she felt like it, to ruin my mood."

"You were seen arguing with her a few times," Holt said. "What was that about?"

"About her getting the fuck outta here and never coming back. But the floozy wouldn't get lost, no matter what."

I looked at Holt briefly. There was enough hate in Pink Fuzz to call it motive.

"Where were you yesterday afternoon?"

"You think I strangled her? Ha! I wish."

"Please answer the question," I said coldly.

"Where do you think I was? Right here, wiggling my ass under video surveillance. The madam can show that to you."

"Did anyone strangle her for you? Seeing how vocal you are about her, if I were a fan or a lover, I might not hesitate."

She broke up laughing, making the tips of the feathers lining her bikini tremble in the shimmering lights. "Can you keep a secret?" she asked, as soon as she could control her braying, testimony of a life of drinking and smoking without restraint.

I nodded, curious about what she had to share that was so private, considering she was showing almost everything she had on a stage, every night.

"I'm a dyke," she replied. "There aren't any men in my life. After these pigs, do you think I can stand the sight of them?" she added, gesturing to some of the customers with an expression of utmost contempt on her face, seeping clearly into the tones of her voice.

"One more thing," Holt asked. "How did you know Maddie was strangled?"

She laughed again, this time less enthusiastically, more like a sardonic chuckle. "Don't you guys watch the news?"

21

Plans

"Who the hell leaked it? DC Wallace will throw a fit." I asked, scampering toward the car in the freezing wind. I wasn't really expecting an answer.

Holt unlocked his car and we climbed inside, then he grabbed the laptop and started searching the internet for the newscast. "There it is," he said, then pushed the laptop closer to me.

The piece of news was less than five minutes long. It included a few seconds shot at the Aquamarine, showing Maddie's body being transported toward the coroner's van, nothing but a shape covered in black plastic. The reporter identified her by name and proceeded in bringing up the governor and his upcoming nuptials with the victim's sister, in an overly dramatic voice that only newspeople have. They probably learn that in journalism school, how to be so theatrical when speaking, and what words to use for maximum impact. Then the reporter proceeded to name Holt and me as detectives in the case, and threw in fifteen-second biographies for us both.

The story then cut to an interview with the governor, who took the media's questions from the doorway of his own home.

"My heart goes out to my fiancée, Caroline, who was Madeline's sister, and to their mother, Mrs. Elizabeth Munroe, during these trying times. I have been personally reassured by Deputy Chief Wallace—"

"Ahh…" Holt interjected with sarcasm, then pursed his lips.

"—that no effort will be spared until Madeline's killer is brought to justice," the governor continued. Then he raised his hand in an apologetic gesture and disappeared inside his house while the reporters clamored, asking questions even after he'd closed the door.

The news piece cut to an interview with DC Wallace himself, taken in the LVMPD building lobby.

"Yesterday was a sad day for Las Vegas," Wallace said, in front of the cameras, "to see a young, innocent life being taken with such violence. Our community is shocked and devastated by this gruesome murder." He paused for effect, struggling to maintain his composure when, in fact, he was beaming in the limelight. He cleared his throat quietly, then continued. "Our entire police force is committed to catching this killer, and we will spare no effort, no expense, until the monster who strangled Madeline Munroe is locked behind bars. Detectives Baxter and Holt are two of the best criminal-hunting minds in our department, and the weight of our entire force is behind them."

Then the news piece ended with the reporter stating that she would keep the viewers posted with any new developments. The video ended, leaving silence in the car.

"What a jerk," I said, referring to Wallace. I was flattered by the way he'd introduced us to the media, but that didn't fool me one bit. "He could barely contain himself in front of the cameras."

"And now you know who leaked it," Holt replied somberly. "That doesn't mean he won't rip us a new one. I don't expect him to admit it."

I chuckled bitterly. "Maybe there's hope. After all, the governor himself mentioned Wallace by name. He must be riding on cloud nine right about now."

Holt gave me a long stare. "I hope you're right."

I paused for a moment, thinking of what we knew about Madeline, what leads we had. Despite Holt's logic, I still believed the spider silk lead had merit, but finding a rapist from eleven years ago, a protagonist in an unreported incident, where no evidence was collected, and no witness testimonies were recorded, made for an impossible task. Spider silk might be strong, but it's nearly invisible. Then my mind jumped to what I'd recently learned about Holt, courtesy of an overly dramatic TV reporter.

"I didn't know you were a marketing major," I said, with a quick chuckle.

"Yeah, can you believe it?" His uneven grin appeared. "Talk about getting lost on the way to your career."

"So... Former Navy, marketing grad, and detective. Is that all I need to know about my new partner?"

His grin died, while he lowered his eyes. "You already know the addict part, so, yeah, that's all there is to know about me."

I let that slide, eager to change the subject. No one stood anything to gain if we couldn't move past his struggle with addiction. "Desert sailor, huh? Where in the Navy?"

"On an aircraft carrier, for six years," he stated, matter-of-factly.

We sat in silence for a while, and I let my mind wander back to the case, and how little information we had, even after interviewing those dancers.

"I meant to ask you before, what was on your mind in there?"

"When?"

"When you were asking Diamond if anyone hated Maddie."

"Yeah," he said with a sigh, then reached for a bottle of water and took a sip. "I was thinking about Mrs. Munroe. If she'd somehow learned her daughter stripped for fun, just how mad could she have been? I believe that's our strongest motive yet."

"Holt, I told you, I didn't read her as a killer," I reacted. "I didn't get that vibe. She was calm, with nothing to hide."

"And yet she does have something to hide. Maddie's rape, for example."

"That happened a long time ago. She might not even think about it anymore, making any signs of deception absent from her facial expression. But this? This would be recent, she'd have emotions about the murder, emotions I didn't sense at all."

"Don't you think the governor might look for another bride if he knew Maddie was a stripper? That could damage his political future. The tabloids would never let that one go."

I let the thought sink in. Holt was right. If the truth about Maddie's favorite pastime came out, it could've been a disaster. It could still happen.

"Okay, but it's funny how you suspect the mother, but not the governor? Or Caroline?"

"Huh… that's an interesting idea," he said. "I didn't think of that. Do you really believe the governor of Nevada would hire a murderer to clean up his family history? I know the guy; he just doesn't seem like that kind of person."

"My gut tells me it's not the witch mother; your gut tells you it's not the governor. Really? That's all we have, after more than a day? We have to do better than this. We need real evidence, witnesses, testimony."

"Forensics are delayed; they said they're due first thing tomorrow. We'll have more then. Financials too."

I scrolled through my inbox, looking for a note from Anne. There wasn't anything from her, but I saw the BOLO that Holt had mentioned earlier, for the thug who stole the murder weapon in the Park case. Frowning and squinting in the dim light, I opened the grainy surveillance photo and looked at the perp's face. He was shown running out of evidence storage, but his hands were empty. He wasn't carrying anything. Where was the gun he'd stolen? I zoomed in as far as my phone allowed and studied him. There was a bulge in his jacket; he might've put the gun in there. For several moments, I stared at his face, burning it into my memory, and wondering whether there was anything I could do about it.

There had to be; the thought of TwoCent walking free after killing a cop was not something I could easily shrug off. But first, I had to ditch Holt.

"Why don't we stop for tonight? You have a meeting to attend," I said, and fished my car keys out of my pocket.

"It's almost eleven," he said, probably getting ready to argue with me, but I didn't let that happen.

"All the more reason to step on it. I'm sure there's still one you can find."

Holt groaned and let himself sink lower into his car seat, then closed his eyes.

"Pick me up tomorrow at seven?"

"Yeah," he said, keeping his eyes closed. "We'll start with the lab?"

"Seven's a bit early for them," I replied, knowing that Anne would text me the moment she had anything. I was planning to text her anyway, later that night, a bit concerned that fingerprint processing took so long. While I could understand the delay when it came to the prints recovered from Maddie's body,

I couldn't think of any logical explanation why those lifted off her phone would've taken so much time. We should've had a result by now.

"Maybe the financials will be in by then," he said, stubbornly refusing to open his eyes. He looked tired, drawn.

"Maybe. Seven in the morning isn't too early for construction though," I said serenely. Holt opened his eyes and glanced at me, and a hint of a smile touched his lips.

"Maddie's father?"

"None other. Let's talk to him first thing, before DC Wallace has the time to say otherwise. Better ask for forgiveness—"

"Than permission," he continued. "You got it. See you tomorrow."

I stepped out of his car into the brisk wind and watched his taillights as they faded away toward the interstate. For a brief moment, I wondered what he thought of me. Except maybe for the suspect beating issue, he must see me as a righteous cop who does everything by the book, someone who is well within her rights to send him to AA meetings, because she doesn't do anything wrong.

If only he knew.

22

Night Prowler

Sometimes, I do what I have to do. Even if it's not my job to do it. Even if I don't have what it legally takes to do that particular thing. Yet I never worry about the procedural maze that confines the parameters of my day job, with concepts such as probable cause, subpoena, warrant, legal search and seizure, and so on, because, you see, I'm after hours. And what I do with my own time is my own choice.

My extracurricular activities started almost two years ago, when Andrew's absence filled the house, leaving me barren and wandering from room to room, searching for something that could no longer be found. My rage, knowing his killer was still at large, made me want to beat the streets, prowling, hunting for that son of a bitch, agonizing for the moment I'd be able to slap some cuffs on him and throw him in a hellhole so deep he'd never be able to see the light of day again.

For the longest time, I couldn't find Andrew's killer, so I settled for the next best thing: Giving my daytime colleagues an unseen nudge, a bit of help in cases that otherwise risked ending up in the unsolved pile, leaving thugs and murderers at large on the streets, to do more harm. Don't get me wrong; I don't plant evidence or assume I know who the perp is just because I'm beyond doing honest police work. No, it's nothing like that, I promise. But if a warrant gets denied on a stupid technicality, or because an ADA is afraid of too much media attention, that's when I put in my unofficial overtime.

My choice that night was to do what was right, what needed to be done. Even if TwoCent was not my collar, and Detective Park's murder was not my case. I didn't know what to expect; I planned on going out there with an open mind. I knew that Nieblas and Crocker were probably out there themselves, looking for the man who broke into our evidence locker, but it wouldn't hurt if someone else looked too. I just needed to be careful not to run into them. And maybe I knew a little bit more about criminal offender psychology, to anticipate where I would find that thief.

The first thing I did that night, as soon as I got home, was to call Technical

Services and ask them to locate TwoCent's cell phone. I gave them my badge number. I held my breath and my fingers crossed for a long minute, then I learned that his phone was pinging at one of the Strip's poshest bars, Slice of Ice. It made sense; he was celebrating, just as I thought he would.

Satisfied, I hung up the call and accessed the known associates database on my personal laptop. A few searches later, I had the name of TwoCent's best friend on the inside, from when he'd done time for manslaughter at High Desert State Prison. The gods smiled on me that night, because his good old buddy, a hulk of a brute going by the nickname Digger, was still locked up serving life without parole for yeah, you guessed it, burying his victims alive. He was still pulling strings from the inside, just like I needed him to. Excellent.

Then I texted Anne quickly, wolfing down a few morsels of Swiss cheese while standing with the refrigerator door open. She texted me right back, with a message that brought a deep frown on my brow.

Still verifying some facts; fingerprints returned a highly unlikely match in AFIS, Anne's text message read. *Double-checking tonight, then I'll have results to you by tomorrow am. We're good?*

Golden, I texted back, then added an intrigued smiley to my text.

It didn't happen often that fingerprint analysis returned a highly unlikely match. What did that even mean? A match was a match, or it wasn't. AFIS either got a hit, or it didn't. I actually couldn't think of another time in my entire career when that had happened, and I couldn't think of a scenario that would fit her findings.

I closed the door to the fridge and swallowed the last half-chewed bite of cheese, then washed my face thoroughly and patted it dry. I stripped down to my underwear, but saved my day clothes on a chair, instead of throwing them in the dirty laundry hamper. Then I put on evening makeup, a tad too accentuated; call girl meets stage performer was the look I was going for. I decided to play up my eyes and went all in with eyeliner, shadow, and mascara. I added a discreet pink to my lips, a stay-in-place lip gloss, and finalized my look with touches of blush on my cheeks and the tip of my nose.

Then I let my long hair loose from the braided bun that comes with being a cop. Long hair like mine can prove a liability if a perp grabs hold of it, leaving me no choice but to lift it up and pull it into a knot at the back of my head. I combed through the long, wavy strands for a good minute, until it regained its shine and started crackling with static electricity. Then I applied hairspray generously from a distance, to preserve its natural bounce.

I walked toward the spare bedroom closet and pulled the doors open, searching for a specific look. A few moments later, I had what I was looking for. Kiki de Montparnasse lingerie, barely there, in bone color. A black, side-slash miniskirt, and a pink sequined, off-the-shoulder, loose top that would hide my gun holster perfectly. I added a few layers of fine necklaces in different lengths and clipped on a pair of long, shimmering earrings. I never wear anything but clip or magnetic earrings; a perp can do some real damage if he grabs and pulls a pierced earring, not worth the risk. The final touch was a pair of open mesh stiletto booties from Christian Louboutin, one of the very few extravagances I could afford out of a cop's salary.

I checked myself out in the mirror, while I thought that if things worked out well, I should charge the department wear and tear on the Louboutins on a personal vehicle mileage expense form. Yeah, like they were ever going to pay. Satisfied with the image smiling provocatively back at me from the wall-sized mirror, I strapped on the smallest gun harness I had, hiding a 9 mil Sig P938 snugged tightly against my ribs.

The next stop was my makeup table, again, where I took a seat in front of the mirror and carefully applied liquid latex to my fingers and palms, let it dry, then applied again. I tested the result, made sure it wasn't peeling off, and, satisfied I wasn't leaving fingerprints anymore, switched off the powerful lights and closed the door behind me.

Then I went into my home office and opened that closet. I pulled aside the clothing hanging there and gained access to the back wall. I pressed toward the side and a panel popped open, exposing the collection I had stashed in there. I had over 150 firearms, twenty-something knives and other weapons, mostly coming from the street, where I'd done the world a favor and confiscated them from various low lives, also in my spare time.

I'm a positive thinker, an absolute optimist when it comes to believing in justice, despite my own personal tragedy; it's what keeps me going. Therefore, I didn't want to leave the house without being prepared for the best possible scenario. I quickly checked the BOLO one more time; the murder weapon in the Park case was a Smith and Wesson M&P M2.0 Compact 9 mil, black. I didn't have that specific gun in my collection, but I had something close, an M2.0 RDS. It takes a trained eye and a close examination to spot the differences. My item was a street "buy," serial number filed off, and I took a few minutes carefully wiping it clean of any prints.

Then I opened a drawer and extracted an evidence bag, put the gun inside, sealed it, and attached a chain of custody tag. I scribbled in a few entries in different pen colors to match the image in the BOLO, then fit the evidence bag into a purse. The lowest drawer on that closet wall held another item needed for my plan to work. I opened it and grabbed a tiny Ziploc bag with several white pills inside, then closed my purse, smiling, anticipating the excitement, the thrill of the hunt.

I was ready for action.

23

Slice of Ice

I'd never been to Slice of Ice before; it's way above my pay grade. But I've heard about it and seeing it didn't disappoint. It's a rooftop dance club, tastefully laid out on two levels. The main terrace overlooks the Strip and its myriad lights. Furnished with leather armchairs and sofas, it looks more like a lounge than an actual nightclub. The dance floor, the bar, and the booths are housed under the upper floor ceiling and an awning, discerningly designed in stainless steel and glass. Lasers, strobes, and LED dynamic lighting projectors hung from that glass-and-metal ceiling, throwing beams of light in perfect harmony with the loud techno beats.

I wandered around the main terrace, but TwoCent wasn't anywhere to be seen. I climbed the curved glass staircase to the upper level, then returned empty-handed to the main level. Just as I was starting to worry he'd slipped away, I caught a glimpse of him, seated in a booth near the dance floor.

It was a semicircular booth in black leather around a small table. TwoCent sat next to the edge, leaning into his elbows and playing with his glass. The thug who'd broken into the evidence locker sat next to TwoCent, in the middle, and a third one, much younger, took the other edge. For a brief moment, I wondered why Nieblas and Crocker weren't all over TwoCent, when it was logical that's where the gun thief would be. But sometimes, working though proper channels slows things down considerably; they might still be waiting for the proper approvals to hang a tail on the recently released TwoCent, to avoid a potential harassment lawsuit the smug bastard wouldn't think twice before filing.

I focused on their booth and took in all the details. A fresh bottle of whiskey had just been opened for them, and the youngest was filling everyone's glasses, while TwoCent was making obscene gestures at some of the dancers on the floor.

"Yo', bring it on, baby, yeah! Shake that booty! Twerk that ass!" TwoCent yelled, trying to cover the blaring music and succeeding, at least from where I stood.

I took a deep breath, feeling the anticipation excitement rush the blood through my veins. I straightened my back and walked toward him slowly, provocatively, slightly tilting my head and swinging my hips. I caught his attention when I was about 10 feet from his table, and as I approached him, I made eye contact, smiling, licking my lips.

He pushed himself back against the leather couch and dropped his hands in his lap. "Whoa, baby," he said, sizing me up. The other two started whooping and catcalling, but I didn't take my eyes off the prize. I approached the table and leaned low against it, keeping my legs straight and my rear end propped up, then came close to his ear and whispered, "Hey, gangsta'," close enough so he could feel my breath on his face. His proximity made my skin crawl, but the thrill of the hunt took that edge off nicely. I'd entered in character, like actors say, and I was living it. I made the high-end Vegas call girl I was playing come to life, real, authentic, irresistible.

He fidgeted in place, grinning like an idiot, while I started to move slowly around the table, looking for the stolen gun. It was a long shot it would be there, but I kept on looking. I ran my finger across the table surface to keep their eyes focused on what I wanted, then against the booth's edge, and tried to see if the one who'd broken into the evidence locker still had that bulge in his jacket. No, he didn't, and through one of those rare moments of pure luck, I saw the gun, sealed in its evidence bag, on the seat, right between TwoCent and the man who'd stolen it. It was unbelievable that they hadn't disposed of it yet at the bottom of some deep hole, but thugs like TwoCent and his gang weren't particularly famous for their intelligence. The arrogant twerp must've wanted it as a trophy.

My smile widened; I knew what I had to do. I just needed to take my time, so they wouldn't be spooked. Slowly, I returned to TwoCent's side and leaned against the table again, tilting my head. "Can I buy you boys a drink?" I asked, ignoring the almost full bottle at the center of the small table.

TwoCent's idiotic grin died, and my heart skipped a beat. He grabbed my arm forcefully and drew me closer.

"Whoa... not so fast, bitch," he said, thrusting his chin forward angrily. "Think I'm a fool? Who sent you?"

I let myself be handled without resisting and continued to smile.

"Digger heard you're celebrating tonight," I said, keeping my eyes riveted into his, while hoping the known associates database was up to date, and that TwoCent and Digger hadn't parted ways after some death match the cops had no idea about. But no, there was no rage, no flicker of fear in his eyes. "I'm the icing," I said, then licked my lips again.

"Holla," TwoCent's grin returned, and he nodded a few times while looking at his buddies, who hollered appreciatively, as if TwoCent's merit had brought me there.

"Just when I thought the night couldn't get any better," said TwoCent, then grabbed my butt firmly.

Calmly, I wiggled myself free of his hand and leaned toward his ear again. "Whoa... gangsta', we got time. Let's party first, all right?" I traced my finger along his tense jaw. "On Digger. 'Go big, or go home,' he said," I added, and cringed when I saw TwoCent frown. He stared at me for a long moment, but I didn't flinch.

"Or die tryin'," he said, and the other two roared with laughter. "Ain't going home for nothing. I'll tell Digger you forgot his words. He'll whup yo' ass."

I raised my hand in the air. "My bad... my bad. Why don't I make up for that, huh?" I stood straight, still making eye contact with TwoCent. "Why don't you name your poison?"

Moments later, I slowly made across the dance floor feeling their eyes on me as I strolled toward the bar, undulating my hips on those high-heeled Louboutins and getting enough unwanted male attention to last me a lifetime. Good; that would keep TwoCent enticed for a while longer.

I ordered their choices and bought a drink for myself too, then made quick work of spiking their drinks with a couple of roofies each, erring on the side of caution. If they woke up with a hell of a headache the next morning, I wouldn't feel too badly about it. Then I carried the tray over to their table, smiling, not skipping a beat.

"Thug Passion for you," I said, and put a tall glass in front of TwoCent. He grabbed it and drank half of it in one thirsty gulp. Good boy.

"Brass Monkey for you," I said, offering the gun thief the second drink. "What's your name, by the way?"

He grinned like a nitwit, showing two missing teeth on his upper left side. "You can call me Colt."

"Abelardo," the third one cackled. "His name is Abelardo. You know what rhymes with that?"

Colt promptly smacked the youngest one with his elbow, but he continued. "Abelardo el Bastardo," he laughed some more, until Abelardo smacked him again, harder. "That's his new street name."

"And a Hurricane for you, um...?"

His smile vanished as he blushed. "Call me Hash," he said, fidgeting badly under my lascivious scrutiny. "I get it, you know, whenever you need it. For you, I might get some for free," he added in a slightly trembling voice, then swallowed hard. That half-pint was more aroused than he could handle, probably blue-balled already.

"Uh-huh," I replied, taking a long sip from my own drink.

"What you having?" TwoCent asked, and I could hear the slurring starting to take over. By tomorrow he wouldn't recall anything from our conversation, not a single word.

"Mojito," I replied, omitting to tell him I'd instructed the bartender to skip the rum.

TwoCent reached for my butt again and almost grabbed it, but I avoided his hand and raised my glass, toast after toast, until most of their drinks were gone, and their pupils nicely dilated. Then I stood next to Hash and said coldly, "You and your buddy need to go take a leak. I wanna sit next to my man," I added, then smiled again.

They didn't think to ask any questions, or disobey in any way, especially after TwoCent waved them away. They stood, a little wobbly on their feet, and disappeared quickly in the throng of dancers. I sat on the leather seat and slid toward TwoCent, then distracted him, pointing at a stunning blonde on the dance floor.

"You know her?" I asked, while I unzipped my purse. "I bet you'd leave me for her in a heartbeat, huh?"

"Nah… would never," he replied, and turned toward me. I groaned in disbelief, then chose another girl to point at. "How about her? That redhead in blue? She's got moves, that one."

He checked her out, bobbing his head with the music, while I removed the gun I'd brought with me from the purse, and put it on the bench. Now there were two guns on the bench between TwoCent and me, and if he turned his head to look, I'd be in trouble.

"That skank? She ain't got nothing on you, babe," he said, starting to slur badly, but still wanting to turn toward me.

"I bet you've done her," I said accusingly, showing him a young African American girl who was giving him the occasional flirtatious eye. He turned to look at her, and took his hand to his sweaty forehead; by now, he was probably feeling the full effects of those roofies.

I didn't have much time left. I grabbed the gun I'd come to recover and quickly shoved it inside my purse, but he sensed my abrupt move and probably remembered something through the fog of his high.

"What you got in there, baby?" he said, and reached for my purse.

I pushed myself away from him, and offered him the other gun instead. "Looking for this?"

"Ahh, yeah," he replied, then grabbed the gun with both his hands. Instead of hiding it in his pocket or something, he put it back on the bench, next to him, and held his hand on top of it for a while. I don't know why I expected more, but I was almost disappointed. Such an idiot, and they couldn't build a case against him without Holt stepping in, or me doing, um, overtime? Amazing.

"Hey, baby," he yelled, seeing I was leaving his side.

I stood and came close to TwoCent's face again, then touched his lips with my finger.

"Hush," I said quietly. "I need to powder my nose, then we'll go wherever you want to go, all right?"

"Uh-huh," he said, then dropped his head on the table.

I made a beeline for the exit but ran into Colt, who grabbed me unceremoniously, almost knocking me off my stilettos.

"Where the fuck do you think you're going?" He was barely slurring; probably he would've needed more than two roofies to do him in properly.

"Ladies room," I replied, clasping my purse tightly.

He frowned and stared at me for a second or two. "It's through there," he said, pointing in a different direction.

"Show me," I said, and he let go of my arm.

I was about to score bonus points. I followed him as he made his way through the crowd. When he entered the small foyer leading to the restrooms, no one else was there, so I took the opportunity and whipped him with the handle of my gun. He dropped like a fly and hit the ground hard, with a loud thump that no one heard.

I opened a broom closet and dragged him in there, with difficulty. He was big, over 250 pounds, and dragging dead weight on stilettos really sucks. But I managed somehow, then, after making sure no one saw me, I closed the door behind me and left in a hurry.

I'd done what I'd come there to do. Now I had to do one more thing: Put the gun back into the evidence locker, without anyone being the wiser.

24

Evidence Locker

It was three in the morning by the time I took those mesh Louboutin booties off my tired feet, in the peacefulness of my living room. The day wasn't over yet, but I smiled to myself every time I laid eyes on the gun I'd recovered: the murder weapon in the Park case, still sealed inside the evidence bag, and, in one of those rare moments when Lady Luck shows her face in the city that lives by chanting her name, with the chain of custody tag still intact.

Now the challenge was to put it back inside the evidence locker in such a manner that it would be still admissible in court, although it had already been reported stolen. Not an easy feat; I still didn't know how I was going to pull that off.

I don't always have a step-by-step plan; many times, I only know what I want, what the end result should be, and I follow my gut as I make my way toward that goal. This time would probably be no different.

I poured myself the cold, stale remnants of yesterday's morning coffee from the machine and gulped it down unceremoniously; I needed a jolt of energy. Then I carefully put on latex gloves, to shield the protective layer that covered my fingerprints, and started to remove my evening makeup. Then I applied fresh makeup, quickly, making it look as if it had been on my face since that morning. A little smudged, the lipstick faded, the eyeliner and mascara completely absent. Then I braided my hair and pinned it into the typical bun I wear at work, making sure it didn't look all that perfect.

Finally, I put on the clothes I'd worn to work all day. They were wrinkled and sweaty, supporting the new act I was playing: a detective putting in long overtime, looking to review evidence in her case in the wee hours of the morning. I expected heightened security at the property locker after the break in: increased manpower, video surveillance, who knows what else. I didn't know what exactly to prepare for.

One more thing needed to be done. I cleaned the table thoroughly with Clorox bleach, to remove all DNA, trace evidence, even the tiniest speck of dust. Then I laid a sheet of new wrapping paper on the table and set the evidence bag on it. Carefully, I took a cotton swab and soaked it in Clorox, then wiped the evidence bag inch by inch. Even if I hadn't left any fingerprints, my DNA was all over it, because it had come in contact with my things, my clothes, my purse, my skin. The only thing I couldn't swab with cleaner was the chain of custody tag; it would dissolve the ink, making the writing illegible. I needed that intact to make the murder weapon admissible in court. I thought for a while, unsure of what to do. Then I had an idea, maybe not the brightest, but the only solution I could think of.

I took apart my razor and extracted a blade, then gently ran it across the label, applying just enough pressure to peel off a thin layer of paper, but leaving the writing on it intact, albeit a little blurred. Any DNA would've been shaved off that label too.

Then I realized I'd done the operations in the wrong order. I'd scraped DNA off the label *after* I'd cleaned the plastic of the bag, but now, particles of that DNA had contaminated the plastic all over again. *Bloody bollocks.* I wiped the shavings away from the table with the swab, then cleaned the plastic all over again, this time using peroxide, to make sure any surviving DNA evidence on that bag would be burned by the released oxygen.

The final step was to unseal a brand-new box of gallon Ziploc bags and slowly extract one. The problem with the polyethylene in bags is that it easily generates static electricity through friction, and static attracts particles from the air, from surfaces, from the hands manipulating the plastic, making it almost impossible to render clean all trace elements. Two long minutes later, the evidence bag holding the murder weapon was sealed inside a new Ziploc bag and tucked inside my jacket.

About twenty minutes later, I was signing in at the evidence locker counter, and commenting about the newly installed bulletproof glass where it used to be an open desk. It made sense, considering that the property clerk who'd manned that station the day before had been tased during the break-in. The night shift clerk didn't smile and didn't appreciate my humor about the events; he was probably feeling somewhat more apprehensive about his job than he used to.

He checked my ID thoroughly, and the only change in procedure I noticed was that he actually looked up my badge number in the system, then compared the photo on the screen with my badge and my appearance. Satisfied, he pushed a button and unlocked the thick wire gate, and I stepped in.

"Know where you're going?" he asked, forcing himself to sound helpful.

"Yeah, I'm good," I replied, eager to disappear from his direct view, and from the surveillance camera feed above his head.

I hurried along endless rows of shelving filled with neatly labeled cardboard boxes holding case evidence. Recent cases were placed together, and I quickly located the Munroe case evidence. A few feet away from that location, yellow tape surrounded the area where the Park case evidence had been stolen.

I looked behind me, visualizing Abelardo grabbing the gun from that case and making for the exit with it tucked inside his jacket. A few yards behind me, the janitor's cart was pulled to the side, almost blocking the entire aisle. I wondered if it was there routinely, or if he left it wherever he stopped cleaning for the day. I approached the cart and kneeled on the floor. Squinting in the dim, fluorescent light, I was able to see where the janitor had stopped mopping the floors for the day. He'd mopped coming from the back of the warehouse, meaning that tomorrow he'd resume work heading toward the exit, then take another row.

Satisfied, I knew what I had to do. I walked a few yards away from the janitor's cart, toward the exit. I listened carefully, then looked all around me to make sure no one saw what I was doing. I checked for newly installed cameras, but out there, in the back of the storage space, there were none. Then I extracted the evidence bag holding the gun from the Ziploc, cautious not to leave fresh DNA on it, and put it on the floor, under the shelf, right next to the edge, where it instantly collected a bunch of dust and particles from the dirty floor. It was barely visible. In the morning, when the janitor would resume his work, he'd find the gun, and everyone would cheer, assuming Abelardo got spooked and dropped it on his way out. Perfect!

I walked back to the Munroe case evidence and opened the box, going through the items one by one. I saw her pink phone, the one that had returned the unlikely fingerprint match in AFIS, and stared at it for a few long minutes. That's how the property clerk found me.

"You okay over there?" he asked, from the end of the aisle, not bothering to walk all the way down to where I was.

"Uh-huh," I replied, then put the phone back in the evidence box, slipped the cover back on, and pushed it back into place. Then I walked briskly out of there, thanked him, and trotted toward the exit.

I didn't dare to smile until I reached the parking lot, still dark and empty although the early light of dawn was starting to chase the stars away from the desert sky. I didn't feel the cold, neither did I care how tired I was; the adrenaline surging though my body took care of that. I had about two hours left until Holt was going to show up on my doorstep, all rested, ready for a new day at work.

Blimey, I done good.

25

The Father

I was still riding the adrenaline high when Holt pulled in front of my house, at seven sharp. I'd had time for a shower and a hefty breakfast, washed down with a solid cup of black coffee, the darkest, meanest I've had in a while. Somehow, I didn't believe green tea was going to cut it today.

I opened the door and greeted Holt, who leaned against the side of his SUV shivering in the cold morning air and looking miserable. He'd raised his collar and hunched his shoulders to keep the cold from reaching his neck. Apparently, no low temperature could make my partner put on a winter coat and a scarf.

I waved and smiled widely, excited with the secret I was keeping and anticipating the moment we'd get the news from LVMPD about the murder weapon in the Park case, about TwoCent going back to the slammer.

"Aren't you chipper this morning," he said, shooting me a mock scornful look. He looked tired, exhausted even.

"Me? Don't know what you're talking about. Let's hit it," I added, climbing into the passenger seat. "Got the address for Mr. Munroe?"

"Kind of," he replied, as a broad frown appeared on his forehead. "He's pouring foundation for the new hotel they're building on the Strip."

"Ah, okay, we can't miss that," I said, knowing exactly what building he was talking about.

Holt's frown lingered, making me curious. I waited for a moment, hoping he'd share what was bothering him, but only silence ensued.

"What's on your mind?" I eventually asked.

"I'd rather go visit Mrs. Munroe first, and I don't really care what form of feces will hit the fan and when. I just want to know if she knew her daughter stripped for fun. That makes her motive stronger than ever. Not to mention Caroline… when will we speak to her? Something tells me that the apple fell very close to the tree with that one. She's marrying a man twice her age, for Pete's sake," he added, sounding more and more frustrated with each argument he made. "If she's willing to do that, who knows what else she'd be willing to do."

"So far, Wallace hasn't learned that we disobeyed a direct order and talked to Maddie's mother, because she probably didn't think to complain about it yet. But if we call on her again, at seven in the morning, with such a line of questioning, I promise you Wallace will be the first number she'll dial. And I don't know about you, Holt, but I've got a mortgage to pay. I'm on probation, and if I disobey a direct order, I'm out in the street."

"What do you think talking to her father is? Testimony of how well you follow orders?"

I groaned, irritated with his perfect logic. Fact of the matter remained I wasn't going to completely stop doing my job, just because I needed to keep my job. I just needed to keep the risks I was taking under a certain limit, at least for now. What a bloody mess!

"I'll take my chances with him," I replied, feeling tension growing in my jaw. "I, too, want to talk to the mother again, but I don't think today is the best day to do it. Let's be smart about things."

He muttered a long oath under his breath and ran his hand angrily over his face, but didn't argue with me. He just shot me a side glance, a quick one, but I still saw frustration in his eyes.

"Let's talk to Maddie's father for now," I insisted. "We still have questions about her life we need answered. Not to mention, I'd rather see the family financials before going back to the viper's nest. When are they due?"

"This morning," he replied quietly, as he turned into the entrance to the construction site. His frown still lingered, and two ridges of tension flanked his mouth. "I haven't seen them yet."

"By the way, the father's got a record," I added, as I got out of the car, stepping carefully into a thick sludge of loose pebbles, mud, and cement. "Eighteen years ago, possession of a controlled substance. He never served any time; he got off with probation."

"You think he might be—"

"Not making any assumptions at this time," I declared, sounding a little harsh, and the glance he threw my way expressed perfectly what he thought about my reply. Maybe it wouldn't hurt if I could loosen up more and share my theories with my new partner, even if unfounded or unsupported by evidence. After all, that's what partners do: bounce ideas off each other, discuss, theorize.

The construction site was fenced, and the moment we stepped through the gate, a worker in coveralls and a yellow hard hat stopped us. Moments later, we made our way to the mobile office, improvised in a portable, prefabricated structure that resembled a cargo container with a door and two windows. That's where we found Mitch Munroe, standing next to a desk covered in blueprints, yelling into his phone, something about concrete trucks being late that morning and how he needed to pour over 120 cubic meters before lunch.

We waited. The moment we showed him our badges, he ended his call.

"Detectives Holt and Baxter," my partner said.

He removed his glasses and extended his hand. "I was expecting you at some point. This is about Maddie, isn't it?" As he spoke her name, his eyes turned dark and the creases on his windburned face deepened. He propped himself against the desk and ran his fingers through his white hair in a gesture of despair. "I still can't believe she's gone, my little girl."

"Do you have any idea who might have wanted to hurt your daughter?" Holt went straight for the gold with that question, usually reserved for the latter part of the interview.

He shook his head, staring at his boots, but didn't say a word.

"Tell us about Maddie, sir," I asked. "What was she like?"

"She was a rebel, my little girl. Nothing like her mother," he added, almost grinding his teeth when he mentioned his former wife, Mrs. Munroe.

"In what way?" Holt asked, feigning ignorance.

He let out a long sigh, almost a groan, riddled with undertones of frustration and disappointment.

"You might have learned by now that my ex-wife sees her daughters as her ticket to greatness, to the ranks of the rich and powerful, and she's shamelessly pimping them to the richest suitor available. My oldest, Caroline, she's her mother's daughter; just like her in every way. I wasn't surprised when I heard she's marrying the governor. I was saddened, even disgusted I might say, being that the son of a bitch is older than I am, but I wasn't in the least surprised."

"And Maddie?" I asked quietly.

"Maddie wasn't like that. She fought back defiantly since she entered her teenage years. Whatever Liz planned for her, Maddie foiled that plan with vengeance and humor. She showed up in ripped jeans at a pretentious fundraiser where Liz was planning to introduce her to a number of rich men. She offered a tube of Bengay to an old perv her mother had her go to dinner with, when she was only eighteen. She was a fireball, my little girl," he added, choked, with an unmistakable tremble in his voice.

I gave him a moment to collect his thoughts.

"Maddie drove her mother crazy, and I was proud of her," he soon continued. "Liz and I argued a lot when the girls were young. I couldn't stomach what she wanted to do with them; turn them into professional wives when they were bright, educated young women I raised to be in control of their own lives. I believed I made enough money to keep the three of them comfortable, but eventually we parted ways, Liz and I, when Maddie was about thirteen years old. Maddie never forgave me for leaving her."

"Why did you?"

"I didn't get joint custody," he replied, frowning and clenching his fists. "I... had a record."

"For what?" Holt asked.

"Prescription pills. I didn't want them showing on my medical record. I was afraid I'd lose my pilot license if I had an official diagnosis. I was young and dumb, what more can I say."

"What kind of pills?" I asked.

"Antidepressants. After living with that woman, trust me, I needed them. But that cost me joint custody, and the judge didn't want to hear my side of it, because Liz can be persuasive. She's a master manipulator. And Maddie... I don't think she really understood why I was leaving her. I was her only ally, and she never forgave me."

He turned toward his desk and started shuffling the blueprints, looking for something. Then he found what he was looking for, a framed photo of Maddie as a teenager, dressed in a yellow cotton dress and laughing in the sun with her arms in the air, in front of the iconic "Welcome to Las Vegas" sign.

"This goes wherever I go," he added, holding the photo in his hand. Then he put it back on the desk and turned away, hiding his trembling chin. "Now this is all I have left," he whispered.

"Mr. Munroe," I said, "we have reasons to believe something happened to Maddie when she was seventeen, while she was working as a lifeguard at the Royal Hall Hotel and Casino. Do you—"

"Damn right I do know something about that," he snapped, "although I wish I knew more."

"Tell us everything you can remember, please."

"Why?" he turned to me, his eyes throwing sparks under a deeply furrowed brow. "What's that got to do with anything, with her death?"

"We don't know yet, but we are looking at any possible motive and anyone who might have harmed her in the past."

"All right," he said with a long sigh, then ran his hand through his hair once again. "She took a summer job at Jim Pelucha's place on the strip, the Royal, although I'd offered her some money. I didn't believe working in a hotel filled with boozers and gamblers was the right thing for a seventeen-year-old, but she wouldn't listen. Being half-naked all day in front of so many men worked just fine for her mother. I always believed she had a finger in that lifeguard job Maddie got that year. As far as I'm concerned, what happened to Maddie that summer was her mother's fault."

I listened to him talk, and wondered why someone so articulate and intelligent kept going back to the same subject. He'd been divorced almost fifteen years, and yet his ex-wife was front and center in his mind as the root of all evil. What if Holt was right, and the woman was as heinous as Mitch Munroe described? Had I lost my touch? Could she be Maddie's killer, and I completely missed that?

"What do you remember about your daughter's summer at the Royal?" Holt asked, trying to steer him back to the subject.

"She didn't tell me much; she barely spoke to me back then," he replied with a pained sigh. "By the time I saw her, after that incident, a few weeks had already passed. I noticed my little girl was different, changed, lost. But her mother didn't let me talk to her about that, and she threatened to suspend visitation rights if I insisted or brought the subject up with Maddie in any way."

"Do you recall anything she might have said?" I asked.

"She didn't say much, that's just it," he said, then paced the small office slowly, with heavy footfalls that resounded in the entire structure. "My guess, she was drugged or something, or too shocked to remember. Even her bruises had almost entirely healed by the time I saw her; I barely noticed anything. But she was different, grim, self-loathing, mature overnight. Her larger-than-life laughter had vanished, and I never saw it again after that summer."

"What bruises?"

His sunburned face scrunched in anger. "She had bruises on her arms, here and here," he said, pointing at his wrist and his mid-forearm. "Maybe she'd been bruised in other places; she wouldn't tell me. She was ashamed; can you believe it? My little girl was ashamed to tell me what happened to her."

"So, you have no idea who harmed Maddie that summer?" I asked, a little disappointed we still had nothing we could use.

He stopped his pacing in front of me, looking straight into my eyes.

"Think about what I do for a living: I pour concrete. If I'd've known, that bastard would be hotel foundation by now, reinforcing the structure with his damn bones."

I saw truth in his eyes, in the way he held my gaze; he meant every word he was saying. I saw his immense sadness for not being there for his little girl, for failing her, for not protecting her when she'd needed it the most.

"Do you think her death is related to that?" he asked, then resumed his pacing.

"We're not sure," I replied. "We're still investigating, and we can't ignore any lead."

My cell phone rang, and I silenced it, unwilling to let it interrupt the conversation. But it rang again, and Holt approached, taking over for me and allowing me to pick up the call.

"This is Baxter," I said, then stepped out of the modular office into the freezing morning air.

"Detective, this is Trisha Downs. I hope I'm not disturbing you."

"Not at all, Trisha," I replied, "what can I do for you?"

"I remembered something," she said, sounding a little hesitant. "I'm not sure if it means anything, but here it is. I told you Maddie was saying that finally someone would believe her, now that she was going to be the governor's sister-in-law, right?"

"Yes," I replied, my interest piqued. "What about it?"

"She usually said that to me when we were at her apartment, when she was watering her plants. She used to play with this potted violet. She used to take the pot in her hands and chant, 'Roses are red, violets are blue, silence is over, I'm coming for you.' That's all," she ended, sounding almost embarrassed for bringing it up.

"Only the violet? Not the lily, not anything else?" I asked, trying to make some sense of what I'd just heard.

"Only the violet, yes. I don't know anything more, I'm sorry."

Maybe there was another message in Maddie's gesture. As through a haze, I vaguely remembered I'd noticed something was different about that flowerpot. I closed my eyes, trying to remember. It seemed stained or something. But now it made sense… Maddie had held that pot in her hands, more than once, and the porous ceramic had absorbed the natural skin oils from her palms, changing its appearance.

But what, if anything, did that mean? I thanked Trisha for the call and went back inside, where Mitch Munroe was telling Holt how he fought for joint custody of his daughters several times after the initial ruling.

"Mr. Munroe," I said, "do you know if potted violets had any meaning for your daughter?"

"I gave her that potted violet, the one she had at her place. I'm assuming that's the one you're talking about?"

"Yes," I replied. "I was wondering if it held any special meaning."

He thought for a moment, deepening his frown. "Not that I know of. She loved all flowers. Every now and then I brought her one."

"You gave her the potted lily and the orchid too?"

"Yes. Why?"

"No reason," I lied, "just trying to understand what she liked and why. How about money? We couldn't help noticing she lived above her means as a young college grad working in an accounting firm."

"When she turned eighteen, my legal obligation to pay alimony ended, but she didn't stop being my daughter. And with a mother like hers, looking to pawn her off... We argued for a while, but eventually she agreed to accept a monthly stipend from me and break away from that woman. Caroline wouldn't hear about anything I had to offer, but Maddie, thank goodness, said yes."

"How much?" Holt asked, and I couldn't help but notice the harshness in his voice.

"Ten grand, on the first of each month," Mitch Munroe replied. "At least one of my daughters didn't have to prostitute herself."

Holt and I exchanged a quick glance, then we thanked Mr. Munroe and left. There was absolutely no point letting him know that, despite the money and support he'd been offering, his beloved daughter took her clothes off on a stage, in a silent scream of rage against herself, against what had happened to her eleven years ago. Against the injustice she'd been forced to accept at the hands of her own mother.

26

Assignment

"I believe it's a safe assumption to say that Mr. and Mrs. Munroe won't be getting back together any time soon, huh?" I said, chuckling quietly, hunched in the passenger seat of Holt's SUV and rubbing my hands together forcefully to restore my blood flow. I hated the cold.

He threw me a quick glance and started the engine, then set the heater to the maximum.

"Yeah, you might say that," he replied, and that crooked grin of his reappeared. "Could you please call the lab and ask what the hell's going on with those fingerprints? I'll drive us to Starbucks for a fix."

I hesitated before making the call, because I'd texted with Anne last night on that topic, but Holt didn't know about it. Instead of calling the lab, I texted Anne again.

Good morning. Any fingerprints for us? my message said.

It took her less than a minute to respond.

Still working on theories. I will let you know ASAP. DNA is still pending.

I shared the text with Holt.

"What the hell theories does she need to work on? It's a damn fingerprint," he snapped. "Either it's in AFIS or it's not, end of story."

"My thoughts exactly," I replied in a pacifying tone. "But if she's reluctant to share the results, she must have a reason. How about the financials? Did you get those yet?"

He pulled over quickly and checked his email. "Nope, not yet. I'll call Gully," he replied, while the frown on his forehead deepened. "It's like a damn smoke curtain is wrapped around this case. We go in circles, chasing our tails, when the lab results and these subpoenas should've taken care of things already. Nothing works the way it should, and it's driving me bonkers."

He dialed the ADA's number, and Gully picked it up immediately.

"Detective Holt," he said, "top of the morning to you, although you're not going to like what I have to do right now."

"What the hell are you talking about?" Holt asked.

"I was instructed to transfer your call to DC Wallace, the moment you called to inquire about the Munroe subpoena. Please hold."

The ADA didn't wait for an answer; hold music filled the car, sprinkled with Holt's curses.

I cringed, anticipating DC Wallace's reaction to the subpoena that threatened his newly founded relationship with the governor and the governor's future mother-in-law.

"What the hell were you thinking?" Wallace said, skipping all pleasantries and going directly for the kill. "Didn't we discuss this?"

"We did, sir," Holt said carefully, "but we've noticed some discrepancies between the victim's standard of living and her income. Things don't add up."

"And the best way to do that is to go after the governor's family with a subpoena request?"

I swallowed, fighting the urge to say the Munroes weren't the governor's family just yet, and felt sweat breaking at the roots of my hair. Did he know we'd spoken to Maddie's mother already? Holt was walking on thin ice with Wallace; we had no clue what he knew, and that made the conversation tricky.

"They'll never have to know, sir," Holt replied. "We just need to take a quick look, to know if there's anything suspicious going on there. After all, this isn't like the typical case, where we interview every family member until we get the complete picture of what was going on in the victim's life."

Wallace didn't respond, and silence grew heavy for a moment.

"And there's no other way to close this case unless you see those financials?" Wallace asked, no longer yelling.

"This will be the easiest way to go about it. We'd eliminate the victim's family and move on to other suspects," Holt said, unperturbed. "For now, we have nothing, and it's already been almost forty-eight hours."

I made a mental note for myself, never to believe a word my partner had to say... he lied like a pro, not skipping a beat. Not blushing, not touching his face, not showing any sign of deception in his body language. A bloody good liar, when he wanted to be.

Another long moment of silence, and I held my breath without even realizing it.

"All right," Wallace eventually said, sounding almost disappointed. "I'll sign off on your subpoena request, if you promise me—no, if you swear to me they'll never find out. The governor cannot know we're looking at his family, do you understand?"

"Yes, sir," Holt replied, "I promise the governor won't know. We'll take a quick look, and no one will be the wiser. Technical Services will pull the financials and we'll review, then move on. It's a promise."

"Baxter?" Wallace said.

"Yes, sir."

"Making sure you heard me," Wallace said.

"Loud and clear, sir." I swallowed again, trying to ease the dryness in my throat.

"What's on your agenda for today?" Wallace asked.

"Um, we need to go back to the victim's apartment again," I replied, frowning. Since when did he care what we did, hour by hour? This case was driving the ambitious weasel crazy. "We have reasons to believe there might be some additional evidence there. We need to pore over that place with a magnifying glass."

"What evidence?" he asked, sounding surprised.

"We don't know yet, sir. It could be nothing," I backed off carefully, not wanting every move we made to be micromanaged by Wallace.

"That place is sealed, Baxter. Rip the seal and put another one in place before you leave, all right?"

"Sure, will do," I replied, while Holt and I exchanged intrigued glances. Why would Wallace waste his time stating the obvious and obsessing over routine details such as door seals? I sighed, thankful for a moment that I was never cursed with his level of political zeal.

"But, before you go there, I need you two to help Nieblas and Croker pick up TwoCent," Wallace added, and I could barely contain a satisfied smile. My extracurricular activities had paid off. Yeah!

"Sir?" Holt asked, confused.

"Well," Wallace said, almost entertained, "the perp dropped the murder weapon on his way out of the evidence locker. We found it this morning. Technically, the chain of custody was preserved, and the gun is still admissible in court. There's a new warrant for TwoCent's arrest, and I need you two to help execute that warrant."

"That's great news," Holt said. "When are they going over there?"

"We have Zebra Team scheduled to break down his door in exactly forty minutes, at 9:00 AM. Be there. Do that first, then do whatever else you need to do to close the Munroe case. Financials will probably be done by the time you bring TwoCent to lockup."

Uh-oh... that was probably the worst idea I'd heard in a while. What if TwoCent recognized me? What if he started running his big mouth and found people crazy enough to believe him?

I pulled the visor down and looked in the mirror. I studied my face in detail, not seeing anything TwoCent might remember from last night: the long, luscious waves of hair; the exotic makeup; the jewelry. No, I looked banal, anonymous, just another cop bulked up in a Kevlar vest and a standard issue jacket. A baseball cap and some shades couldn't hurt though.

"Sir, if I may," Holt said, "you have Zebra Team and both Nieblas and Crocker. What do you need us for?"

"We have no way of knowing how many armed perps we'll find at TwoCent's residence. Just making sure we're not screwing this up, Detective. Be a team player for once, will you?"

"Yes, sir, understood," Holt replied.

Wallace ended the call without any other comment, and we stared at each other. It didn't make sense. Zebra Team, LVMPD's elite SWAT team, should've been more than enough to bust a street thug and his buddies. But an order was an order, at least once in a while.

"Anything amusing, Baxter?" Holt asked, probably seeing the smile fluttering on my lips.

"Yeah... I was thinking we should follow at least some of the DC's orders."

"Yeah, no kidding," he replied. Then he checked the dashboard clock and pulled up TwoCent's address. "No time for coffee," he announced somberly. "Let's bust that piece of crap, then we'll stop for a hot one."

27

House Call

TwoCent's property was a few miles west of the Strip, in an affluent neighborhood where Porsche Cayenne and Cadillac Escalade were among the most common brands of vehicles parked in front of triple car garages, making me wonder what kind of vehicles were worthy of being hosted inside. Tall, brick fences, many times exceeding 10 feet, obliterated the view into the backyards of those houses. Looking at the front of TwoCent's house, the casual visitor could envision the large backyard with a pool and a covered patio, and maybe green lawns nourished by automated sprinkling systems to keep the desert dust at bay.

By the time we arrived, Zebra Team was already taking positions around the property, moving quietly and communicating exclusively via hand and arm signals. Two men stood near the main door holding a battering ram, ready to breach. Nieblas and Crocker were steps behind them, weapons drawn. Holt waved at them, and, from a distance, I thought I saw Nieblas scoffing angrily and making a dismissive hand gesture in response. Three other Zebras were ready to breach the fence by the gate, and from there to enter the house through the back door.

We turned our radios on in time to hear Nieblas give the order.

"Breach, breach," he said, and the two men at the main entrance slammed the battering ram into the door, near the deadbolt. The door gave, and the two men took the ram out of the way, letting two other Zebras enter the premises first, closely followed by Nieblas and Crocker. We trailed behind them, guns in hands, ready to fire.

The first thing I noticed was the heavy smell of booze and sweat, thick enough to be revolting. Stale smoke filled the room, our tumultuous entry making it swirl and thin out under the oblique sunrays that pierced the lowered window blinds.

TwoCent slept splayed on a leather sofa, face down, his left leg hanging loose, almost touching the floor. El Bastardo had collapsed in an armchair, his jaw slack and leaking a thin trail of saliva. Hash had crumpled right on the floor, near the sofa. Another thug, unrecognizable beyond a pile of dreadlocks and some yellow baggy pants that didn't even cover his underwear, had fallen asleep with his head propped on his arm, seated at the kitchen counter, inches away from a few cocaine lines drawn carefully on the black marble.

The noise we made busting through the door startled everyone, and a ruckus of shouts, cusswords, and guttural sounds filled the room. TwoCent scrambled to get off the sofa but tripped and fell to his knees on the thick oriental rug. Nieblas took position in front of him, pointing his service weapon at his face from 3 feet away. I stayed behind, not really that eager to get any closer to TwoCent.

"Hands in the air, asshole, you're going back to the joint," Nieblas said.

"Wha—whatcha doin' in my crib, man?" TwoCent said, stuttering badly. "This is police brutality!" He wiped his mouth with the back of his hand, then grabbed his forehead and cussed. "Man, my head's about to crack open... I need a doctor."

"Hit the deck, face down," Nieblas ordered, but TwoCent was too confused to obey.

"What you bustin' me for? Y'all sprung me loose yesterday, man. You got no murder weapon. You got nothin' on me," he added with a wide grin, and his eyes shot a glance toward the coffee table, where, on the lower shelf, I saw the gun I'd nicely wrapped and delivered for those boys the night before.

Crocker followed his glance, then approached the table carefully. "Gun," he said, and picked up the evidence bag with a look of confusion on his face. "What the heck is this?" he asked no one in particular, holding it up in plain view.

One of the Zebras had cuffed Abelardo and brought him forward, holding him tight by the arm.

"This?" Nieblas replied, after examining the gun through the clear plastic of the evidence bag. "I don't know what this is supposed to be. The tag's fake, the weapon isn't the right one. It's a street piece, no serial number; it's been filed off."

"Ha!" Crocker reacted. "I think our Mr. TwoCent has been duped by his lieutenant. This piece of crap," he continued, grabbing Abelardo by the arm, "forgot to tell TwoCent he didn't have the marbles to swipe the real piece from police evidence. He left his mug on our video for no reason at all."

I watched Holt as he followed the exchange with amusement, then I turned toward TwoCent. He'd turned pale, as whatever brainpower he could summon processed the information, and the implications sunk in.

TwoCent hopped to his feet with unexpected agility and turned to Nieblas. "What the hell are you sayin', man?"

"I'm saying freeze right there, asshat."

TwoCent didn't listen. He took another step forward, toward Nieblas, who took a step back. Holt approached from the side, holding his gun trained on the perp's chest.

"You sayin' this ain't the right gun?" TwoCent asked in a high-pitched voice, confused beyond the point of realizing he was about to confess to another crime: conspiracy to steal evidence in an open case.

Nieblas broke out laughing. "That's right, wiseass. The murder weapon you used to kill a cop is still in the evidence locker, and you're going down for it. Now hit the deck before an accident happens and you wind up dead. My finger's itching badly."

TwoCent stared into emptiness for a split second, then turned to Abelardo, cuffed and held a few yards away. "What'd you do, *ese?*" he bellowed. "Played me for a fool? You're gonna die in the slammer, *pedazo de mierda.*"

"I swear to you," Abelardo said, shooting glances of pure, primal fear at everyone in the room. "I swear to you on my mother's eyes, this was the gun."

"I'm gonna kill you slow, *de puta madre,*" TwoCent said, narrowing his eyes and taking another step toward Abelardo.

Holt put his gun into the holster and grabbed TwoCent from behind by the arms, then threw him on the floor, face down. He straddled him, under the gunpoint of Nieblas' weapon, then cuffed him and lifted him back on his feet.

"Collaring another man's perp again, Holt?" Nieblas asked coldly. "Once wasn't enough for you?"

"Just doing what I'm told, Nieblas," Holt replied, unperturbed. "Just following orders."

I swallowed a chuckle. Holt was devious, dangerously smart. Now Nieblas was left wondering why his superior officers had sent Holt to assist in his case. Nieblas was probably going to second-guess himself for the rest of the day, at least.

"Wait a minute," TwoCent hollered, struggling to break loose from Holt's grip. "Call the police," he shouted, "I've been mugged! This ain't the right gun," he said, then he looked at me fixedly, frowning.

I didn't flinch; I stared him right back with a frozen glare. Nothing this piece of crap was going to say would make any difference. The cop killer was going to go to jail for a long time.

A faint flicker of recognition passed through TwoCent's bloodshot eyes, instantly replaced with fear. "I been drugged, and I been mugged! I need da police!"

They hauled Abelardo out right behind TwoCent, and the entire time TwoCent hollered death threats and Abelardo sobbed and pleaded with the cops to put him in a different car. My work was done; it had been done since five in the morning.

I found Holt and beckoned him toward the car, eager to start searching Maddie's apartment. This entire thing had been nothing but a tremendous waste of time, squandering us precious hours while Maddie's killer was still at large, and our investigation, instead of yielding answers, only uncovered more questions.

28

Violets Are Blue

I was relieved to see Holt driving us to Starbucks first. The lack of sleep from last night had caught up with me, and I struggled to keep my mind focused. He came out of the coffee shop with two steaming venti cups and a bag of pastries, and I grinned widely, anticipating the treat.

"Any news?" he asked, as he climbed inside the vehicle and handed me the pastries.

"Not a peep from anyone," I replied, between two large bites from a warm croissant, "not from Anne and not from the lab either."

"Damn," he muttered with his mouth full, "your friend better have one hell of an explanation for this delay."

"Uh-huh," I said, wondering myself what could possibly justify fingerprint analysis taking almost two full days, maybe more. But I trusted Anne like no one else, and I knew her professional integrity was beyond anyone else I've worked with. She'd tell us what was going on when she'd be ready. Anne didn't like to speculate; my guess was that whatever match she'd found in AFIS posed more questions than answers, and Anne never called me before having definitive findings.

"Don't tell me the fingerprints returned a match and it's the governor," Holt said with a chuckle, "and now they're all scrambling, thinking how to deal with it."

"Ha," I reacted, "wouldn't that be something." I took a big gulp of hot coffee, burning my throat in the process. "I seriously doubt that our governor would kill someone with his own hands, but I guess you never know."

We soon arrived at Maddie's Spring Valley apartment building, and the same jittery superintendent materialized to greet and escort us before we could reach the main entrance. He must have spent his entire days watching the traffic; otherwise I couldn't explain how he knew we were coming. Just like yesterday, he scampered ahead of us, showed us to the apartment and gave us the key, while averting his eyes the entire time. Then he vanished without saying a word.

Holt was about to rip the seal and open the door when he noticed the seal had been cut neatly along the doorframe, making it appear intact when, in fact, someone had been there ahead of us. Someone not cops, someone who couldn't replace the broken seal with a new one. Holt touched my arm briefly to get my attention, showed me the cut seal, then we both pulled out our weapons and entered the apartment cautiously.

We stopped in the hallway, listening for sounds, but there weren't any. Then we split up. Just like before, I took the living room, then went into the kitchen, and Holt went into the master bedroom. Nothing seemed touched or out of place. I heard Holt go into the second bedroom, and I went into the small, hallway bathroom; no one was there.

"Clear," I said, and holstered my weapon.

"Clear," Holt replied, then joined me in the kitchen. "Any ideas?"

I shook my head. "Let's take a look at that violet, then we'll find the super and ask him if he'd seen anyone. That man behaves like he's wanted for murder, or as if his tenants are. If anyone set foot in here, the super will know."

Holt laughed. "Yeah, damn right. Do you want to bring Crime Scene in here, to lift some prints?"

"I don't think the person who knew to cut the seal on the door the way it was cut would enter this apartment unprotected and leave fingerprints behind. It does, however, make me think we definitely missed something, and someone else knows to be after whatever it is that we missed."

"This apartment hasn't been searched yet," Holt stated the obvious, confusion seeping in his voice.

I nodded. "Maybe he knew exactly what he was looking for, and he didn't need to ransack the place searching for it?"

"Maybe," Holt replied with an intensifying frown. He probably disliked uncertainties just as much as I did.

I slipped on a glove and took the potted violet in my hand, examining it closely. There wasn't any dust on the exterior of the pot, consistent with someone handling it frequently. The saucer showed deposits where the pot had leaked water and soil, and evaporation lines, quite common for plant pot saucers. Nothing out of the ordinary, except possibly the reddish hue of those evaporation lines. They should've been a dark gray, considering they came from the black topsoil inside the pot, but there was definitely an unusual color to them.

"Get me a fresh garbage bag," I asked Holt. His eyebrows shot up, and he gestured with his hand. "Open some drawers and you'll find them." Men... When practical sense was distributed in our chromosomes, it must have been stored exclusively in X chromosomes, not in Y.

He found one and laid it flat on the kitchen table, and I placed the potted violet gently on it, making sure not a speck of soil was lost. I took the saucer from the shelf and put it on the table, then pointed at the reddish residue to show Holt my observation.

"See? There's a—"

I heard a noise, but I didn't have time to react or understand what it was, because Holt leapt forward and threw me to the ground under the weight of his body, knocking the air out of my lungs. I heard a gunshot, then something ripped through my leg, and I screamed. Then I heard Holt's weapon, two shots in rapid sequence. I saw a man drop to the floor and remain motionless, as blood gushed from the wounds in his chest. Faintly, as if I were dreaming, I remembered I'd locked the apartment door after coming inside. My eyes stayed riveted to the unknown man's face, as disconcerting thoughts circled my brain. We'd cleared the apartment; where had he been hiding? How come we missed him? Who was he, and what did he want?

"Are you all right?" Holt asked, forcing me to look at him.

"I'll live," I replied groaning, and tried to lift myself off the ground. I was dizzy, nauseous, and could barely breathe. My left calf throbbed with pain, and I felt blood trickling from the wound, soaking my pants. "Where the hell was he? Where did he come from?"

He pointed toward the open closet near the front door. "In there. We fucked up, Baxter. We didn't check everywhere."

Holt gave me a hand, easing my back off the floor and helping me lean against the kitchen table leg, then he took a quick look at my wound and dialed our dispatch.

"This is Detective Holt, Homicide. I need a bus at my location, on the double. I have an officer down. Send some backup and the coroner's van; the shooter's down permanently."

"ETA on that bus is fourteen minutes, Detective," the dispatch said.

I cringed. The pain was intense, but bearable. By the way it felt, the bullet had cut through my calf, through and through, missing the bone. However, I was losing a lot of blood, and the thought of waiting fourteen minutes for someone to show up was a little scary.

Holt searched my eyes then nodded once. "That's not acceptable, dispatch. Kill that bus call."

He hung up, then picked me up from the floor as if I were weightless. He made for the door, but I stopped him. Maybe whoever was trying to get to the evidence before us hadn't had the time to search the place yet, but there was no telling they wouldn't try again.

"No way I'm leaving that behind," I said, pointing over his shoulder at the potted violet on the table.

"Jeez, woman," he groaned, "we're about to leave a police-involved shooting dead body at an unsecured crime scene, and you care about a potted plant."

He put me down gently on the couch, then took another fresh garbage bag and packed the pot, the saucer, and the other bag in it. He held it in the air for a moment, confused, probably debating how he was going to carry me and the bag with only two hands.

"No need to carry me," I said, "it looks worse than it is. I'll lean on you and hop my way to the car. Give me your arm."

"Nonsense," he muttered, then gave me the bag and lifted me up in his arms again. Within a few steps, we were outside the apartment, making our way to the exit under the long stares of the neighbors who'd been rattled by the gunfire.

"Go back inside your apartments, people. There's nothing to worry about," Holt said. Then, seeing the super, he added, "You, please make sure no one enters the premises until the other cops get here."

"Y-yes," he stuttered, keeping his eyes riveted to the ground.

I groaned, hiding my face against Holt's chest.

"What's going on?" he asked, and picked up his pace.

"It's the adrenaline wearing off, Holt," I lied, then reconsidered and told him the truth. "I don't think he's much of a resource to guard our crime scene."

I peeked over Holt's shoulder and saw the superintendent standing in front of the apartment door, arms crossed at his chest, looking the part. Thankfully, the backup unit pulled in at the curb just as Holt loaded me into his car.

"What do you have, Detective?" one of the cops asked.

"Crime scene upstairs, unit 212; coroner's been dispatched. I'll be at Spring Valley Hospital if anyone's looking to get our statements. My partner's been shot."

"Understood. Anything specific you need us to be watching for?"

"There might be evidence in that apartment," I replied while Holt was getting behind the wheel. "Critical evidence that someone is willing to kill for."

29

Aftermath

Getting shot sucks; that's the understatement of the day. In all fairness, getting shot in the leg, with no bone or major blood vessel involved counts as sheer luck, although from where I was standing it didn't look that way. Scratch that... I wasn't standing, I was lying on my back on a stretcher that a bunch of people, talking in a mixture of codes, acronyms, and English-sounding words I didn't quite understand, were pushing as fast as they could on endless corridors, making me queasy. They acted as if I'd taken three 45s to the chest, not one 9 mil in the calf.

Then someone wearing surgical attire finally bothered to speak to me, appearing ghostly against a flood of powerful light.

"Don't worry about a thing, Detective, we've got you covered," she said, and her voice sounded alarmingly young. "We'll have you out of here in no time."

I squinted, as I looked at her eyes, hoping to find the wrinkles of countless years of experience as a trauma surgeon, but found only youthful skin and a lot of confidence in a pair of beautiful green eyes.

Then I fell asleep, right after feeling a needle poking my vein, and woke up after what seemed like barely moments, to find myself patched up, my wound dressed tightly, and my favorite pair of slacks cut right above the knee. For some reason, I felt anxious, eager to run out of there. I tried to sit up, but a gentle hand pushed me back against the pillows.

"Not so fast, Detective," I heard a man say, "You owe us an MRI before we let you go. Your partner said something about possibly hitting your head when he threw you to the floor. How many fingers do you see?" he asked, popping his hand in front of my face, maybe 10 inches away from my nose.

For some reason, the answer required some effort. "Three." Then he shined a flashlight into my eyes and I hated that, as if the light pierced all the way into my brain, about to trigger a migraine.

"Your pupils are responsive, great. What day is today?"

"The day I was shot," I replied dryly. "Come on, let me go already." He frowned and didn't budge, so I had to humor him. "It's Tuesday, November 20.

There, happy?"

"Maybe," he replied, but there was no talking him out of that MRI. Thankfully, thirty minutes of claustrophobia later he helped me into a wheelchair and signed off on my release.

"Should we call someone for you?" he offered, and I turned my face away from him, feeling the emptiness nested inside my chest growing, engulfing my entire world.

"No, there's no one you can call. Just get me a cab—"

"There's no need for that," I heard Holt's voice, and, for some unexplainable reason, my heart swelled. "Now you're a real cop," he added, then grabbed the handles of my wheelchair and started pushing me toward the exit. "You got the scars to show for it."

I let him load me into the SUV while my recently anesthetized mind wandered. Who was the man who shot me? By now, Anne had him on one of her slabs, and his fingerprints were being matched against those found on Maddie's body, on her cell phone. By now, she had an identity for the mysterious shooter, who'd come to Maddie's apartment without carrying any ID, only a loaded gun. What was he looking for? What were we missing?

I made a promise to myself to go back to that apartment and turn it inside out, when my eyes dropped on a white garbage bag on the car floormat, next to my feet. I smiled. Maybe the evidence was right there, with us.

Holt pulled into my driveway and gave the house a quick look. It was completely dark; I lived alone. By the quick frown that appeared on his brow, then vanished just as quickly, he understood that. He opened the car door for me, but I stopped him before he had a chance to lift me.

"I have crutches, in the hallway closet. I broke an ankle skiing a few years ago. Here, take the keys, they're easy to find."

He stood for a brief moment, as if considering it. Then he scooped me up from the car seat and took me to the door. I had the keys in my hand, and I unlocked it, then squeezed the handle down. He pushed the door open and entered, then put me on the sofa, in the dim light coming from the driveway.

"Thanks, Holt, I'll be fine from here," I said, eager to be on my own again, afraid of how vulnerable I felt.

He gave me a doubtful look and blatantly ignored what I said. He closed the main door, then went to the fridge and started digging inside, making me cringe, as I remembered the kitchen sink filled with dirty dishes and the almost empty fridge.

"There's evidence in the car, Holt. Please bring it inside."

He scoffed quietly, but obeyed and brought the plastic garbage bag inside and set it on my kitchen counter. Then he resumed his search through my fridge, unabated, whistling a movie theme song I couldn't place.

"What are you doing?" I asked, although I knew the answer quite well, and the glance he shot me expressed clearly what he thought about me treating him like an idiot. He trotted over to the coffee table and found the remote, then turned on the TV.

"That should keep you entertained and quiet for a while," he said with an uneven, mischievous grin, then resumed scavenging through my fridge. He pulled out a carton of eggs, butter, a bag of shredded cheese, and a bottle of wine. A few minutes later, I tasted one of the best omelets I'd ever had, puffy and cheesy and smooth, probably worth at least 700 calories, but who cared? I savored it, taking the occasional sip of wine, welcoming the warmth that soon spread through my body.

As soon as he cleared the table I tried to stand, but my wound smarted badly, and I promptly lifted my foot in the air. It wasn't going to take any weight on it tonight if I wanted to be limping my way through life tomorrow.

"The doctor said to keep you off your feet for a few days," Holt said. "As in bed rest."

"Really?" I reacted angrily. "With that killer out there? Hell, no. I'll be fine. Please pick me up tomorrow morning at seven. Business as usual."

He shook his head, laughing quietly in disbelief. "You're a stubborn woman, Detective Baxter. Last time I checked, I could work a murder investigation on my own for a day or two. Won't be the end of the world, and the killer won't go free. I promise you that," he added, and his eyes darkened in silent rage. "He had a cop shot; he won't get away with it."

"So, you believe the guy at the apartment wasn't Maddie's killer, that it was someone else? That's what I think... I agree."

"Uh-huh," he said quietly. "Maddie's killer executed the crime perfectly. He moved flawlessly in a hotel full of tourists and managed to leave no witnesses, no usable video. Even now I struggle to explain why someone so thorough left behind fingerprints; maybe he didn't expect us to be able to lift them off her body or to find her second phone. But the man who shot you managed to fumble whatever the heck he was doing in a small apartment with only two people in it. It's not the same guy."

He was right, concise and thorough in his analysis; I liked that. I nodded and sipped the last of the wine, eyeing the empty bottle with a sigh. "We screwed up royally clearing that apartment. Where the hell was he hiding?"

He shrugged. "Don't know. He could've waited us out though. A few more minutes and we would've been long gone."

"What if he was after the same thing?"

"You mean, that?" he asked, pointing at the garbage bag on my counter.

"Precisely. Let's take a look," I said and tried to stand again, but a wave of weakness had me give up mid-movement. I fell back against the sofa cushions and squeezed my eyes shut for a moment, then tried to pretend that nothing happened.

He threw me a concerned glance. "Nope, you need to sleep. It will be there in the morning. Come on," he insisted, "it's a potted plant, for Pete's sake. It's not like it holds the secrets of the universe, and it's not like it's going to walk out of here on its own. I'm willing to bet good coffee against a spoonful of topsoil we won't find a thing in there, just dirt. Who knows what Madeline was thinking?"

I was preparing my counterargument when he scooped me up in his arms again, and this time I didn't fight it. I let my head buckle and lean against his chest, and listened to the rhythm of his strong, steady heart as he climbed the steps to my bedroom.

Once on the second level, he hesitated for a moment, but then found my bedroom and set me on the bed. I watched him as he pulled the covers aside, then tucked me in without a word, leaning over me to set the pillows just right.

I didn't think clearly in that moment; all I knew was that he was about to leave, and I couldn't let that happen. I couldn't let the darkness back in, even if for another hour. I breathed in his scent, the heat coming from his body, and felt the forgotten feeling of eagerly anticipating, of needing a man's touch. I grabbed his lapel.

"Holt," I whispered, and gently pulled him closer.

His eyes opened wide and searched mine for a long moment. "You drive me crazy, Baxter," he moaned, then crushed my lips with a scorching, imperative kiss.

30

Clichés

I woke aware of a dull pain in my calf; within a split second, I remembered how I got it. Then I remembered everything else that had ensued, and I opened my eyes widely, welcoming the daylight and hoping I'd only dreamt it. No, Holt was there, in flesh and blood, asleep with his leg thrown over mine and his head nested on my pillow.

Bollocks.

I'd screwed up royally, and the only thing I could think of in my defense was the meds they'd given me in the hospital yesterday. Because someone like me, cerebral, almost cold even, doesn't shag men only three days after she met them, no matter how attractive they might seem. I'd never done that before, not even once. Must've been the meds. Or the wine. Or both.

He's my bloody partner, a voice screamed inside my head, probably my formerly absent common sense, and I couldn't think of anything to say to silence that voice. What was done was done and soon to be forgotten, although it had been quite memorable I had to admit, feeling my cheeks on fire as I recalled last night's activities. *Damn it to bloody hell!*

I decided to put some distance between us and tried to get up. My hair was entangled around his arms, under his head, caught against his skin. It took some doing, but I managed to pull myself free without waking him, then stood with difficulty. My leg still smarted, but not as badly, and, if I only put weight on my heel, it was bearable. I got dressed quickly, then hopped my way down the stairs and into the kitchen.

I started a pot of coffee, still beating myself up over last night. Had it been worth it? Ruining a perfectly good professional relationship over a roll between the sheets? With a cocaine addict, no less? What the hell was I thinking? I groaned with despair and covered my mouth with my hand. There were millions of ways this could go badly, and not a single way I could think of in which it wouldn't. Call me a pessimist, but fraternizing within the force is frowned on for a reason.

Fraternization, my arse… this was shagging. Who was I kidding?

I poured myself a cup of coffee and gladly sat at the counter, taking the weight off my leg. I stared at the garbage bag, wondering if I should wait for Holt to wake up before opening it and decided not to. If he could solve a murder on his own, as he'd recently offered, I could very well examine a potted plant by myself.

I pushed the coffee out of the way and pulled on latex gloves. Then I opened the bag carefully, tearing it along the seams to make sure not a single speck of evidence was lost. I took the wilting, potted violet in my hands, and turned it around slowly, examining it on all sides. I was looking for something written, a scribble on the bottom of the pot or something like that, for no rational reason.

"Having fun without me?" Holt said, speaking softly behind me. I startled, unaccustomed to having someone in the house. There had been no one since Andrew. *Bloody hell.*

He leaned forward and kissed my neck. "Good morning."

I cringed, dreading the moment I had to face him. Could I possibly make this anymore awkward? *Get a grip, Baxter,* I willed myself, then turned and nodded, keeping a straight, distant face.

"Ah," he reacted, and his smile vanished. "You've decided to be a cliché."

That word set my anger on fire, no warning, no fuse, nothing.

"What other choice do I have, huh? We're partners, Holt! It's a disaster waiting to happen, nothing else," I snapped, and he took a step back as if I were physically hurting him. "We... I made a mistake," I added, lowering my voice and veering my eyes away from him. "Let's just pretend it never happened."

He shook his head in disbelief. "Is this what you really want, Baxter?" He searched my eyes, but I kept staring at the floor. "Look at me straight and tell me that's what you really want. I felt something different last night."

I forced some air into my lungs, wishing the entire thing were over and done with. Then I willed myself to look into his eyes and say the few words that could put last night permanently into our past. Words wouldn't come to mind though, not the right ones anyway, not while looking at his boyish smile and remembering how those lips felt on my body. I choked, tempted to throw him to the floor and have another roll with him before calling it quits. I cleared my throat quietly and summoned all my willpower to keep a straight face, but failed miserably and turned away.

"That's what I thought," Holt said in a low whisper. "Then why do it, Baxter?"

I let a pained sigh escape my lips. "Because we'd be vulnerable," I said, thinking of his addiction, of the hidden storage space behind the back wall in my closet, of our jobs. "Because we'd stop being Holt and Baxter, good or bad, however the hell we are. We'd become something else I'm not ready for, I'm not looking for."

"All right, I'll respect that," he said, after a long moment of heavy silence. Then he pulled a chair closer to the counter, across from where I sat and waited, looking at the evidence laid in front of us.

I grabbed the potted violet and resumed my inspection. I showed him the stains, then I showed him the bottom of the pot, where the reddish hues were more pronounced.

"Isn't that ceramic powder or something?"

"We'll find out soon enough," I said, and grabbed the plant gently and pulled it out of the pot. I gave it a gentle shake, to loosen the soil from the roots, and examined them carefully. There wasn't anything there but whitish, entangled roots. Probably Anne would find out more, in her lab. She'd determine the source of the reddish deposits within seconds using a mass spectrometer.

Then I looked at the pot; it still had an inch of soil inside, so I flipped it upside down. Loose soil fell into a small pile on the plastic sheet, and with it, a rusted key.

"Well, hello there," I said, picking it up. It was small, smaller than a house key, larger than a padlock. Most likely, a safety deposit box.

"Speaking of clichés," Holt chuckled. "Key under the flowerpot? It can't get any more cliché than that."

"It was inside the pot, for what that's worth," I said, still studying it. I loosened some dirt from it with my gloved fingernail, hoping for a name, some identifier we could use. Other than the number 801 etched in the metal, there was nothing we could use. "We need to trace this as soon as we can. I'd call it a priority. Maddie played with it when she sang how she was going to expose her attacker. I believe we might find his name in that safety deposit box."

I turned to look at Holt, whose quasi-permanent smile hadn't reappeared in a while.

"I have a few ideas," he said. "People are creatures of habit."

I waited for him to continue, then shot him an irritated glance. What was he waiting for? An invitation?

My cell rang, and I picked it up on speaker, recognizing Anne's caller ID.

"Need to see you both in my office," she said, skipping through all pleasantries.

"You got the fingerprint results back?"

"We're a one-stop shop here," she joked, without putting any hint of a smile in her voice. "We've got everything you can possible want, and more."

31

Coroner's Report

I limped badly on my way to Anne's office, touching the wall for balance and refusing Holt's extended arm for what I thought were obvious reasons. Obvious or not, that didn't keep him from insisting I lean on him.

"No, sorry," I whispered, since we were almost to Anne's office door, "I need to do this on my own." I hated thinking how awkwardly it had all become; if it weren't for last night's adventures, I would've accepted his arm without hesitation.

I held on to the doorjamb for as long as I could, then to the door itself, and finally grabbed the back of a chair, across from Anne's desk. She lifted her eyes and measured me from head to toe, then gazed at me critically.

"Why aren't you using crutches? Didn't that doctor tell you to keep your weight off your leg for two days?"

I swallowed. What was it, these doctors all did things the same way? Was there a single possible regimen for a gunshot wound to the leg? She hadn't even seen my injury, but she knew exactly what the other doctor had ordered, what I chose to ignore. So bloody unnerving. I breathed, trying to subdue my irritation. Anne didn't deserve any of it, and neither did Holt.

"Guilty as charged, your honor," I quipped, but her eyes stayed cold, clinical, inquisitive. "Let's hear it," I said, deflecting to a subject that had kept both Holt and me intrigued, almost anxious over the past few days. "What's the big deal with those fingerprints?"

She opened a file folder and skipped forward a few pages. "First, the man who shot you. We've identified him as Rudy Camacho, twenty-nine. Want to see the body?" she asked, gesturing toward the refrigerator on the wall at her left.

I shivered. The man who tried to kill me, lying on a cold, metallic drawer, with a fresh Y-cut sewn on his chest. I still remembered seeing his face hit the floor in Maddie's apartment, and his eyes turning glassy behind long strands of dark, sweat-clumped hair. "Um, no," I replied. "I'll pass."

"All right," Anne continued. "Double tap to the chest; one slug hit the inferior vena cava, severing it completely. I have his tox screen and trace evidence still processing. Nice shooting, Detective," she added with a quick glance toward Holt.

He nodded slightly.

"Mr. Camacho wasn't a match for the DNA or fingerprints lifted from the victim. I know you were probably hoping for a different finding, but he isn't the killer you've been looking for." She paused, waiting for us to ask any questions, but we had none. First, I wanted to look at Camacho's background, pull his priors, his financials, and his phone records. Then I might have some questions.

"Next, I have the DNA evidence in the Madeline Munroe murder case," she continued. "The fluids found in the hotel room match Dan Hutzel, Madeline's boyfriend. He was also the father of her baby. No surprises there."

Holt jotted down something in his notepad, while I waited for her to continue. After almost three days, there had to be more.

"DNA swabbed from underneath Madeline's fingernails and from the tip of her broken shoe heel didn't return a match in CODIS. Find me something I can match it against, and I will."

Holt paced the office quietly, keeping his hands in his pockets, seemingly deep in thought. I shot him a quick glance, but he was looking straight at Anne. He appeared tense, and the furrow in his brow deepened with every bit of new information we gathered.

"That's a bummer," I replied. I'd held high hopes for those DNA results, and we had nothing.

"Tox screen was clean," Anne continued. "Traces of marijuana in her blood, so minimal I believe she might've smoked a joint a few weeks ago. She wasn't a habitual user. Blood alcohol was under the limit, at 0.052 percent. Maybe she'd had a beer or two that day. I have stomach contents—"

"Fingerprints, please?"

She shook her head, disapproving of my impatience, then flipped the pages back in the file until she found the right one.

"AFIS had a match for the fingerprints we lifted off Madeline's body. Same person left prints on her second phone, the one recovered from the hotel laundry room. The problem is with the identity we found in AFIS, a forty-five-year-old man by the name of Raymond McKinley, from Provo, Utah."

I frowned, not seeing what the problem was.

Anne closed the file and interlocked her fingers on top of it. "Raymond McKinley was reported missing twenty-one years ago. He disappeared on the way home from his favorite watering hole, only six months after being released from prison."

Holt and I exchanged a quick glance. Now that was a problem. Why would someone who'd disappeared twenty-one years ago suddenly materialize to kill a young woman in Las Vegas?

"What was he collared for?" Holt asked.

"He tried to rob a bank, rural Utah style. Got in there with his gun in his hand, but dropped it at the security guard's first request."

"A loser then?" Holt asked.

"You could say that, based on his MO," Anne replied reluctantly. She hated labeling people, calling them names. In her own words, repeated to me several times over the years, it was unprofessional, and many times a practice that led to hasty or wrong conclusions being drawn.

"Were there any partners in the attempt?" I asked, thinking of what could have caused Raymond McKinley to vanish.

"No, just him, based on the information I received from the detective who worked his case. He's retired now, but still remembers McKinley. You have his contact info in here," she added, tapping on the file folder with a long, thin finger.

"I have to ask this, and I believe I already know the answer," I said, "but how sure are you this McKinley is the right match?"

"Now you understand why it took me so long to give you the report. I repeated the procedure three times, and the prints from Maddie's body match the ones on her phone to perfection. We have more than enough data points to call it a positive match, by all current standards in forensic science. I looked at it again, and again. Based on these fingerprints and the record found in AFIS, your suspect's name is Raymond McKinley."

"All right," I sighed, "I'll put out a BOLO." It was standard procedure, but it didn't make much intuitive sense. We needed a break, and we weren't catching one, no matter where we looked.

"Sure, go ahead," Anne said, with a dismissive gesture, "but I've seen this type of thing before, and you'll be wasting your time."

"Where?" I asked, leaning forward and putting my elbows on her desk.

"CIA," Holt replied somberly. He leaned against the wall and crossed his arms at his chest.

"Spook IDs for intelligence assets," Anne confirmed with a nod in Holt's direction. "Fake identities for deep undercover cops, the types that would pass a thorough background check, even a federal one. DEA uses those a lot. Or WITSEC, for a few critical federal assets, not for everyone who's turned state evidence."

Whoa, that was a game changer. I leaned back against the chair, processing the information. What the hell was going on? From what we'd learned about Madeline Munroe, her life didn't exactly jive with covert identities and espionage. She was a young accountant with a dysfunctional family and a troubled personal past, nothing more. Were we missing something?

"I thought they used dead people for those covert identities," I said, unable to shake a feeling of dread that had nested in my gut.

"They normally do, but in certain sensitive cases they use missing persons, especially if it's believed that someone will conduct in-depth background investigations on that particular subject," Anne replied. "In such situations, the identity of a real missing person is used, one who shares a number of common physical traits with the protected asset, such as age, gender, race, and certain physiognomy traits."

"You're saying you could tell me what my suspect looks like?" I asked, feeling hopeful for the first time that day.

"Not in any detail," Anne replied, "and not with any certainty. I believe it's safe to assume that someone who goes through that much trouble to get a new identity will pay attention to details that could otherwise blow his cover. Nevertheless, it's still an assumption."

"Okay, I got that," I replied impatiently. "What does the perp look like?"

"He's early to mid-forties, Caucasian, average height."

"And that's it?" I asked in disbelief. "That's all you can tell me?"

Anne nodded. "Everything else can be altered. Eye color, hair color and length, even body mass. But if it's of any use, this is the photo we have on file for McKinley. Keep in mind it was taken more than twenty years ago." She opened the file and pushed it toward me. I looked at the photo and saw a regular guy who could've been just about anyone. Great.

"What if the real Raymond McKinley decides to appear?" I asked.

"His bones are probably bleaching in some Utah ravine, never to be found," Holt replied. "These people don't leave things to chance."

"These people?" I asked in a high-pitched voice. "What do you know about it?"

"Four years with a Special Warfare Group," he announced calmly. "I know a thing or two."

I frowned, suddenly wondering what other secrets he was keeping. So, he wasn't just a former Navy guy, he was a former SEAL. It's always the quiet ones who surprise you the most. Maybe he was also married and had a bunch of kids. Then I caught Anne's gaze, as she studied my reaction, and the glint of amusement in her eye. *Bugger.* So much for keeping last night a secret, soon to be forgotten. Few things could be kept from the keen Dr. St. Clair.

"I made some calls," Anne continued, as if nothing happened. "As far as the respective organizations were willing to share, Raymond McKinley isn't an active CIA cover, although I wouldn't be surprised if they weren't exactly truthful. He's definitely not an active police undercover case, because the search for his fingerprints didn't raise any alarms. WITSEC won't cooperate for the obvious reasons, and the FBI wouldn't even talk with me, no matter how many favors I called in."

"What about private?" Holt asked. "Could this be a sophisticated contract killer who took a cover identity and did it so well, we can only think government and black ops?"

"I don't see why not, Detective," Anne replied.

"But then, if he's that sophisticated, why leave fingerprints in the first place?" Holt asked. "That I don't understand."

He had a point. "Okay, so let's take a moment here," I said, feeling my mind spinning with suspects and scenarios. "Holt, you still think it could be the mother?"

"Uh-huh," he replied, "I still believe there has to be motive for any murder. The mother, the sister, anyone who stood to lose big from Maddie's lifestyle jeopardizing Caroline's future as the governor's wife had motive. Even the governor himself could be a suspect."

Anne gazed at him intently. "This will make for an interesting investigation," she said. "I can barely wait. You're assuming one of these high-profile people hired a contract killer?"

"Something like that, yeah," Holt replied. "I know you don't believe it was the mother," he added, turning to me, "but at least let's assume it's possible, at least for now."

"Okay," I replied. "I'll give you that, but I'm still interested in finding out what happened to Maddie eleven years ago. Especially now," I added, extracting from my pocket a small evidence bag with the key we'd recovered from the bottom of Maddie's potted violet. "By the way, we have some evidence for the lab, the pot from where this was recovered; we'll leave that with you, if that's okay," I asked Anne.

"Anything in particular I should be looking for?"

I shrugged. "Not really. Just anything that doesn't belong."

"How does that connect with this?" Holt said, pointing first at the key, then at the coroner's report. "Let's assume you're right, and someone from Maddie's troubled past has resurfaced for whatever reason. How does that tie into covert identities and contract killers?"

He had a point. There's a principle of logic, called Occam's razor, that stipulates the simplest, most direct explanation tends to be the correct one. And Occam's razor agreed with Holt's list of suspects. Rich, powerful people are more likely to be the ones hiring top-notch contract killers, not those poor dancers from the Kitty's Whiskers nightclub; he was right about that. A current, immediate threat to Caroline's ascension into the role of Nevada's First Lady, not to mention the White House, made more sense as motive for murder, than something almost trivial that happened eleven years ago, something no one knew or cared about except Maddie. Occam's razor agreed with Holt's scenarios, not with mine. And still, it didn't feel right. Razor or not, my gut said otherwise and wouldn't be silenced.

Holt started pacing the room again. "I usually leave your office with a working theory, Doc. This time, we don't have that luxury. Do you have anything else we could use?"

Anne thought for a moment, looking at us above the rim of her glasses. "I can't draw any conclusions for you; I can only give you facts. The fact is that someone with knowledge, power, and access replaced Raymond McKinley's ten-print card in AFIS with another set of prints belonging to a man who's alive and well, killing people in our city. Someone with skills, based on what you've told me, someone who wouldn't hesitate to pull the trigger on a cop, whether personally or via proxy. That's your suspect, Detectives. That's as good as it gets. But you can go ahead and put out your BOLO. I've been wrong before."

"Really? How many times?" Holt asked, and that crooked grin stretched his lips a little.

"Once," Anne replied dryly. "Only once."

32

Trouble

"When has she been wrong before? About what?" Holt asked, the moment we climbed into his SUV. The man was more interested in gossip than a seventy-year-old cat lady, but curiosity is a great asset in a good cop, although it can get annoying at times. At least he was predictable, and he made one hell of an omelet. At the thought of that, my mouth started watering.

"Do you know what she was talking about?" he insisted, intrigued by my silence.

Of course, I knew every detail, albeit not firsthand. When she and Andrew were serving together in Afghanistan, she was called to identify and examine the body of a Taliban terrorist, killed in a mission to capture the head of the Taliban's operations in that valley. The Marines believed they'd succeeded in their mission. It was in the early days of using DNA collected through CIA-mandated vaccination programs, so she didn't have much to work with, other than old, blurry pictures and unreliable witness accounts. She signed off on a report identifying the corpse lying on her table as Omar Abdul Wasiq, the intended target of the USMC incursion in the area. Satisfied they'd achieved their mission, the colonel withdrew the teams from that valley.

She'd been wrong.

The man on her table was Omar's brother, Amir. The real Omar, blinded by rage over the loss of his brother, attacked a military convoy a few days later, leaving no survivors. That was public knowledge, more or less, captured in Anne's service record. Rumors said that was the incident that altered the course of Anne's existence, responsible for her choice of career as a coroner, and the reason why she was so intense, so focused in her office or at crime scenes.

Not public knowledge was that right after she'd found out about her innocent yet consequential error, she'd woken Andrew in the dead of the night, and the two of them, together with two other comrades in arms, flew a chopper behind Taliban lines and brought back Omar himself, alive and ready for questioning. Considering she flew an unauthorized mission, the best her colonel could do for her was leave the facts out of her file, to keep her from getting courtmartialed.

Knowing what Anne would've wanted me to do under the circumstances, I looked into Holt's eyes and lied. "No idea," I said, without skipping a beat.

He gazed at me for a moment. "Yeah, right." He wasn't buying it.

That's what happens when people grow too close together: trouble. Only trouble can come out of that, and I wished against all reason that I'd remembered that fact last night, before pulling him toward me. Before shagging my partner in less than seventy-two hours since I'd met him. Bugger… that had to be some kind of record.

Within minutes, we arrived at the precinct, and I limped miserably next to Holt, but accepted his arm for support. I figured we'd be less conspicuous that way, although crutches would've been much better. I sat at his desk and logged into the system with my Henderson credentials. Then I typed in all the information I had for the BOLO and released it, while Holt got us fresh coffee.

Upon his return, Holt checked his email, then snatched the keyboard from under my fingers. "We have the Munroe financials," he announced cheerfully.

"Which ones?"

"All of them," he replied, "but I'll start with the mother. That's where I think we're going to hit jackpot. You'll see." He opened the attachment named "Elizabeth Munroe Financials."

We scanned quickly through the many activities on the account, taking note of any patterns and unusual transactions.

"This woman burns through a ton of cash, every month," I said. "Where's it coming from?"

"I saw a first-of-the-month deposit from a brokerage account."

"Let's see if it repeats," I said. Holt scrolled back another month, and there it was. First of last month, twenty grand deposited. "Okay, then, if she's not in financial distress, why does she pawn off her daughter?"

"Because she wants more," Holt replied grimly. "Some people are like that; they can never have enough money, or power, or prestige, and there's nothing they wouldn't do."

"There," I said, then pointed my finger at an unusual transaction, a twenty-five thousand dollar cash withdrawal. "This is your jackpot, and I hate to admit it."

"Ha," Holt exclaimed, "I told you! She paid someone to off her daughter."

"I don't know about that, twenty-five seems a bit low for murder, don't you think?"

"Maybe," he admitted reluctantly. "I know a few scumbags who'd do it for ten."

"I'm guessing lowlife caliber, not pro grade, like we've seen with our perp."

"Yeah," he replied, frowning. "Let's check Caroline and Maddie."

We pored over every line of banking and credit card transactions going back three months, for both Maddie and her sister, and didn't find anything worth noting. Maddie's bank statements showed the monthly cash deposits her father had told us about, and Caroline was spending everything she was making on wedding arrangements, mainly bridal stores of all sorts. None of the three women had taken care of catering, or any other high-ticket item related to the wedding. Probably the governor had that covered with his staff.

"We have to talk to her," Holt said, speaking about Elizabeth Munroe. He grinned widely. "I have some questions for that witch."

"You do realize we have to run this by Wallace, right?" I said, grabbing the edge of Holt's desk to pull myself to my feet without tensing my calf muscle. "The moment we ask her about that twenty-five-grand cash withdrawal, she's going to scream bloody murder and call the governor. And guess who Nevada One is going to call."

"Wallace will allow it, considering these financials," he said, stapling the printout together, then offering me his arm.

We made our way to Wallace's office, but the door was closed, and the lights turned off. We asked his assistant and found out he'd been out of the office since about ten. Then I tried his cell phone, but it went straight to voicemail.

"How do we reach him?" I asked his secretary.

"I'm sorry, I don't know how long he'll be out of reach. I'm told he's on a—"

"Detectives, what do you need?" I heard a voice behind me, and I turned. Assistant Sheriff Dunn stood impatiently, holding an open folder in his hands, while a young intern held a few more.

"We were looking for DC Wallace, sir," I replied.

"You look familiar, Detective…" he said, almost apologetically, measuring me from head to toe.

"Baxter, sir. Just transferred in from Henderson this week."

"Ah, you're that Baxter," he said in a somber tone, while his brow furrowed. Not the reaction I was hoping for.

"We're working the Munroe case, sir," Holt intervened. "We need DC Wallace's authorization to interview the victim's mother. We have questions regarding certain financial transa—"

"Do you always ask for permission for the interviews you conduct?" Dunn said, frowning and drilling Holt with a long stare. "Do you need a deputy chief holding your hand while you do your jobs?"

"No, sir, but this is a politically charged case, and DC Wallace has requested we keep him apprised of developments."

"Ah, I see," Dunn replied, barely containing a smile. "I've sent Wallace to attend a public function in my place; he won't be available for another few hours."

"Thank you, sir," Holt replied, getting ready to leave.

"No need to wait though," Dunn added, "I'm sure he won't mind. Be respectful, go by the book, but ask your questions. Interview whomever you need to."

"Understood," I replied, maybe a little too enthusiastically, because Dunn gave me a long stare before we could turn around and leave.

"Detective Baxter," Dunn called, "if I can have a moment."

Holt and I exchanged a quick glance, then Holt went on his way, and I turned back toward Assistant Sheriff Dunn, showing a confidence I wasn't feeling.

"Sir."

"I'm told Internal Affairs wants to have a word with you."

I felt a pang of anxiety rippling through my gut. This was serious trouble.

"Is this about yesterday's shooting at the Munroe apartment?"

"I don't know what it's about, Detective. Show up, know your rights, be careful what you say."

"Understood, sir."

He turned and left without another word, just a quick nod in my direction.

Know my rights? My mind screamed in panic. They must've captured on some video camera the stunt I pulled in the evidence locker. Or maybe that piece of crap, TwoCent, woke up from his hangover and remembered what went down and with whom. Maybe his first call from lockup was to his old cellmate, Digger, who must have sworn on his life he hadn't sent him any hooker. Maybe he spilled everything he knew, and he knew enough, about what I'd done, about what Holt had done on his first arrest.

I needed some time before talking to IA, some time to collect my thoughts, to think of what I'd say, how I'd respond to any questions they might hit me with. I hesitated in front of the elevator, my finger hovering between the two call buttons. Up meant IA's office. Down meant Holt and the interview with Maddie's mother. And time to think.

I pressed the down button, and let out a long breath of air. A killer on the loose trumps any paperwork IA needs to keep themselves busy with.

33

Conspiracy

The butler opened the door for us and held it patiently, holding his other hand ceremoniously behind his back. I thought I noticed a glint of amusement in his dark irises; I smiled back, but that glint disappeared as if never there. He showed us to the living room and announced us by name.

Mrs. Munroe sat on a wide leather sofa, cream colored to match the wall décor and the Persian rugs, with an open magazine in her lap. I had to admire her jacket, an Akris, if I wasn't mistaken, something definitely above this detective's pay grade. It looked good on her, the bold colors bringing contrast to her otherwise pale skin and lending a sense of stylish youthfulness to her overall attire. The fashionista in me envied her for a moment, albeit a fleeting one.

"Thank you for seeing us, Mrs. Munroe," I said, and she nodded once, without smiling.

"Make it quick," she said. "As you can see, I'm busy." She flipped another page of the magazine she was browsing with a stern look of defiance on her face.

"Only one question then," Holt said coldly. "Almost three weeks ago, you withdrew twenty-five thousand dollars in cash from your checking account. What was that money used for?"

Her jaw slacked for a moment, then she squinted her eyes, throwing darts of pure venom.

"How dare you look into my accounts? What gave you the right?" She stood and approached Holt, with her fists tightly clenched in front of her chest, slightly trembling. She drilled him with her glare, but he didn't flinch. Thankfully, he didn't flash his condescending smile either, probably aware of how that would've fueled her anger.

"We had a subpoena," he replied calmly. "The courts saw fit that we examine your financials."

"You dragged my name in front of a judge? Now, on the eve of my daughter's wedding? Who put you up to this?"

A sickly shade of gray colored her face, and she started pacing around Holt like a hungry hyena.

"There's the minor issue of your daughter's death that we needed to investigate," Holt replied, and I had to bite my tongue to keep quiet. Holt could be quite wicked when he wanted to be, but scorning Mrs. Munroe was probably a bad idea. "Your daughter Madeline, remember her?" he asked in the most innocent of tones.

"Damn you people, for dragging our good family name through the mud like this. It's all political, I know it. A lot of bad people want my son-in-law replaced, you know, and you're working for them, doing their bidding. Damn you."

"Either way, ma'am," I said, "we have a subpoena, and you need to answer some questions. When someone is killed, large amounts of cash changing hands is considered suspicious activity, and all we want to do is clear your name, nothing more."

"Ah, so now I'm a suspect too? You think I killed my own daughter?" She stopped in front of me, with her hands propped on her hips, her eyes shooting fiery glares above the narrow, rectangular lenses of her Chanel glasses.

"Well, did you?" Holt asked, and the woman froze in place, as if suddenly turned to stone. Then she straightened her back and turned slowly to face him. When she spoke, her voice was calm and ice cold.

"This conversation is over. Contact my lawyer for any of your ridiculous questions; he'll deal with the likes of you." Then she beckoned the butler to show us out.

In the vestibule, the butler held my jacket for me, then moved to the side and opened the door. As we were about to step outside, he stopped us.

"Excuse me, ma'am, I believe you dropped this," he said, holding out a crumpled piece of paper.

For a split-second, I tried to remember if I'd left anything in my jacket pockets, and I knew I hadn't; intrigued, I smiled and thanked him as he passed the note to me. I shoved it in my pocket and didn't look at it until Holt had put the SUV in motion and turned the corner.

Then I took out the piece of paper and read the name written on it in rushed cursive. "Emilio Macias."

"Who's that?" Holt asked, frowning slightly.

"Apparently, a lead in your jackpot scenario. Yet another suspect. Have you noticed how many suspects we keep finding in this case?"

"That was bound to happen," Holt replied. "It's a charged case. A victim with a troubled past who lived a double life. Politics and political alliances to top it off, and the most manipulative woman I've ever met, holding the reins." He chuckled lightly. "I'm surprised there aren't more."

"Well, I have to admit Mrs. Munroe's recent transactions surprised me quite a bit. I thought I'd developed a sense for killers, after so many years of being a cop. If it turns out she's the killer, I'll have to get my radar checked," I said bitterly.

I always relied on my gut for a sense of direction, to guide me where to lead an interrogation, or which one of two suspects to pursue first. That gut wasn't just a sixth sense; it was augmented by my ability to read microexpressions and body language, to spot the moment a guilty suspect's pupils dilate in fear, or what particular words she speaks when she can't force herself to look me in the eye. With the Munroe matriarch, I felt as if my senses had been thrown off, like unshielded, electronic-measuring instruments in the presence of an intense electromagnetic field.

I knew precisely what that meant; if evidence proved she was the killer, then Mrs. Munroe was a true psychopath, one who doesn't display any of the normal body language tell signs when lying, manipulating, or feeling guilty, because psychopaths can't feel remorse nor fear. That scenario made more sense than the one in which I simply missed seeing the signs, but I still wasn't sold to Mrs. Munroe being the killer. Something was off, but I couldn't put my finger on it.

"You still believe someone from Madeline's past has emerged now and decided to kill her?" Holt asked.

"That scenario makes more sense to me on an instinctive level. On a logical one, you win."

"We'll both win once we collar the doer, whoever he or she might be," he said somberly. "But if you want to place a bet, I'll be happy to honor it and get a chance to even the score."

"What do you mean?"

"You might have already won the bet we made over the potted violet. It did hold an answer, more than I'd expected anyway."

"We don't know what that key opens yet, and what we'll find in there. I, for one, am dying to find out."

"We have three options," Holt said, stopping on the side of the road, close to a four-way intersection, most likely an unintended metaphor. "We have the opportunity to interview Caroline, the vic's sister, but we have to do it fast, before DC Wallace returns and has the time to stop us. I'm not saying he will, but he might. We have the key, and I believe—"

"We have this," I said, showing him the crumpled note from the butler, "and this is urgent. I want to find out what this means, before Elizabeth Munroe gets the chance to mess things up for us."

"Right." He unscrewed the cap off a water bottle, then offered it to me. I shook my head, and he downed the entire thing in a few thirsty gulps.

I pulled the laptop closer and did a quick background check on Emilio Macias.

"Oh," I reacted, the moment the screen displayed his background information.

"What?" Holt asked, leaning toward me to see the screen. I turned it partly his way.

"He's, um, unexpectedly attractive," I replied, feeling my cheeks heat up a little. "But he's got a record a mile long, mostly nonviolent stuff," I added quickly, scrolling through his list of charges. "A few con jobs, some drug dealing, a couple of thefts, then he moved on to assault and battery, for which he served a few years."

"I hate him already," Holt replied, and the double meaning of his words made me chuckle. "Do you have a last known address?" he asked.

"Yeah, in North Las Vegas," I replied, and before I could add anything else, Holt had turned on the siren and lights, and was flooring it toward the interstate.

34

Hired Help

The sound of the siren made it difficult to carry on a conversation, and for a while, we were quiet. But then, I asked the million-dollar question.

"Do you think we should question the governor?"

Holt threw me one of those side glances he liked to pair up with a crooked grin.

"Madeline was thrilled about the marriage, because she believed that would bring the opportunity for her to seek justice for what had happened to her," I added. "What if she'd already spoken to him?"

"Or what if the governor learned about Madeline's secret life and decided to clean up anything that could keep him from moving on to the White House?" Holt replied. "If we can prove he knew about Kitty's Whiskers, we can prove motive. You know, career politicians run background checks on an entire family before marrying into it. Look how little time it took us to find out about Maddie. I'm willing to bet—"

"All right, all right," I replied, raising my hands in the air to stop the flow of arguments coming from Holt. "I thought you liked the mother for it."

"Like you said, this case is ripe with suspects, a real maze of leads," he replied, frowning deeply. "I'm keeping an open mind, that's all."

"Okay, let's deal with Mr. Macias first, then we'll pay the happy couple a visit."

I almost blurted that I'd need to talk with IA before we did anything else that day, but I kept my mouth shut. There was no good reason why Holt should worry about the rat squad instead of keeping his mind on the case.

A few moments later, we were banging on a dirty apartment door on the third floor of a cheap housing building in North Las Vegas.

"Open up, police," Holt shouted, pounding on the door again.

We listened intently and heard the sound of rushed footfalls moving back and forth through the apartment, bumping into furniture, then we heard the toilet flush. I stepped to the side and pulled my weapon, while Holt kicked the door open.

"Freeze," he shouted, and Macias stopped in his tracks, dropping the small plastic bag he was holding and raising his hands.

"What you got here, huh?" I asked, holstering my weapon and sliding on a glove. I picked up the baggie from the floor, holding it with two fingers. "Coke? Meth?" It was always the bloody drugs, wherever I turned. I felt a familiar wave of rage singe through my brain, another notable moment for Dr. Beville.

"N-no, please," Macias said. "They're not mine, I swear," he added quickly, his eyes shifting from Holt to me and back, desperately looking for someone who could believe his lies.

"That's not why we're here," Holt replied, and grabbed him by the collar, then slammed him against the wall. "I'm here about the cash you got from Elizabeth Munroe," he said in a menacing low tone, close to his ear. "Those twenty-five thousand dollars you got a couple of weeks ago."

That's when I saw it, real fear, dilating his pupils to the max. He probably couldn't even see us straight anymore; we were a blur of terror to him.

"I—I don't know what you're talking about," he said, stuttering badly, almost whimpering.

"What if we could pretend we never saw this?" I said, showing him the bag of drugs I still held in my hand. "We're not after you, we're after her, and you know the drill, who talks first gets to walk."

Holt shot me an amazed look. We weren't authorized to offer a deal like that; we needed an ADA to sign off first. But I wasn't going to let this one slip through our fingers either. Well, the rule book said we should've collared him for the drugs, and, while in holding, squeeze everything out of him about the Munroes. In reality though, we ran the risk of having the lovely Mrs. Munroe lawyer up that perp before we even got to central booking with him, and that was a risk I wasn't willing to take.

He stared at me with rounded eyes, his pupils still enlarged, and his jaw a little slacked. "Really?" His voice was high pitched yet strangled.

"Really," I replied. "But you have to spill everything right now, all of it, in the next five seconds, or the deal is off the table."

"Yeah, yeah, okay," he replied, and Holt eased his grip a little. "I didn't do nothing, you know. She never showed up."

"Who never showed up?" Holt asked.

"The old lady's daughter," he replied. "I swear she never showed."

Holt and I exchanged a glance.

"Okay, what were you supposed to do?" Holt asked patiently.

"I was supposed to scare her off, nothing more."

"How, exactly?"

"You know, pick her up, show her a good time, then rough her up in her hotel room. That's what the old lady said, rough her up, so she'll behave. No broken bones, no need for stitches. Just a few bruises."

"How generous of her," I replied, suffocated with anger. Unbelievable, that a mother would do something like that. Although, if anyone in any line of work could say they've seen it all, that's homicide detectives after about ten years of tenure or so.

"Did she say why she wanted Madeline roughed up?" Holt asked calmly.

"Uh-huh," Macias replied, nodding vigorously. "She said her daughter had been whoring around, bringing shame to the family, and she wanted someone to put the fear of God into her, so she'd never whore again. She said I could... you know, do it rough with her."

Holt slammed him against the wall again, without a word.

"I swear, that's what she said," he repeated, still nodding.

"Then what happened? You got overly enthusiastic and strangled her? Is that it?"

"No, no," he shouted. "She never showed up, I swear!"

"Walk me through what happened, step by step," I said.

"I followed her online, on Facebook, friended her, chatted, then made her promise she'd meet me for dinner. That was the plan. But she never showed up."

"Where was she supposed to meet you, and when?"

"Sunday night, at four, on the terrace at that sushi place on Flamingo. They have space heaters out there, it's nice."

"And what happened?"

"She never showed, I told you already," he repeated, seemingly frustrated with how many times he'd said the same thing to us. "I was there from a quarter to four, until about half past five. I... didn't want to have to give the old lady her money back, so I waited."

I took out my phone, ready to call Technical Services and ask them to pull video surveillance from that sushi place. If they confirmed, Macias had an alibi for the time of death, but he was still on the hook for conspiracy. "Wrap up this piece of shite, will you, partner?"

"Gladly," he replied, then turned Macias around and started cuffing him.

"Wait," he shouted, wriggling to break free. "You said I'd walk if I talked, right?"

"I said, 'who talks first gets to walk first,' as in 'reduced sentence,'" I replied serenely. "You must have misheard. We'll tell the DA you cooperated, and we'll try to skip the drug charge this time, but you're going down."

"I didn't do nothing," he screamed, while Holt moved him down the stairs and toward the car.

I strode behind them smiling widely, and that smile lingered on my lips until I climbed into the car.

"What's so amusing?" Holt asked.

"Oh, I'm just anticipating the moment we're going to read Mrs. Munroe her rights; we have her on conspiracy to commit assault. What do you think she'll want to wear in lockup?"

35

Legacy

I still limped badly behind Holt as he walked Macias to central booking, but my wound was healing faster than I'd hoped. Dr. Green Eyes had done a good job cleaning and closing it, and I expected I'd stop touching the walls sometime before the end of the day, despite the unrelenting throb in my left calf.

Macias had entertained us the entire time with his display of emotions, spanning from rage to denial to having a complete meltdown on the back seat of the SUV, but he hadn't added anything new to what we already had. He wasn't the right material to pull off the highly organized crime we'd witnessed on the video surveillance tapes from the Aquamarine. AFIS had his fingerprints from prior collars, and they weren't a match. He was just a small time con artist who'd graduated to some violence due to a stint behind bars, and some skills he'd acquired while in residence upstate.

The three of us stopped in front of the elevator bank in the main LVMPD building, and I decided it was as good a time as ever. I pressed the up button and took a sharp breath.

"Would you mind booking him by yourself? There's something I got to do upstairs. It might take me a little while."

A frown ruffled Holt's brow. "Anything I should know about?"

I hesitated for a moment, tempted to lie, but didn't.

"Um… they have some questions."

"About what? Yesterday's shooting?"

"No idea."

He gave me a long stare, but then my elevator arrived, and I nodded briefly his way before the doors closed.

Internal Affairs was organized in a separate suite, complete with a suite door and a receptionist. I greeted her with a smile, but she didn't smile back. It was probably in their code of conduct: Don't smile, and don't be pleasant with your colleagues.

I shrugged it off, while continuing to smile, just to spite her. "I'm Detective Baxter," I said. "I was told IA wanted to speak with me?"

She typed a few keys into the computer. "Yes, Lieutenant Steenstra wants a word with you." She stood and walked from behind the reception desk. "Follow me, please."

She opened the door to a small conference room and showed me inside.

"I see you don't have your rep with you. Would you like me to call someone?"

I frowned, considering it. Assistant Sheriff Dunn had recommended it also. What the hell was going on?

"No, I'm fine," I said, then sat down where shown, happy to take the weight off my leg.

"All right," the receptionist replied. "She'll be a few minutes."

The door closed, and I breathed, expecting to be left waiting for a while, in typical police interrogation procedure. But Lieutenant Steenstra took less than two minutes to walk through that door.

I hadn't met her before. She looked sharp in a navy blue pantsuit with a light blue shirt, and she offered a quick smile before sitting down with an open file folder laid on the table between us. Then she stared at me, with an enigmatic, yet amused, smirk on her lips, probably waiting to see if I flinched. It took me all the willpower I had inside me to keep from fidgeting in my seat, to steady my eyes from turning sideways, afraid they'd become transparent and she could see every thought in my mind, every little thing I'd done. By the way she waited, by the confidence in her demeanor, they had something on me. I wasn't sure what, but I was positive that file folder held a few unpleasant surprises.

Steenstra was the first to break eye contact, a small win.

"We need your help, Detective," she said, and I had to force myself to contain the sigh of relief I felt rushing out of my lungs. Instead, I nodded, showing just the right amount of interest in my eyes.

"What can I do for you?" I asked, then cleared my voice quietly. My throat had constricted all of a sudden, making my voice sound raspy, broken.

"You've been partnered with Detective Holt. How's that going?"

I shrugged. "All right, I guess. I only met him four days ago." They couldn't possibly know about last night; there was no way, unless Holt had walked in there himself and told them. He'd never do that.

"Good," Steenstra replied. "We want you to continue to stay his partner and build a solid relationship with him."

My eyebrows shot up in genuine, unfiltered surprise.

"What's this about?" I asked, while a feeling of uneasiness crept down my spine, bringing a chill.

"We have reasons to believe he… mishandled some evidence in the last case he worked on," Steenstra said. "Specifically, a kilo of pure cocaine has gone missing," she added, seeing my inquisitive frown, "on the way between the crime scene and the evidence locker."

Bloody hell, Holt… it better not be true.

I scoffed quietly. "Did you ask Holt about it?"

Steenstra hesitated a brief moment. "No, we did not. He'd obviously deny it, and we'd like to save time here, Detective."

"He could explain what happened, address your suspicions. Why not give him a chance, before having his partner sicced to spy on him?"

"Why don't you leave these matters of procedure to Internal Affairs, Detective? We're asking for your help, and that's all you need to know."

There it was, a suffocating wave of blood-red anger rushing through my veins and taking over my brain.

"Well, was he the only one at the scene?" I asked, leaning toward Steenstra. "Was he alone with the cocaine bust for any length of time? Who recovered the drugs, and who signed the chain of evidence tags? What made you suspect Holt, over who knows how many other cops present at the scene?"

"Detective," Steenstra called, raising her voice, but I wasn't finished.

"And how did you figure the coke was missing? Did some perp tell you, and you decided to take his word over a seasoned detective?"

Steenstra stared at me again, this time somberly. She didn't bother to reply to any of my questions, and I felt the pang of fear unfurling in my gut. Then she opened her folder and extracted an enhanced print taken from the surveillance video inside the evidence locker.

"We draw conclusions from facts, Detective," she said, talking softly, as one would to a child who needs to learn a life lesson. "For instance, here we have you, on camera, in the evidence locker at almost five in the morning, going through the case evidence for the Munroe murder. All legit, apparently. Yet we could choose to believe that there is a correlation between your presence there that night and the murder weapon in the Park case, conveniently found by the janitor the very next morning. You know, the weapon that allowed us to take that cop killer to court after all."

They knew! How the hell did they know? Or maybe they didn't, and they were toying with me. Cops are mandated to lie and manipulate facts in any way they choose during an interrogation. I'd better remember that.

"I don't understand," I replied calmly.

"Sometimes, good people do things a certain way to make sure criminals don't get away with their crimes, even if that means breaking protocol or stretching the line of the law until their actions fall inside the right category."

I nodded slightly, unsure how to react.

"Are we on the same team here, Detective Baxter?" Steenstra asked. "If we are, we could help each other. You have, um, issues on your record that could go away forever," she added, upping the gambit. "I'm sure I don't need to remind you what those are."

My throat constricted again, and I felt my palms sweat. I nodded.

"Excellent," Steenstra said in a cheerful voice. "I'm glad we understand each other. Someone in your position is very vulnerable, and we're here to make sure you don't take the wrong step."

And there it was, the explicit threat to complement the bait. If I played, I'd get my record cleared up. If I didn't, they'd throw me to the curb like an old shoe that no longer fit. I was cornered, squashed against the wall, with nowhere left to go other than being a rat squad spy. I felt bile rising in my throat and the urge to throw up. Thankfully, I didn't have to keep a straight face for much longer. Steenstra thanked me for my cooperation, then showed me to the elevators.

I didn't stop until I reached the second-floor ladies' room, where I locked myself inside a stall and unloaded my restless stomach, then gasped for air like someone who'd been under water for too long. I looked around for something to punch, but there weren't any options; just tiled walls and a metallic door, both guaranteed to resist my anger unscathed yet add new injuries to my body. I grunted and swore out loud instead, then pulled myself together somewhat, enough to throw some cold water on my heated face and get ready to see Holt.

What the hell was I going to tell him? Finding a good lie wasn't an issue; I'd always had a talent for that. But the question that really troubled me was, had Holt really taken the coke? I had to get my own computer and look at the case evidence, see what had happened. Or I could ask Holt directly, share with him what the IA was after, and give him a chance to be considered innocent until proven guilty, to explain himself. But he was an addict, a cocaine addict no less.

What would I want, if the roles were reversed? *Oh, bloody hell, Holt.*

I finally extricated myself from the ladies' room, after a good look in the mirror showed my makeup intact and a decent control of my emotions, and limped my way toward Holt's desk. He saw me approaching, and cut the distance in half with a sprint in his step.

"Is everything okay?" he asked, letting worry furrow his brow.

"Yeah, just some whiplash from that, um, thing I have on my record. The perp I beat up."

"This will cheer you up," he replied, then showed me a computer printout. "I have Madeline's safety deposit box."

"How come?" I asked, relieved by the change in topic.

"People are creatures of habit and essentially lazy. She did her banking with First National, and there was a high probability she kept the box with them also. They confirmed that it's the type of key they use, and that Madeline's box number was eight zero one."

I smiled, feeling excitement dissipating the dark cloud that had been looming around me since I'd spoken with Lieutenant Steenstra.

"Wanna go for a ride?" I asked, then grabbed the arm he was offering.

Almost thirty minutes later, we were shown to box 801, one of the larger containers, and I held my breath as I turned the rusted key in the lock. The bank representative gave us the room, and I slid on a glove before opening the box. I took one look inside, and my breath caught.

36

Testimony

"Bloody hell, Madeline!" I exclaimed, then cheered loudly, as I saw the plastic bag with clothing. "If this is what I think it is, you're a smart cookie!"

"Yup," Holt said, "That's got to be the clothing she wore the day she was assaulted."

He picked up a small, colorful notebook, the type used by young girls as diaries, the only other item found in box 801. He opened it and flipped through several pages.

"Yeah, that's the evidence," he confirmed, "and there's more. Her account of what happened."

I opened the bag carefully and sifted through the items inside, without removing them from the bag. It had been sealed tightly and most of the air removed from it. Any speck of dust, hair fiber, or particulate could help us identify her assailants. She'd put in there a miniskirt; a green, cotton top with the Royal Hall logo; bra; and panties.

"Excellent," I said, then closed the bag carefully. "Roses are red, violets are blue," I recited my own version of Maddie's little poem in a sing-song voice, "the wait is over, I'm coming for you."

Holt pulled his chair next to mine and opened the notebook on the table, so we could both read. It felt as if Maddie was right there with us, giving cursive testimony of the day that had changed the course of her life.

I don't know who will read this, or if anyone ever will, Madeline's diary said, *but I'm terrified I'll forget what little I can remember. Most of what happened is already gone, and I don't know where to start. I'll just write it as I can, whatever facts I still recall, in the hope that someday, someone will want to hear my story.*

I took a summer job at the Royal Hall Hotel and Casino, as a poolside lifeguard. Don't laugh; I might be thin, but I'm strong, my lifeguard certification is legit, and the pool isn't that deep. I wasn't particularly fond of all the catcalling and rudeness I got from some tourists, but there aren't that many jobs a seventeen-year-old can work in a hotel and casino, and in Vegas, it's either that or fast food.

Underage staff isn't supposed to serve liquor, but that didn't mean I didn't have to.

Everyone works to please the guests, our boss says, and whatever they ask for is what they get. As a lifeguard, I was required to sit in the chair or walk the deck and watch the pool, but, in reality, I had to do more than that. I brought poolside drinks to whoever asked, for a share of the tips. I rubbed sunscreen lotion on hairy backs and tried not to get pinched while doing it. I waited on the poolside cabanas whenever the waiters weren't available, and the customers needed something.

That's how they saw me. The three of them shared a cabana, lounging on the white beds, drinks in hand, laughing and cursing and making obscene comments. They beckoned me, and I had to respond; one of them was the hotel owner's son.

Then I brought them drinks, cold beers. One of them had some joints, and they lit up; I recognized the smell. He wore a hat, one of those white beach hats with a black ribbon, the kind that looks like straw but isn't really. Then they wanted more drinks, and they refused to let the regular waitress serve them. They asked specifically for me, and I had no choice but to go.

Over the next hour or so, I brought them beers and shots and witnessed them get drunker and louder. One of them grabbed my arm roughly, as I was putting the drinks on the table, and I squealed and tried to pull away. Then the boss's son said something to him like, "I believe it's time you joined our gang for real. Do you got what it takes?"

The man in the hat cheered along and said, "Yeah, it's initiation time, man, you have to."

The one who'd grabbed me refused at first, but he didn't let me go either; he still crushed my arm in his grip. "No way. Here? You have to be crazy or something."

"Or drunk," the boss's son replied, and they all guffawed so loudly, everyone turned to look. "No, not here, you wiseass, I got a suite upstairs."

The three of them brought their heads together and whispered for a while, and I didn't catch any of that. From what I could tell, the man who'd grabbed me argued about something with the other two, but they were daring him, pushing him, and he eventually gave in, even became excited about it.

I didn't know about what at the time. If I'd known, I would've screamed my lungs out until someone would've helped me. But I didn't, so when the boss's son ordered the other man to let go of my arm, I felt grateful and thought that was the end of it. Then he asked me to join them for a drink, a cold soda or something. I hesitated, eager to get away from them, but he insisted, said he had special guests, and I was embarrassing him in front of his friends, his own employee refusing to drink a cold Coke with them. I obliged.

That's when I think they must've slipped something into my drink. I became dizzy, almost unable to stand, and they made room for me to sit next to them on the side of the bed. I remember realizing there was something wrong with that Coke. They pushed me to drink all of it, but I stalled, and when they weren't looking, I spilled it against the side of the bed, knowing that the foam would absorb it.

Then one of them, I don't recall which one, offered to take me inside the hotel lobby, where there was air conditioning, so I would feel better. I didn't fight it; I couldn't. It was as if my arms and legs were made of soft rubber. I just obeyed, holding on to his arm for balance, and hearing the other two laughing behind me.

The next thing I know, I was in a hotel suite, a top-floor fancy one, lying on my back on the bed. I was pinned down, and when I tried to stand, I felt a man's strong grip on both my wrists, lifted above my head. I remember looking at him to see who it was, but I couldn't see his face clearly; everything was a blur. This man had a birthmark, a dark triangular shape on the inside of his left forearm, that was close enough for me to see clearly. I'd recognize that birthmark anywhere. It looked like this.

Madeline had inserted a drawing of an elongated triangle, filled with numerous lines to color it dark.

Then I'm afraid I don't remember much else, no matter how hard I try. I woke the next morning inside an empty hotel room, dressed the way I'd been the day before, as if nothing had happened. But it had happened. I was in pain and bleeding and had bruises all over my body. I remember running away from there, scared they'd come back.

I don't know who they were; other than the one who was my boss's son, I didn't recognize anyone else. I never went back to that hotel, and my mother said I should never talk about what happened, not with anyone, not ever. She told me that as a minor I can't file a police report without her consent, and she didn't want my future ruined over something so trivial. She's very ambitious for us, my mom.

It wasn't trivial to me, and I wish I had the nerve to go against her wishes and talk to someone. I watch enough TV to know what I'd want to remember, if one day someone will care enough to listen to me.

They were white, all three of them, and in their late twenties, maybe thirty years old. They seemed close, touching one another, patting one another on the shoulder, mock-punching one another. They seemed to have money. Not as in millions, but enough money to feel good and do whatever they wanted. They all wore dark shades, so I never saw their eyes.

That's all I remember for now. I'm sorry.

I closed the diary and remained silent for a moment, choked, reeling from having heard Madeline's testimony beyond death. Then I turned to face Holt.

"I don't know about you," I said, "but if I were one of these wankers, and I learned that the girl I raped had a sister who's about to marry the governor, I'd get a little scared."

"Maybe," Holt replied, cupping his chin in the palm of his hand. "Statute of limitations has run its course for this assault, you know that."

"Can we at least talk to the hotel owner's son?" I said, then stood with difficulty, ready to leave.

"Absolutely," Holt replied.

We got to the car, and he grabbed the laptop and started a search. It was freezing, but I waited for him to finish the search, eager to find out if my theory was correct.

"Aaron Pelucha is the name," Holt said. "He's forty years old, which made him twenty-nine at the time of the assault. He's the owner of the Royal Hall Hotel now; his father passed away five years ago. But we can't go anywhere near that guy; he'd lawyer up before we get to say our names."

"There has to be a way, Holt. We'll think of something," I said, already having an idea, but unwilling to jump the gun just yet. "Let's drop these clothes at Anne's first, then see what the ADA suggests we do."

Holt didn't reply; instead, he turned on the engine and peeled away from the curb. Then he dialed a number from the car's memory.

"Hey, Gully, I need a favor," he said, the moment the ADA picked up.

37

After-Dinner Plans

We'd just dropped Madeline's clothing at Anne's office when Gully called us back with bad news.

"I caught Judge Hayden right before he left for the day, and he laughed in my face," Gully said, sounding frustrated on the phone. "I was kind of expecting that, but I thought maybe we had a chance."

"What did he say?" I asked, frowning and fidgeting in my seat. My stomach growled and hurt, still upset after the earlier meeting with IA, and we'd managed to skip lunch altogether. I needed good news, not bad.

"The statute of limitations on the alleged assault has long since expired, and we already knew that," Gully replied. "He said there's no basis for questioning Aaron Pelucha, because there's no evidence linking the alleged assault from eleven years ago with Madeline Munroe's murder, and we can't interrogate Pelucha on a crime we can no longer prosecute. He's off the hook."

"So, we got nothing?" Holt asked.

"In his honor's own words, 'Get me some evidence to link the two cases, and you can bring him in front of a grand jury.'"

Holt and I exchanged a quick glance, then thanked Gully and ended the call, leaving silence to engulf the car for a long, disappointed moment.

"What do we know about Pelucha?" I eventually asked.

Holt pulled the laptop over and started typing.

"He's clean; no priors. He's not in the system at all." He slammed the laptop shut with a frustrated sigh loaded with unintelligible oaths. "What do you want to do next?"

I leaned my head against the cold window and looked outside for a while, letting my mind wander. It was dark already, and the myriad lights and colors of Las Vegas had come to life. Traffic was thin; it was one of the least busy times of the year, the week before Thanksgiving, when people normally choose to spend time with family instead of gambling and partying on the Strip. I like this time of year in Sin City; it feels like the city is all mine to explore, even if it's cold and dreary. Only this time, I wasn't enjoying it as much, knowing Madeline's killer was out there, doing whatever the hell he wanted instead of rotting in jail.

My thoughts went back to Madeline and what had happened to her eleven years ago. Whenever I thought of that smart girl, saving her clothing in a clean bag to serve as evidence at some point, my heart filled with admiration and rage at the same time. Admiration for the girl who was silenced, but not defeated. Rage for that mother of hers, who'd lied and manipulated her into not filing a police report. I almost asked myself what kind of creature does that to her own daughter, but I already knew the answer: Elizabeth Munroe was a sociopath, certifiable.

I closed my eyes, trying to visualize the hotel pool, the cabana with the three drunken men, the young Madeline trying to free herself from their grip. She didn't stand a chance, poor kid. Just two nights ago, I'd turned three badass thugs into putty with two roofies each. There's no escaping the power of Rohypnol; Madeline had been smart enough to realize it and spilled some of her drink, so she could remember at least some details about her attackers. I would like to have met the smart, gumptious Madeline Munroe; she was special.

Then my thoughts went to her attackers. Three men... one was Aaron Pelucha, who gave her the roofie and talked her into entering the hotel. The second had a birthmark on his arm, "the triangle," and he'd pinned Maddie down during the assault. And the third man? I decided to call him "the grabber" for now, because he was the first one to grab Maddie's arm, and, per her father's testimony, to leave bruises on her skin.

The three men were close, in Maddie's own words. There were ways in which we could find Aaron Pelucha's close associates from a decade ago. Facebook was maybe one way, then witnesses of all kinds, such as seasoned hotel workers, colleagues, other friends, and neighbors. Not easy, and definitely not fast enough. Madeline's killer could disappear five times over by the time we'd finish looking into Pelucha's background. Not to mention if we tipped him off, he could let the other two know we were coming.

We needed something else, faster, better, foolproof. We needed Pelucha squeezed tightly in a corner, ready to spill everything that he'd done eleven years ago, and with whom. We needed him vulnerable and afraid.

I felt Holt's touch on my arm. "Earth to Baxter? What do you want to do next?"

"Eat dinner, and you're buying," I replied.

"Yes, ma'am," he replied enthusiastically, and his boyish grin reappeared.

Damn it, Holt, wait 'til you hear what I have to ask you.

In front of a good meal, my resolve to discuss the IA investigation with Holt dispersed completely, and I found myself enjoying his company, afraid that the atmosphere would turn to ice the moment I'd open my mouth. Instead, we discussed the Munroe case at length, bounced ideas back and forth, going through every lead we could still follow, every bit of evidence we could hope to find, and every person we could talk to. Some things, of course, I kept to myself.

We hadn't had the chance to speak with Caroline or the governor, but the motivation to see them was dissipating, deprioritized by the new evidence that we'd uncovered in Maddie's safety deposit box. Instead, I wanted to find a way to drag Pelucha into an interview room, scared and willing to talk.

But how?

I needed time alone to work things out.

I watched Holt sign the check and forfeited my last opportunity to ask him about the last time he'd used cocaine. I smiled, and I thanked him, while a fleeting thought passed through my mind. If anyone ever asked why we'd gone out to dinner together, I could always say I was following IA's orders, to get close to my partner and earn his trust. Isn't life funny that way?

Once we stepped outside in the biting cold, reality took over. I had work to do.

"You need to attend a meeting, I believe," I said, as I climbed into his car. "Drop me off at my place, please. I'm wiped."

The smile in his eyes vanished. He started the engine without a word, and I dozed the entire time, knowing that I'd probably be busy for most of the night.

He pulled into my driveway and offered to help me inside, but I was quick to reject his offer, afraid that if I had him in the privacy of my living room all my plans for the night would fall apart under the pressure of temptation. Visibly disappointed, he waited to see me get to the door, then drove off and disappeared around the corner.

38

Incursion

The first stop was the kitchen counter, where I started a big pot of coffee, then fired up my laptop. There wasn't much about Pelucha online; probably a security measure that most public figures engage to keep stalkers and weirdos at bay. I did find a few photos showing him in various locations inside his hotel, including his office. I memorized the layout, as much as it came across in that photo.

The second search was more productive; it had to do with the floor layout plans for the Royal Hall Hotel and Casino. I needed to know where Pelucha's office was located. The best guess was a remote suite, rather large, housed on the second floor in the southeast corner. He could also have one of the penthouse suites, like many other hotel owners, but there was no way of knowing which one. I needed Lady Luck to smile in my direction.

Satisfied with the odds, I downed the rest of the coffee and went upstairs, holding on to the rail with both hands as I climbed each step with difficulty. I probably should've stayed off my feet for the night, but, courtesy of Mr. Pelucha's transgressions, I had a different agenda.

I changed my clothes after long moments of hesitation in front of the closet. I couldn't wear my first choice, a little black dress with heels, because my wound dressing showed, and limping would've made that outfit awkward. Walking on heels strains the calf muscle, and I wanted my sutures to stay in place for a while longer. The second choice was black jeans with a black T-shirt and black sneakers, accessorized by a NV Energy utility cap and an ID tag that took me almost thirty minutes to manufacture. I kept my hair tied in a bun and adjusted my makeup to make me look pale and tired. That wasn't difficult at all, considering the black circles around my sunken eyes and the pallor in my cheeks. The final touch was applying latex to my fingers, and improvising a tool bag out of what I had on hand.

I stocked the bag with tools of the trade, extracted from behind the closet wall. A professional grade lock-pick set. A handheld, digital alarm code breaker, in case I ran into any security systems at Pelucha's office. A thermal imaging camera that worked with my phone.

I drove my own car to the Royal Hall and parked it underground. I walked across the garage to the main elevators, then spent a good thirty minutes on the main floor, taking the pulse of the foot traffic, noticing how security moved around, and the locations of surveillance cameras. Then I took the escalator to the second floor and made my way toward the southeast corner in the steady gait of a tired worker, called to check on something. Shoulders hunched forward, slightly lowered head, one hand shoved in the pocket.

I turned into a corridor and the noise of the casino subsided. The area was engulfed in darkness, barely lit by safety lights. At the far end of the corridor was a massive, double, glass door. I stopped and pulled out my phone, already fitted with the infrared camera. I looked and saw nothing out of the ordinary; just a deserted administration office suite, long after hours. No security guard lurking in the darkness, no laser beams crisscrossing in the air. It made sense; the vault and all the secure offices were in the basement. This was Pelucha's official office, where he saw his business guests.

I looked around and saw two surveillance cameras pointing straight at the door, but decided to act as if nothing was wrong. Most likely, the security staff was focused on the casino floor cameras this late at night, and I was planning to be in and out of there in less than two minutes.

Then I looked inside through the glass door and located the alarm control panel. It was sophisticated, but nothing my device couldn't handle. The biggest risk was having someone walk in on me while it did its job flickering red and green LEDs, or being seen on video by one of the many security personnel employed by the hotel.

I took a deep breath and steadied my hands. I felt excitement at the thought of doing this, but also a bit of fear. Getting caught could land me in jail, just like any other perp, but I didn't let that fear stop me. Maddie's killer belonged in jail, and I wasn't going to let anything, or anyone, stop me from putting him there. I took out my lock-pick set and made quick work of unlocking the door, then disarmed the alarm system in less than fifteen seconds. Then I started searching for Pelucha's own office.

It wasn't hard to find, the only one with massive, wood-panel doors and labeled with his name in gold letters at the side. I opened the door and stepped inside, closing it after me. It was pitch black in there, but I put on infrared goggles and moved with ease around the room. Then I grinned widely when I saw the door to his private bathroom.

I entered and closed the door gently, then removed my infrared goggles and turned on the light. There were some hair fibers on the counter, but neither had the follicle attached. I groaned and started opening drawers until I found what I was looking for. A comb, with a few strands I could pluck and pack inside a small evidence bag. Satisfied, I turned off the light and quietly made my way toward the exit.

I heard them before I actually saw them, two security guards on patrol, chatting and chuckling over the latest episode of *Game of Thrones* and a rather unusual sex scene in it. I crouched behind a large sofa and waited for them to move on. They stopped in front of the suite door and projected the beams of their flashlights inside, still talking, but going over every inch of space. Fortunately, they didn't think to try the door handle. After a long minute, they moved on, and I breathed again.

It was almost two in the morning when I dragged Anne out of bed and into her office. She came without complaining and didn't raise an eyebrow when I handed her the hair fibers for analysis.

"Want some coffee?" she asked, putting on her lab coat and powering up her equipment.

"Nah," I replied, swallowing a yawn. "If you cut me, I bleed coffee," I chuckled. "I'll make you some, though."

The machine beeped twice when it finished brewing, and I poured Anne a cup, then topped it off with fresh cream, as she liked it. Then I put it quietly on her desk, not daring to interrupt what she was doing.

"You got yourself an occasional amphetamine user," Anne said, lifting her eyes from the computer screen and looking at me. "Nothing else."

Everyone in this city was a bloody drug user. What the hell happened to people? Only this time, it worked in my favor.

"How about DNA?" I asked, rubbing my eyes with my fists, struggling to keep my eyelids peeled open.

"It will take me a few hours to compare with what I have from Madeline's clothes," Anne replied.

"There was DNA on her clothes?" I asked, feeling energized.

"Two donors," Anne replied. "One left semen on her skirt and panties, the other left epithelials. None of them were in CODIS, but I can compare them against this new sample. Whose is it, by the way?"

"Aaron Pelucha's," I replied sheepishly.

She shot me an inquisitive glance, and I pasted a guilty smile on my face, staring at the floor.

"Then I won't log this into evidence," she said calmly, as if it were normal procedure. "I'll run the DNA match, while you can crash over there," she gestured toward her two-seat couch.

She didn't need to insist, and the moment I felt the soft cushions under my head, I was fast asleep.

After what seemed like only a few moments, she woke me with a gentle squeeze of my shoulder.

"Pelucha's not a match to either DNA sample recovered from Madeline's clothing," she announced, sounding a bit disappointed, despite a hint of excitement in her eyes.

I shot Anne a bleary look. What was she excited about? I'd kept her up all night, and for nothing.

She approached the sofa and crouched to be at the same eye level with me.

"While you snored, and trust me, you did snore, results came back from another DNA match I was running."

I perked up and sat on the side of the couch, rubbing the nape of my neck, willing my brain to wake up. Which DNA match test was she talking about? What was I missing?

"Tell me," I said, feeling my throat parched.

"I ran both samples found on Maddie's clothing against our killer's DNA, recovered from her body."

"Oh," I reacted, taken by surprise.

"What, you thought I forgot about that?" Anne said, continuing to smile. "The rapist is your killer, Laura. You were right. The semen DNA found on Maddie's clothing is a full match to the DNA recovered from underneath her fingernails and the tip of her broken heel. Now you go find that bastard."

I leaned and kissed her cheek with a loud smooch.

"Thank you, sweetie, you're the best."

On my way out, I checked the time; it was almost seven, and Holt was probably up by now. I called, and he picked up immediately in his sleep-filled voice that I remembered so well.

"Hey, partner," I asked, "know any K9 officers who could do us a favor?"

39

Harassment

"You want to do what?" Holt reacted, then cleared his voice to rid it of the sleep that clung to it and made him sound a little hoarse. "This is not okay on so many levels."

I took a deep breath, forcing myself to stay calm. If I wasn't going to share the whole truth with my partner, he had no way of knowing Pelucha was a confirmed drug user, and he must've thought what I was trying to do was a desperate shot in the dark, not a slam dunk.

I'd just finished sharing the news that I got from Anne earlier, and he refrained from asking how I came to have the report before seven in the morning. He admitted his theory had been wrong; Maddie's mother wasn't the one we were looking for; just a regular, heartless sociopath. Holt admitted defeat, happy we were closing in on our real killer. Only we had no idea who he was, not yet. And for that, we needed Pelucha.

I willed myself to be patient and work through his objections, one by one.

"Listen," I said, lowering my raised voice and hiding my escalating frustration. "I'm not saying we'll collar Pelucha for possession. I'm not even saying the dog will sniff anything on him; maybe he's clean. All I'm saying is we might get him scared enough to cooperate. That's all. Wanna give it a try?"

He hesitated for a while, and I heard him sigh quietly. "It's harassment, partner."

"Maybe," I said, "but from where I'm sitting, it's just a well-orchestrated coincidence."

"You got balls, Baxter. Has anyone told you that?"

I could hear him laughing on the other side of the call, and he was probably rolling his eyes too.

"I grow what I need, Holt. Right now, I need Pelucha in a room with us, even if only for fifteen minutes."

"All right," he said, sounding more enthusiastic than resigned. "This is so crazy far‑fetched, it might actually work. I'll call Wong."

On the way to the Royal Hall, I stopped and picked up a Danish to make my stomach settle. It was rather dry and stale, probably a leftover from yesterday's batch. I wolfed it down, nevertheless, while I promised myself I'd let Holt cook me another omelet as soon as we wrapped this case up.

Then I took my position near the hotel's main entrance, leaning casually against one of the large pillars and watching the drop-off lane. Soon, if we had any luck on our side, Pelucha would be dropped off by his driver, in one of the three SUVs he had registered in his name.

I waited almost an hour in the freezing cold, wondering how a place like Las Vegas could be so scorching hot in the summer and manage to seem arctic in the short-lived winter, when temperatures rarely dipped below freezing. Perceptions, and the force of habit, that's what it was. At least the sky was clear, and the dreariness of that London-like drizzle was long gone.

When I saw Pelucha's SUV turn the corner, I hid behind the massive pillar and radioed Holt.

"Go now. Over."

"Copy," his confirmation crackled in.

Officer Wong and his companion, K9 Officer Dakota, appeared from behind a parked tourist bus, walking briskly toward the entrance. Wong, a young officer who was thrilled to help two seasoned detectives in whatever it was we were trying to do, hurried a little, afraid he was going to miss Pelucha. The plan was to have the K9 cross Pelucha's path inconspicuously, but then signal the presence of drugs. Dakota, a large yellow Lab, trotted quickly along the hotel's wall, and, for a brief moment, seemed to be timed perfectly to meet with Pelucha right in front of the entrance.

Only the driver called Pelucha back to the car; he turned and climbed back inside. Cool as a scoop of ice cream in November, Officer Wong stopped and had the dog examine a large trash can, until Pelucha got out of his vehicle again.

This time, Dakota came close to Pelucha, sniffed the air, then sat on her wagging tail. That was the signal for Officer Wong to intervene, while Holt and I approached in a hurry.

"Sir," I said to the baffled Pelucha, "would you mind stepping to the side?"

He complied, seemingly confused and increasingly aggravated, judging by the tension in his upper lip and the deepening frown in his brow.

"What is this about?" he asked, after shooting a fleeting glance at our badges.

"Are you in possession of a controlled substance, sir?" I asked serenely, hoping that Pelucha had the mentality of a habitual drug user: never leave home without a fix. I watched his eyes closely, as he registered the question, and saw the flicker of fear in his pupils. Bingo.

"Let me call my lawyer," he said, and reached into his pocket.

"Hands where I can see them," Holt bellowed, with his hand on his weapon, and Pelucha flinched.

"I don't think you want me dragged in cuffs out of here," Pelucha threatened, glints of rage sparkling in his eyes. "You have no cause, nothing."

"The dog sniffed drugs on you, and that's enough cause to justify a search, blood tests, the whole shebang," Holt replied.

Pelucha softened like a piece of microwaved butter, within seconds. "Any chance we could, maybe, look the other way, officer?"

"It's detective," Holt replied in a low, menacing tone of voice. "We might do you that immense favor, if you do us one too."

He nodded spasmodically. "Sure, anything."

"Tell us the truth regarding an incident that took place in your hotel, eleven years ago," Holt continued.

There it was, another flicker of fear dilating his pupils and making him swallow hard.

"I don't know what you're talking about."

"Oh, I think you do," I replied. "The assault of Madeline Munroe."

"The, um, girl who was killed the other day?" he replied, feigning ignorance quite well.

"You could choose to do the right thing, Mr. Pelucha," Holt said, whispering closer to his ear. "You could tell us who the other two men were in a room with you when Madeline was assaulted, eleven years ago."

He shook his head violently, and the glint of fear in his eyes intensified.

"I have no idea what you're talking about, but I think my lawyer will need to be present for anything you want to ask me."

"It was your room, Mr. Pelucha, your suite, where it all happened," I insisted. "Surely you must remember."

"Sorry… lawyer. Now. Or let me go right this instant." He was growing increasingly determined and sure of himself. We'd missed the moment.

"We have evidence that puts you at the scene of an assault, but it doesn't indicate you as the main perpetrator. There's no need to cover for them; the statute of limitation has expired. Who were they?" I asked.

"How many times do I need to tell you? I know my rights, and I'm not saying another word without an attorney present. End of conversation."

"Too bad," Holt replied, after shooting me a quick glance. "You had the chance to be a hero today, to do what's right, be the good guy for a change. But hey, whatever, suit yourself."

He let go of Pelucha's arm, who immediately stepped away from him, arranging his sleeve.

"We'll get warrants for your property, for your blood, and we will get you, Mr. Pelucha. These dogs, they're never wrong. Then we'll drag you in front of a grand jury, and you will have to testify."

"I'll take my chances," he replied, his arrogance and self-confidence intact. "Have a nice day, officers," he added with a hint of sarcasm, making me realize he used the wrong title for us on purpose. Then he walked into his hotel and disappeared.

We thanked Wong and went back to Holt's car. I felt defeated, out of options. We'd had one chance and blew it.

"I wonder how long," Holt said, starting the engine and cranking up the heat.

"What do you mean?"

"Until Pelucha's complaint will trickle through the channels down to us, in the form of DC Wallace screaming and threatening, maybe even firing us."

"Ah, that," I replied, turning my face away from him. "Not long, I assume."

I felt guilty as hell for dragging not only my partner, but Officer Wong too into this mess that could cost them a lot. Sometimes I'm impulsive like that, and I don't know when to stop. I wanted Maddie's killer caught so badly, it clouded my judgment. Hearing from Anne how close I was to catching him only made things worse. But no, no excuse. The things I choose to do at night, on my own time and dime, should never cross into the realm of day, where other people can be harmed.

40

Consequences

"We bluffed, and we lost," Holt said in a pacifying tone. "At least we tried, partner. Chin up. I put in for a warrant to bring Pelucha in."

I still couldn't bring myself to look at him, especially since he was encouraging me, making me feel even worse. But what was done was done, and I forced some air into my lungs. Maddie's killer was still out there, and we needed to stop feeling sorry for ourselves and get back to work.

"There's another lead we could follow, the guy who shot me," I said. "It should take us all the way to the killer."

"Rudy Camacho?" Holt replied. "I think I saw his financials come in. Let's take a look."

He fired up the laptop and dug through some emails.

"There's no unusual financial activity. If he's been paid for the job, he's a cash-only business," Holt said. "I'll check priors next."

The phone rang, and I saw Gully's name on the display.

"I think I'll put in for a transfer," Gully shouted in lieu of a greeting. "While I still have a job! What the hell were you thinking?"

"What are you talking about?" Holt asked serenely, but threw me a glance that showed his concern.

"I'm talking about the stunt you pulled on Aaron Pelucha. That's harassment, all the way. You can't just put a dog to sniff someone without cause and then manufacture cause on the fly."

"We didn't put the dog there, it just—"

"Happened? Don't insult me, Detective Baxter. I've seen a copy of the coroner's report. I know what you're gunning for, but this isn't the right way to do it. The courts are still debating whether a dog's alert constitutes probable cause. This debate has been going on for years, and what, you think you solved it? You didn't even bother to call and ask?"

I didn't think it was a good idea to say anything, and Holt remained quiet as well.

"Since *Florida vs. Harris*, we've heard all the arguments about how the dog's reliability comes into question when obtaining a search warrant. I don't expect you to quote case law, but I expect you to follow the rules. This wasn't sanctioned, and you know it. Judge Hayden threw me out of chambers so fast, my head's still spinning. He thinks I was in on it with you, helping you get leverage on Pelucha instead of getting a subpoena for a grand jury."

"I'm sorry, Gully, I really am," I said, trying to mend whatever was left of our working relationship. It was my fault, all of it.

"Sorry, my ass. Why did you send me in there without telling me the facts? You set me up, Baxter." He breathed, a long, pained, frustrated sigh. "Pelucha's probably going to sue now, and that's on you, both of you," he continued. "You just served him a harassment settlement on a platter, and he's got grand-an-hour lawyers who'll eat us alive."

Then he hung up before we could say anything, leaving us engulfed in guilty silence. I couldn't think of anything left to say.

"He'll come around, eventually," Holt said, sounding unconvinced. "He's not a bad guy."

Then he pulled the laptop closer and continued digging into Camacho's background.

"Camacho, he was an upstanding member of the community," Holt said, trying to ease the tension in the air. "B&E, battery, assault. Did his dime and got released for good behavior." He rubbed his chin. "Huh… quite quickly, I might add. Only served two and a half out of ten."

"I guess this is the only lead left," I said, failing to hide my discouragement. "It doesn't help that you put two in his chest before we could question him, but—"

"What the hell, Baxter?" Holt reacted.

"You're right," I replied, raising my hand in a pacifying gesture. "I never even thanked you."

"For what?"

"Everything," I replied, averting my eyes. "For saving my life. For taking care of me. For this," I added, making a desolate gesture at the space between us, a symbol of the trust he'd placed in my decisions and the consequences of that trust.

"Don't mention it," he muttered, riveting his eyes on the laptop screen. "I'll pore over every inch of this scumbag's life until we find out who hired him. People like him, when they're into cash, they talk about it and do stupid stuff."

I nodded. It wasn't much left for us to go on, except… there was something nagging me about Camacho's background. Something didn't add up. Someone like him doesn't behave that well on the inside. No one does, not enough to shave almost 80 percent of their sentence off.

"How come he was released so soon?" I asked. "Did he turn state's evidence?"

"Good behavior, says here, no mention of any testimony," Holt replied, shifting through screens. "Ah, what do you know," he said, and a crooked grin appeared on his face. "Guess who signed his release."

I encouraged him with a head movement.

"None other than our friend, Judge Hayden," Holt replied. "He's also the one who signed his sentencing. He put him in, then he got him out. Let's go to the judge and ask him to help us; maybe that will mend some fences."

He shifted into gear and closed the laptop lid, while a troublesome thought whirled in my mind. I'd never worked with Judge Hayden; another judge was working with the Henderson ADA. But since I'd been assigned this case, I'd heard his name a lot.

"How old is he?" I asked, and as I voiced my question, I felt my gut churn, as if I'd awakened a bad omen.

"Um, about forty, I guess," Holt replied, shooting me an intrigued glance. "Why?"

"Do you believe in coincidences?" I said, then grabbed the laptop from its holder and opened a browser window.

I remembered last night, when I'd done my research about Pelucha, that I'd seen photos of him with various officials at certain events and fundraisers. No one in particular had caught my eye, because I had no reason to look for anyone in particular. Now I did.

"Holy shit, Baxter," Holt replied. "You can't be serious."

"Is this him?" I asked, and turned the laptop screen his way. It displayed a photo of Judge Hayden in chambers, wearing his black robe.

"Yeah, that's him."

"Lately, I've been feeling like we're being toyed with," I said, while my fingers danced on the keyboard, typing in another search. "Maybe not all our requests were warranted, but he definitely hasn't been too helpful in this case."

"Maybe," Holt said, frowning deeply. "But he approved the subpoena for the Munroe financials, didn't he? It wasn't like he said no to everything we've asked for."

He was right, but I felt that wave of excitement a good hunter feels when she smells blood. I kept on searching, sifting through hundreds of images I found posted online.

"Look," I said, and this time he pulled over to the side of the road. He took the laptop from me and stared at the screen, where I'd displayed a photo of Pelucha with Hayden, both wearing tuxedos. The image was captioned, "Joining hands against domestic violence." The two men smiled at the cameras while shaking hands, surrounded by a group of other people, including Pelucha's glamorously clad wife.

Unconvinced, Holt shook his head. "Baxter, these people do this kind of thing all day long. Fundraisers, political events, you name it. Everyone wants a piece of what Pelucha has to donate. That's nothing."

"Hayden's the right age, Holt," I insisted. "I think we've got something here. Let's just look into it, no matter how thin it might seem."

"It's beyond thin, Baxter, it's imaginary. I know the judge; he's not the type."

41

Orders

"All I'm asking for is ten minutes of your time," I insisted, and Holt gave me a long stare, followed by a sigh of frustration.

"We're wasting our time, I'm telling you. What do you have against him, other than circumstance and coincidence?" he asked, slightly frowning despite apparent calm.

We'd returned to the precinct and huddled in front of his desktop computer, in the middle of the crowded bullpen, and that meant we had to argue in whispers, considering the name of the person I wanted to investigate. Nothing made me angrier than having to whisper, for some unexplained reason. Maybe something for Dr. Beville to obsess about.

"He got the guy who shot me out for good behavior in a fraction of the time he was supposed to serve. Don't you think that buys him some credits with the perp? Maybe he didn't have to pay Camacho for the deed; he just called in a favor." I insisted. "Hayden's the right age, and—"

"He's forty years old and Caucasian, for Pete's sake, and so are millions of others, Baxter. I know the judge, and I'm telling you, he's not our guy."

"Not all those millions locked paws with Pelucha on camera, you know."

Holt raised his hands in the air, ripe with frustration. He mumbled something, some indecipherable oaths, but I thought I'd heard the words, "stubborn woman," mixed among them.

"Ten minutes, that's all I'm asking for. If I had my own desk and computer, I wouldn't even be asking. I only have basic systems on my personal laptop."

"Okay," he groaned, "all right. No one says no to you and lives to tell the story, huh?" he mumbled, while logging into various databases.

"Pull Pelucha and Hayden's backgrounds, side by side. Let's see if they intersect anywhere."

We reviewed every bit of data available, from neighborhoods, friends, and former addresses, to schools and tax records.

"Aha," I said, excited to find something. "They both went to Northwestern University in San Francisco, at roughly the same time. Pelucha did business administration. Hayden was a law student. See here?" I tapped gently on his screen with my fingernail.

"Wait a second," Holt whispered, "Hayden went to school a year before Pelucha, and Pelucha dropped out during the second year. There's nothing there."

I scoffed and took the keyboard from him. After a few more minutes of frantic search, I gave up.

"Nothing… no fraternities, no activities, nothing. Pelucha could afford to live in a rental in town. Hayden lived on campus. They might've met, but they haven't left a trace for us to find. But I'm guessing they did; they were both from Las Vegas and in a strange town, relatively far from home."

"I don't remember hanging out with juniors when I was in college," Holt said. "No one really does, unless those juniors are girls."

"Even if they were from your hometown? Or filthy rich?"

"Even. In college, all I cared about were girls and parties," he confessed with a guilty, crooked smile. "Maybe that's why I'm not a marketing executive right now, forking millions in pay instead of stretching the ends to make them meet on a cop's salary."

I couldn't help but smile. Holt had his charm, and I bet he was quite popular with the girls in college; I can't imagine many said no to him, and the thought of that irritated me like an exposed tooth nerve. But then again, maybe I was biased, being that I'd joined their club.

"Okay, I give up," I replied, rushing to erase the image of a young Jack Holt surrounded by oversexed college girls in cheerleader attire. As far as the Hayden–Pelucha connection, maybe he was right, and I was grasping at straws. It was time for us to focus on what we could find, not waste any more time. "Let's go back to Camacho and his background. What do we know?"

"Why does Henderson take credit for this precinct's activities?" DC Wallace asked, appearing out of nowhere, startling me. I turned, at the same time as Holt, to find him standing behind us, tight-lipped and tense. By now, he'd probably learned we'd spoken to Madeline's mother against his specific orders, and he was also aware of the stunt we pulled earlier that morning in front of the Royal Hall. By the look on his face, we were beyond screwed… I cringed, feeling my heart beating against my chest like a caged bird trying to escape.

"I'm not sure what you mean, sir," I managed to say, sounding almost normal.

"The BOLO on Raymond McKinley," he replied. "We're about to announce to the media that we have a suspect, right? That BOLO should be issued with Las Vegas origination, not Henderson."

"That's on me, Deputy Chief," I replied, with an apologetic smile. "I'm still using my Henderson credentials; I haven't been assigned new ones yet."

"Holt, change the BOLO to be under your name," Wallace said, dismissing my explanation with a wave of his hand. "What else have you got? From what I hear, you've been really busy. I've seen the reports… all of them." His face scrunched, as he said those words, making it very clear how he felt about our recent performance.

"We're still piecing together what happened eleven years ago," I replied, steadying my voice as I spoke. "Dr. St. Clair confirmed that Madeline's killer is also her rapist from back then. Pelucha won't talk, and the judge won't sign the warrant. We need to iden—"

"Raymond McKinley, right?" DC Wallace asked, but it wasn't really a question; it was a statement, or even better said, an order he was giving. "Fingerprints don't lie, Detectives."

"Well, they could lie," Holt said, "if Raymond McKinley's identity is being used as a cover for a government operative or even a contract killer. We're looking into—"

"Nonsense," he replied coldly. "We have a press conference scheduled in thirty minutes, during which I will name Raymond McKinley as the suspect, and congratulate my two senior detectives for a job well done."

"But, sir, I believe we still have a lot of unanswered questions," I said, and cringed when I heard my own strangled voice. Lame… my mind processed what conceding meant, having Wallace happily close the case without ripping us for insubordination, because that's what it's called when a ranking officer tells you not to do something and you do it anyway. The only problem? It also meant letting a killer get away with murder. It meant there would never be justice for Madeline's death.

Wallace's brow ruffled with pronounced ridges. "I believe the governor and his family deserve to grieve in peace, and that won't happen until this entire circus is over," he said bluntly, making lots of heads turn and look our way. "Guess whose beliefs carry more weight, Baxter," he added, and the threat in his voice was clear.

"Y-yes, sir," I said, and Holt echoed my response.

"I'll assign your new case tomorrow," he added. "Until then, Baxter, take some R&R. You didn't take any time off since you were shot, did you?"

"No, sir," I replied, frowning slightly at the sight of an IA officer approaching Wallace quietly. I recognized him from my recent visit upstairs; he was a rookie, probably a messenger waiting for Wallace to finish with us.

"Then go," Wallace said. "And you, Holt, IA wants you to pee in a cup; random drug test. You haven't done one this year, right?"

"No," he replied, and I watched how blood drained from his face. He looked at me, a look of despair, silent, anguished. Then he lowered his eyes to the floor, resigned to his fate. He knew he wasn't going to pass the test. He knew he was finished.

Bollocks, Holt… what the hell can I do?

42

Test

Stunned, I watched the IA officer chatting casually with Holt about something to do with parking spaces and an initiative to have them permanently allocated to officers. Holt wasn't reacting; his head hung, and his shoulders were tense. They stood right where Wallace had left them, only a few feet away from me, on the other side of a row of desks.

I leaned against Holt's desk and breathed. My mind raced, thousands of thoughts colliding at the speed of light. Holt was a good cop; he didn't deserve any of that shite. It was bad luck; bad timing, especially now, when he was going to AA meetings every night, and, as far as I could tell, was keeping clean. A few more days, and the last trace of cocaine would've been flushed from his system and he'd test negative. Then, on the other hand, what did IA know about him that made them so sure he'd test positive? Was he being tested randomly, like it's normal procedure with cops? Or was he being hunted for that kilo of cocaine that supposedly went missing during one of his busts? After all, an addict is an addict; he'll do or say anything, and couldn't be trusted. Was he really, at heart, an addict?

It also crossed my mind that since we'd taken on the Munroe case, we'd run into an interesting assortment of roadblocks and apparently unrelated events, all slowing our investigation, wearing us down. The IA, forcing me to spy on my partner. The judge, refusing to work with our assistant district attorney to find a legal way to interview Pelucha and get to the bottom of what had happened eleven years ago. Now Internal Affairs again, going after Holt in what seemed more like an execution than anything else.

Then another, more troublesome thought started nagging me. Who else would've known better where we stood with our investigation than the judge who kept rejecting our requests? Who better positioned to sic IA on Holt than a judge? He wouldn't've had to do much to set the wheels in motion; a quick call to a friend, nothing more. Yeah... who else than a judge, and probably Holt would've dismissed my theories yet again if he heard them, despite the fact that the coincidences kept piling up in blatant defiance of Occam's razor.

Unfortunately, the night before I'd chosen to enjoy a lighthearted dinner instead of discussing these things with Holt, instead of giving him the heads-up and an opportunity to explain the missing kilo of coke. Now all I had to go on was my gut.

Holt raised his eyes from the floor and looked toward me. As our eyes met, I mouthed, "stall." He nodded almost imperceptibly, a different kind of frown touching his brow. Then I heard him say to the IA officer, "Let me grab a Coke or something; I just went in there. If I don't hydrate, it could take a while." The officer smiled awkwardly and made room for Holt to take the corridor toward the kitchen area.

I shook my head, unable to believe myself and what I was about to do. Casually, I walked toward the coffee machine at the side of the bullpen and spent a few moments in front of it, then left with a paper cup covered with a lid, handling it as if it were full. Just as casually, I stepped into the ladies' room when no one was looking. A few moments later, I came out of there with the same coffee cup in my hand, walking toward the kitchen and feigning absentmindedness.

I paced myself so that I'd run into Holt halfway through the corridor as he was returning to the bullpen, in an area I knew was poorly covered by video surveillance. When we were just a few feet away from each other, I looked around and saw the IA officer chatting with someone from Human Resources, a young blonde with long, wavy hair and an enviable figure. He was all into her, excellent timing.

I made eye contact with Holt then drew his attention to the cup I was holding. His eyebrows shot up, but he nodded slightly. We walked past each other without stopping, without skipping a beat, and the paper cup landed from my hand into Holt's pocket with a slick move I learned ages ago on the streets of London from an old gypsy woman. Seconds later, I was brewing a cup of coffee in the kitchen and fixing it with a lid, getting ready to show myself on all the bullpen cameras with the same cup in hand, as I had before.

By the time I returned from the kitchen, Holt was walking toward the men's room with the IA officer by his side. He pushed open the door to the restroom, but stopped in his tracks when the officer wanted to follow him inside.

"I think I can tinkle on my own, thank you very much," Holt said coldly.

"It's procedure, I'm sorry," the officer replied with a shrug, appearing a little frustrated.

"Really? That's the way you treat a cop with more than fifteen years on the job? What the hell would I do in there other than pee in the damn cup you gave me?"

"In case someone else is in there, that's all," the officer replied, sounding irritated. "I'll be the one signing the affidavit, not you."

"There, check if you need to," Holt said, holding the door open for the officer. "Knock yourself out."

Satisfied, the officer came out a moment later and invited Holt to proceed. Then he stood in front of the door, keen on not letting anyone else use the facilities while Holt was in there. Perfect.

I kept myself busy at Holt's desk running background searches on Camacho, to see if I could find any leads connecting him to anyone else. Then I searched for known associates and shortlisted a few names, including his former cellmate from the time he served upstate. I was deep into reading about the circumstances of Camacho's arrest when I sensed Holt approaching.

"So?" I asked, as if I didn't know the answer. Several cops were within earshot, but due to the circumstances, I didn't want to whisper or draw any unwanted attention.

"All good," he replied, "we're ready to go. It was one of those instant results test cups."

"Ah, the wonders of modern technology," I said, and quietly sighed with relief.

We didn't speak another word until we were in the car, engine running, ready to leave the LVMPD parking lot.

"Baxter, I—" Holt started to say in a hesitant, choked voice.

"Don't mention it," I replied, unwilling to hear him thank me. I still wasn't sure I'd done the right thing, or that I'd actually got away with what I'd done.

For now, I didn't want to think about it anymore, afraid I'd come to my senses and ask myself what the hell I was thinking. But I had different, more urgent priorities at the center of my mind. Regardless of what Wallace had ordered, I still had a killer to catch. I wanted to spend time somewhere quiet where I could start figuring out why no other leads made sense to me except Judge Hayden, and what in bloody hell I was going to do about it.

"Where's your meeting tonight?" I asked, sounding a bit harsher than I'd intended.

Holt grabbed the wheel with both hands, squeezing hard until his knuckles turned white, and replied, only slightly louder than a whisper. "Community center. Why? Want to come?"

I sensed a touch of bitterness in his voice, but I decided to ignore it and focus on the more pressing matter I had on my agenda. Maybe if I gathered some more data, my partner would be willing to take another look at Judge Hayden as a suspect. If he put aside his personal perceptions about Hayden, he'd see what I saw.

I tilted my head and smiled. "Do they have Wi-Fi?"

"Probably, but I wouldn't hold my breath for too much speed."

"It'll have to do," I replied and buckled up my seatbelt. "Let's go."

43

Photo

I found a table inside the Community Center where I could set my laptop and work, a small, cracked, and dirty sheet of splinting plywood screwed on four metallic legs. I had to be careful, so the splints wouldn't do a number on my cashmere sweater, but it worked just fine for me. The center was almost deserted; it was late, and, except for the AA meeting, nothing much was going on.

I fired up my laptop and, while it loaded and established a Wi-Fi connection, I let my weary mind go over the facts once more. What did we really know, beyond any reasonable doubt? We knew that three men assaulted Madeline Munroe eleven years ago. Although only one of the three had apparently raped her, in my eyes they were all equally guilty. We knew the rapist who'd left semen behind was the same person who'd killed Maddie. We knew that out of the three men, one was Aaron Pelucha, the instigator and facilitator of the assault, the second had a birthmark in the shape of a triangle on his left forearm, and the third was the rapist and killer.

We didn't have any conclusive evidence involving Judge Hayden. In Holt's own words, all I had was circumstantial, coincidental at best. But it was a growing pile of facts. The judge was the right age and knew Pelucha; they went back, possibly since college. The judge had signed a very early release for Rudy Camacho, the career criminal who ambushed us at Maddie's apartment, the man who didn't hesitate to fire his weapon on two cops. To me, all those coincidences were more than enough to keep me there, in that poorly lit Community Center, looking for more information on his honor.

If Judge Hayden was one of the three men in the Munroe assault eleven years ago, which one was he? I needed DNA to find out, but I couldn't exactly show up on his doorstep with a swab in my hand, asking him to be a team player and waive his rights. However, if he had a certain birthmark, say, a triangle-shaped one on his forearm, I should be able to find that in a photo somewhere. Something told me his honor took off his black, long-sleeved robe on occasions.

I quickly found his Facebook page, but it was restricted only to his friends, and those weren't many. I opened the list and examined their faces. They seemed to be mostly family members with the same last name, and others with avatars showing group photos with kids and dogs and whatnot. One avatar had a dog's portrait instead of a person's, and the name didn't have anything in common with the other names; nothing I could use.

Toward the end of the judge's friends list, a smiling, age-weathered face grabbed my attention. It belonged to a Mrs. Lenore Hayden, seventy-six-years-old per her own profile. Maybe it was his mother or a close relative. Someone I could use.

I loaded the database search screen and looked up Hayden's background. His mother's first name wasn't Lenore, but the old lady with kind eyes in his friends list had some familial resemblance. I pulled up her background in the database. She was the judge's aunt, more precisely his father's sister. Out of all his Facebook friends, Mrs. Lenore Hayden would probably have the easiest password to crack.

Yeah... I might've omitted to share, I'm a bit of a hacker too, also in my spare time. Don't imagine the NSA is pining for me; no, nothing that spectacular. I do break access codes with relative ease, just like I open physical doors in the analog world. I don't believe any door, physical or cybernetic, should keep me from finding if his honor has a birthmark on his arm; if he's innocent, he has nothing to worry about; I'll disappear just as discreetly as I poked around.

If Hayden does have the mark, then we'd have some solid evidence to justify a warrant for questioning him in connection to Madeline's murder. If he doesn't... well, that would mean one of two things: he could be the killer, but we won't know that for sure without his DNA, or he could be completely innocent and uninvolved in the case, like Holt's been swearing that he is. I bet Mrs. Lenore Hayden has access to tons of the judge's family photos.

I spent the next fifteen minutes or so sifting through databases for everything there was to know about Lenore. Her husband had died a few years ago; I jotted down his birthday and his name as possible password hints. She had two cats, Nibbles and Panther, jotting those names down as well. She was born in Sausalito, another entry for my notepad.

You see, I'm not the type of hacker who has written password-breaking software, or who can build back doors into systems and people's digital lives. I use psychology to give me an edge, that's all. And the older the target, the more likely I am to break their password. Younger people are tough; their values are shifting dramatically, making them difficult to profile and even tougher to code-break, and they don't fear a lengthy, complicated password.

I opened a secure browser window via proxy, using Lenore's last known address as server location. That's because most large technology platforms track the physical location of their users as a security measure, and might shut me out if they see multiple failed login attempts from an unknown location. Then I tried a few passwords, and luckily got the right one before the system shut me down for security purposes. Most systems allow three, maybe five failed attempts before they block that account, but Lenore loved Panther more than she cared about Nibbles. Good to know.

I was in. I browsed to the judge's photos, then sighed. There were thousands of them... Apparently, the judge's wife had very little else to do than post every meal, every purchase, every kid's bruise or school mark or test result, every single day. I started scrolling through them quickly, looking for photos featuring the judge wearing short-sleeved attire. A few minutes later, my eyes were watery, and I was seeing the images through a blur, understandable after the sleep deprivation that I'd subjected myself to recently.

I rubbed the nape of my neck to shake the drowsiness off and wished for another cup of tea, or even coffee, while still scrolling through endless screens of family photos. I'd seen some with the judge in short-sleeved polo shirts, but they weren't the right angle, or his left arm wasn't showing. But the thing that drove me crazy the most was how genuinely honest he looked in those photos. Carefree, happy, a family man, and an upstanding member of the community. But I knew, deep inside my weary gut, it was all a façade.

I scrolled away, minute after endless minute, photo after photo, until I found what I was looking for. A group picture, taken with the judge's extended family at a cottage they'd rented in North Carolina a few summers ago. They all waved for the camera, short-sleeved arms raised in the air, and one of those arms bore the mark, an elongated, triangular shape right where Maddie's written testimony said it would be.

"Gotcha," I whispered, and saved the photo in my personal files, then signed off of Aunt Lenore's account.

44

Talking Trash

The AA meeting came to an end, and the crowd started trickling through the poorly lit hallways, Holt among the last of them. A few hung behind in small clusters, chatting in subdued voices. I read the signs of their personal battles written on their faces: drawn eyes, pallor, hunched shoulders, lowered gazes. By comparison, Holt didn't appear he belonged, not among those struggling, yet undefeated, anonymous figures. I respected all of them, him included, for having the willpower to refuse the lousy hand that life had dealt them and reclaim their destinies.

Holt took a seat across from me at the table and, for a second, I caught a glimpse of the weariness in his eyes until he remembered to hide it. He avoided my glance, and a tentative, unconvincing smile tried to stretch his lips.

"Any news?" he asked in a quiet voice.

"And then some," I replied, and he immediately perked up.

"Shoot."

"Before I show you what I got, you have to understand that sometimes I won't be able to tell you anything regarding the provenance of certain pieces of information."

"You mean, like a confidential informant? We all have those," he said, frowning a little, intrigued.

"No," I replied, "it's more than that, but I can't go into any details, and you have to trust me when I say I can't, and it's not personal."

He gave me a long stare, then sighed quietly and nodded. "Sure, partner, you've earned it. Tell me what you got."

"I looked into Judge Hayden's background, because I had my suspicions, despite your vote of confidence for the man."

"Ah," he reacted, letting himself lean back against the chair. "Don't tell me you found something."

I pulled up the photo on my laptop's screen, then turned the screen around so that he could see it clearly.

"Judge Hayden and family, a few years back in North Carolina. Notice that left forearm."

He squinted and drew closer to the screen, then studied the image for a long moment.

"Son of a bitch," he muttered. "That's one hell of a coincidence."

"What? You still think it's a coincidence?"

He ran his hand across his face, as if to wipe away the web of tiredness and refocus.

"No," he eventually admitted. "I, personally, don't. But everyone else will. Birthmarks might be unique, but not against a teenager's description and doodle in a diary. They'll want more before going in front of a judge and accusing him of gang rape."

"No one's going to accuse him of anything; that time has passed. We'll settle for the name of the third man, the killer."

"Even for that we need evidence. Leverage," he added, then closed the laptop lid and grabbed it and offered me his arm. "Otherwise he'll decline having any knowledge of what we're looking for. But I've got an idea."

"Where are we going?" I asked, limping along with renewed difficulty. An entire day spent on my feet brought a dull, throbbing pain to my calf, and a burning sensation along the suture line every time I put weight on that foot.

"Tomorrow's Friday," Holt said, with an evil grin that brought a deeper furrow to his brow, "it's garbage day in half the city. I bet his honor has a trash can at the curb."

I was thrilled with Holt's idea, and at the same time, embarrassed I hadn't thought of it myself. A trash can that was left for the city to pick up could be searched without a warrant; the evidence collected was admissible in court, including DNA, and household trash is ripe with DNA. Saliva on food scraps and bottlenecks, epithelials on wrappers and packaging, on paper cups and plasticware. It didn't have to be perfect; all we needed was to establish probable cause to secure a warrant for Hayden's DNA and get the leverage we needed to get the name of Maddie's killer.

He started the engine and turned the heater to the max, but I couldn't stop shaking; it felt as if my blood had turned to ice. I couldn't recall the last time I had something to eat, and I would've given anything for a hot meal. However, nothing seemed more important than getting my hands on his honor's DNA.

Holt threw me a quick glance and took the next interstate exit, heading into the city.

"Where are we going?" I asked, seeing we were entering the wrong neighborhood.

"To dinner," he replied. "You look like you could use a few calories." He must've read my mind, or maybe he felt the same way.

"How about the trash can we were going to pilfer?"

"It'll still be there."

He stopped near an Asian place on Spring Mountain Road. Moments later, an older Chinese woman who bowed a lot showed us to a small booth. He didn't wait for the menu; he ordered hot tea for both of us and a sauce with a name I didn't catch. The woman bowed again and disappeared.

"What was that? The sauce?"

"A fix for tired, overworked people," he replied, and his boyish grin was back. "She'll bring you a small cup. Just forget it's technically a sauce and eat it like it's soup. You'll thank me tomorrow."

As soon as I tasted it, I couldn't stop. It was delicious, and very hot, both temperature and spicy hot. No one really knows what's in those sauces, but I recognized a few ingredients: soy, sesame seeds, green onion rings, garlic, and, by the thickness, it definitely had cornstarch. It must've had enough pepper to corrode stainless steel, as it packed a serious punch. Each mouthful left a trail of heat all the way to my stomach, and, from there, warmth spread quickly into my bloodstream, as if it were alcohol.

"No need to wait 'til tomorrow," I said, licking the spoon after I'd finished the sauce, "I'll thank you today. What's it called?"

"Chanming Sauce. It's her late husband's recipe, and she named it after him. Chanming was his name."

"Charming," I replied, feeling warmth traveling through my veins and taking the pain away. "I'll remember it as charming sauce."

"Hot and sour soup is next," he replied, and a glimpse of concern appeared in his eyes. "How are you holding up?"

He reached forward and touched my hand. I didn't pull back; I welcomed his touch. But then my mind started wandering, worrying. Maybe it was best to talk to him about the Internal Affairs investigation now, when I had the time to tell him what was going on.

I started talking about it at least twice, or at least I wanted to, but he changed the subject every time. Exhausted, I didn't have the energy to fight him, to call on him to focus and hear me out. Tomorrow would be best, after I had a few hours of sleep.

A delicious cup of hot and sour soup and almost half a plate of sizzling beef made me yearn for a warm bed. I could barely keep my eyes open.

"Let's do garbage duty before I pass out," I mumbled, climbing in the passenger seat.

"Uh-huh," he replied, with an uneven grin at odds with his frown.

I couldn't recall leaving the parking lot. When I woke up, the dashboard display said 3:37AM, and we were parked on a small street, a posh cul-de-sac.

"Where... are we?" I asked, licking my dry lips and swallowing with difficulty.

"Ah, good morning," he quipped. "See that house over there, with the brown garage doors?"

"Uh-huh."

"The property, as well as the trash can in front of it belong to Judge Hayden. The only issue I'm having with what we're about to do is that we'll stink up the car."

I waved away his concern with a gesture of my hand. "It's November, and it's freezing. I don't think it's that ripe. Let's go steal us some garbage," I replied, feeling more excited than I'd anticipated.

I'd never had anyone take part in my after-hours activities before, and this wasn't really one of them. What we were doing wasn't illegal; it was going to be mentioned in the official case report. But it felt as if it were one of my illicit incursions, and I savored the jolt of adrenaline I felt as I was approaching the judge's house.

The house was completely shrouded in darkness, and we retrieved two large bags without waking anyone up. A dog barked somewhere in the distance, but that was the only sound disturbing the serenity of the elegant neighborhood. That and Holt's engine revving as we drove away from of there.

I texted Anne as soon as the car was in motion, a quick message apologizing for the late hour and asking her if she'd be willing to run a DNA test. Her reply came almost immediately; she was on her way.

"Okay," Holt said, pulling to the curb on the interstate ramp and turning halfway toward me. "No coroner I ever worked with would consider being dragged into the office in the dead of the night to do me a favor and run a test that could technically wait until tomorrow. I think it's about time you told me what's really going on with the two of you."

I groaned. He had to ask about everything, curious as a cat, unwilling to let things go. I weighed my options, considering I still wasn't in a mood for sharing my personal history with him. I could see how his knowledge of certain things in my past could make it awkward between us; I decided to lie. It made sense.

I was about to serve him a well-thought-out piece of fiction, but it didn't feel right. To some extent we were alike, Holt and me. We did whatever we had to do to collar our perps. We had a strong sense of right and wrong and keenly observing minds. Lying to him felt almost like insulting him for no reason other than doing his job, being perceptive, and giving a damn.

"I wish you'd let this one go," I said quietly, not willing to lie after all. "Just know we go way back, that's all. It's a long story I'd rather not tell."

He searched my eyes, and I held his glance until he turned away and drove off. The silence between us didn't make me uncomfortable, only a little sad. I'd met him merely a few days ago, and he was already turning my world upside down. Maybe Jack Holt was a recipe for disaster, my own personal brand, in case I didn't know to keep my distance, and, obviously, I didn't.

We didn't speak another word until we got to Anne's office. It was almost five in the morning, the darkest moment of the night, right before the light of dawn. Being in the coroner's office at that time of night seemed eerie, even to me, and I'd been there before on occasions when my after-hours hobby required Anne's skill and attention. Holt appeared uneasy as well, probably unsure how Anne felt about his presence.

She looked at us from head to toe with clinical thoroughness and frowned.

"You shouldn't be on your feet," she admonished me, in the tone of a concerned parent. "What brings you here?"

"These," Holt replied, showing her the two garbage bags that he'd brought from the car. "Baxter thinks we'll find DNA that matches one of Madeline's assailants from eleven years ago."

"Baxter thinks, huh?" I snapped, instantly angry. "You're doing this just to humor me, is that it?"

"Damn it, Baxter, that's not what I meant! I just—"

"Save it, Holt," I snapped. "Maybe if you were more open-minded, we wouldn't be chasing our tails, talking to the wrong people and wasting time. We're already off this case, in case you forgot."

"Don't you think I know that?"

"You two need to stop," Anne said calmly, glaring at us from behind the lab table where the two bags of trash lay open. "I look at you two, and all I see is a long list of health risk factors. Poor nutrition, sleep deprivation, exhaustion. Need I say more?"

I swallowed my inexplicable bout of anger and lowered my eyes. I couldn't understand, for the life of me, why I was ripping at Holt with such energy, after he'd been nothing if not supportive and collaborative, even caring. Maybe Anne was right, and I was tired beyond being rational. Or maybe there was something else I didn't want to admit, an anger with myself for every time I remembered the night we spent together and wished, against all reason and my own personal resolution, for another one just like it. Bloody hell.

"There," Holt said, pointing at an empty paper cup. "I recognize these. The judge drinks this brand of coffee every day. I've seen it on his bench."

Anne gave him a quick glance before picking up the colorful paper cup with two gloved fingers. Then she made quick work of dusting it for prints. A few moments later, AFIS confirmed with a chime that the prints on that paper cup belonged to Judge Leland Hayden.

Anne swabbed the cup's edge, then cut the tip of the swab and let it sink in a test tube filled with clear liquid. Then she opened the drawer of a complicated-looking piece of equipment and placed the tube in there.

"It will take a while," Anne said. "How urgent is this?"

"Very," Holt replied. "Officially, we're not working the case anymore. The higher-ups have named the suspect."

"I saw that on TV," Anne replied, "and didn't buy it for a minute. I wonder if the governor laid any kind of pressure on our police force to quickly solve the case. It's possible, you know."

She checked the readings on a machine, then pushed some buttons, and the machine started whirring quietly.

45

In the Fishbowl

"Thank you for taking the time to speak with us today," I said to Judge Hayden, conveniently forgetting the slew of invectives he'd poured over us on the way in. He was seated in the fishbowl, one of our interview rooms, at the height of his entitled indignation, with pursed lips and chin thrust forward, throwing glares of pure rage from his bloodshot eyes.

I sat across from him and didn't avert my sight. I let him glare at me all he wanted, and took it all in, even smiled at times. The angrier he got, the more likely he was to make a mistake. I threw Holt a quick look and saw he was ready to proceed. He and Hayden had known each other for many years; it must've been difficult for Holt to be there, to interrogate someone he'd worked with all that time. Someone he'd believed was innocent with all his heart, until only yesterday.

I opened the file lying on the table and extracted a printout of the DNA match result.

"Your DNA was found on Madeline Munroe's clothing after she was assaulted by three men, eleven years ago. One of those three men was you. There's testimony speaking to your role during the assault."

"Even if I knew what the hell you're talking about, does the term *statute of limitations* mean anything to you?" Hayden said, his voice loaded with disdain.

"Oh, we're aware of that," I replied, smiling widely. "All we want from you is the identity of the third man, the one who actually raped Madeline, while you were busy immobilizing her. He's wanted for murder, and there's no statute on that."

He stood and took two steps toward the door, but Holt got in his way, standing firmly with his arms crossed at his chest.

"I'm not some poor schmuck you can play with until you get your way, Detective. You either charge me or let me go. I know the law, and I know I haven't committed a chargeable offense. This conversation is over."

"We can get a subpoena and drag you in front of a grand jury," I said. "Because you're familiar with the law, I'm sure you know that the state is entitled to your testimony. We will get the identity of the third man, sooner or later, and we will get it from you."

"I don't know what you're talking about, Detectives."

"How about this, for chargeable offense?" Holt asked, his voice low and menacing. "You've been stonewalling this investigation since day one, and done nothing but keep us from getting the evidence and the testimony we needed to catch the killer, a person who you personally know. You failed to recuse yourself from a case you had a history with, and—"

"This is insane," Hayden snapped. "You're insane. I have no knowledge of what you're talking about."

"And we're going to charge you with obstruction of justice," Holt continued, unabated.

"I'm getting out of here right this moment," Hayden said, speaking with his teeth clenched. "Or I won't say another word until I have a lawyer present."

"You don't have to say anything you don't want to," I added with an angelical smile, "I'll just say a few things. You see, we understand the rape issue has run its course, and we can't pursue charges for it, but there's nothing keeping us from leaking it to the press. They'll just love it."

I paused for a moment, letting my words sink in. As they did, Hayden sat back on his chair, defeated.

"You wouldn't," he said in a whisper. "I'd sue you and everyone who would say a single word about an unproven, unsubstantiated claim. You have nothing."

"I have evidence that proves you were smart enough to only leave epithelials on your rape victim, not semen. I have proof you're a rapist, one who got away with it and managed to be a judge all these years. They'll disbar you so quickly, they'll want to pay for overnight courier express to let you know."

"You can't do this," he said, sounding choked. "I'm entitled to a formal hearing. I have rights—"

"Maybe so," I replied calmly, "but I'm willing to bet that yesterday was the last day of your career as a judge. If you don't cooperate."

"She wins these damn bets every time," Holt added, with a quiet chuckle. "She cleans up, so that you know; I've learned it the hard way. I wouldn't bet against her."

A rap on the one-sided window got our attention. Holt opened the door and looked outside, then beckoned me to follow him out of the room. Really bad timing; I'd just broken Hayden, and he was about to start talking.

I only took three steps on the corridor behind Holt until we ran into a livid DC Wallace.

"What the hell are you two doing? I thought I pulled you off this case," Wallace asked, keeping his voice low, but throwing fiery glances at the both of us.

"We have DNA evidence that puts him at the scene of Madeline's rape, sir," I argued, "proving he at least touched the victim enough to leave epithelials on her clothing. He's the one who can give us the identity of the third man, and a simple DNA match test will prove that third man's the killer. We can subpoena

Hayden and Pelucha and bring them both in front of a grand jury."

"But you already have the identity of the third man, Baxter," Wallace pushed back. "It's Raymond McKinley, isn't it? From Utah? That's what we agreed, and that's what you had me tell the public, only yesterday. You'd better not give me a different story today."

I made an effort not to shake my head in his face. Wallace lied like a son of a bitch, since he was the one who forced the McKinley story on us against our objections, then rushed into the limelight to announce the news that put him in the governor's good graces. But then again, he also told us to drop the investigation and just stick to tracking down McKinley, while Holt and I didn't hesitate for a second before disobeying a firm, direct order. The perfect recipe for a reprimand or even termination. Lovely… but it wasn't like I didn't see it coming. We'd known that the moment we dragged the judge into the interrogation room, Wallace would throw a shit fit. I almost chuckled, thinking how shit fit sounds way better than shite fit. American cusswords have their charm after all.

"What the hell is so funny, Baxter?" Wallace bellowed. "Insubordination?"

"No, sir, I apologize," I replied quickly, lowering my glance and looking as humble as I could manage, while my blood flash-boiled in one of those sudden anger spells of mine. He was being an arse, and that drove me crazy. The lack of logic, the refusal to see the weight of the evidence, and to let that evidence lead to the conclusion of the case was infuriating. All he cared about was some misplaced political interest, so petty and self-centered it made me want to puke.

"How sure are you about Hayden?" Wallace asked, somewhat more subdued.

I raised my eyes, unwilling to believe his change in attitude. I'd said nothing that convincing. I was stunned and slack-jawed.

"Very," Holt replied, in my place. "One hundred percent positive."

"Okay," Wallace said with a long sigh. "I'll babysit this interrogation. I don't need a fuckup from you two, with a judge no less. You've threatened him with obstruction, but you can't prove a thing. He had valid, lawful reasons to deny those warrants; you didn't have probable cause for any of them."

We followed Wallace back into the fishbowl, and Hayden's brow furrowed when he recognized the deputy chief.

"I'm just here to observe," Wallace said. "Please continue."

Bloody hell. The moment was gone, and Hayden had resumed his earlier arrogant demeanor, unwilling to budge. He'd had enough time to think things through and build a strategy, while we were arguing with Wallace outside. But I forged ahead, nevertheless.

"So, are you ready to retire and move to another city, your honor?" I asked serenely, looking at him directly to see the impact of my words. He barely reacted, just a tiny dilation in his pupils, so tiny I would've completely missed it, if it weren't for the contrast with his blue irises.

"I have nothing to say," he replied, seeming unnervingly calm. "I don't know what you're talking about. Maybe it's time to tell me what that so-called evidence is you're talking about."

Oh, crap. If we were to present that evidence in court, we'd probably lose. The epithelials were found on the girl's clothing and could've come from anywhere, including casual, innocent transfer during an activity such as the judge helping Madeline up after she'd fallen by the pool. Even if some skin cells were found on her panties, cross-contamination could explain that away in a millisecond. As for the birthmark, and Hayden's role during her rape, that was based on the testimony given by a girl who'd admitted she'd been drugged with a substance that caused memory loss and altered perceptions. That's what I would've argued for the defense, and his arrogant honor had figured it out for himself.

"You have two options at this point," Holt announced, as if he were talking about Chinese food items from a menu. "You can risk a fair amount of backlash from the media and the community, once we leak the evidence we have, and the heartwrenching testimony left by Madeline from beyond her death. You think we can't prove much in court, and maybe you're right. But the public opinion court we can control. That's your option number one, where you refuse to share the name of the third man and face whatever we decide to throw at you: subpoenas, grand jury, movie rights for Maddie's story. You'd be finished, and the truly innocent victims of your decision to not cooperate would be your family. Your wife and children, having to learn and live with the reality that their husband and father is a rapist."

He paused for effect, while Hayden lowered his head into his hands.

"Then," Holt continued, "there's option number two. You give us the name of the third man, and the secret of your transgressions stays buried here, between these walls. You'll be allowed to retire gracefully and continue your career in private practice for as long as you like. I hope you do understand that we can't let you be a judge anymore."

Hayden looked at Holt, then at Wallace, and finally at me.

"Choose carefully," I added, "and make it quick. This offer won't be on the table for too long."

He shook his head. "I'm sorry, I can't."

"You can't? Or you won't?" Holt pushed.

"I can't," he repeated, sounding desperate.

"Whatever you're afraid of, we can protect you," I offered. "You know that. We can work with the DA and get a full immunity deal on the table. If you're afraid of the third man's retaliation, we can put you in witness protection until the trial is over. He won't know a thing until his murder trial."

He scoffed quietly. "You have no fucking clue what you're talking about. It's time you get me that lawyer now. This conversation is over."

46

Hooky

I followed DC Wallace out of the interview room, biting my lip so I wouldn't start cursing out loud in a perfect mix of American and British profanity, including some original phrases I could've come up with effortlessly, after being forced to let Judge Hayden walk.

"Let it go, Baxter," Wallace said. "I'm not really that convinced he took part in the rape eleven years ago. All you have is circumstance and an unreliable piece of testimony."

"But, sir—"

"You had your shot, and he didn't talk. Don't leak a word to the press, or do anything stupid. Are we clear on that?"

"Yes, sir," I replied, not taking my eyes off the small-print pattern woven in the carpet.

"I have the assistant sheriff's approval to mark the case as 'looking for main suspect,'" he added. "Any objections?"

I couldn't bring myself to respond, but Holt nudged me discreetly and answered for both of us. "No, sir, we're good."

"What about a grand jury?" I insisted. "I still believe we should subpoena both Hayden and Pelucha for their testimonies and hold them in contempt if they don't talk. We shouldn't give this up, sir, with all due respect. We're letting a killer walk free."

Wallace turned to look at me. He seemed dispassionate, not exasperated as I expected.

"I like persistence in a cop, Baxter. But what, if anything, do you really have to support your request for a subpoena? That girl was roofied. She thought it was her boss's son, but how certain are you it was Pelucha? You don't have enough hard evidence to support a subpoena. They'll deny ever taking part in that rape."

"If you give us one more day—"

"No, Baxter, you've had your chance, and you've done good work, both of you. Now everyone in this country is looking for Raymond McKinley, and we'll find him. Until then, I'm assigning you both to assist Nieblas and Crocker with another homicide investigation."

I felt Holt tug at my sleeve and that shut me up, just as I was getting ready to plead with Wallace some more. It was one thing to pester my boss at the risk of my own career, it was another to drag down Holt with me.

"Understood," Holt replied. "Who's the vic?"

"A homeless woman they found earlier today under the interstate overpass at Cheyenne. There's a lot of ground to cover, so get going already," he replied, throwing the last words over his shoulder as he walked away from us.

By the time we wrapped up the paperwork and left the building, heading out to the new crime scene, DC Wallace had gathered a bunch of reporters in the building lobby and was making a statement.

"The search for the suspect will not cease," he was affirming, as we hurried by, "until he is found and held accountable for the heinous crime he has committed."

Nauseated and frustrated out of my mind, I didn't say a word, and neither did Holt, for most of the ride to the new crime scene. I noticed the tension line in his jaw, the way his muscles danced in knots under his skin, the way he drove with unnecessarily abrupt, rugged moves.

"What's on your mind?" I asked.

He didn't reply immediately, as if he needed a moment to figure it out.

"We've been tricked," he eventually replied, "but I can't figure out how."

"I take it you're not buying the Raymond McKinley story?" I asked with a light chuckle.

"Hell, no," he said. "What I believe is that both Hayden and Pelucha are covering for someone." He glanced at me quickly, then turned his attention to the road ahead. "Someone they're afraid of, someone powerful enough to make their issues go away."

"You mean, like someone who could easily associate a ten-card to a different identity in AFIS? That kind of someone?"

"Yeah, exactly," he replied, sounding grim. "Someone powerful enough to make sure that this particular judge, Hayden, got all the related case warrant and subpoena requests. One hell of a coincidence, don't you think, when there are thirty-two criminal court judges in Clark County?"

I stared at him in disbelief. I hadn't thought of that. Landing a certain judge for a case was the luck of the draw, subject to how their schedules rotate though court dates and other duties. I'd just taken it for granted, that Hayden was "our judge" for the Munroe case.

"Yeah, I looked it up," Holt continued, "that many. So how the hell did it happen, unless he got the case routed to him somehow?"

"I, um, don't really know how cases are assigned to judges," I replied, bitter with myself for having missed an important clue. "This is our next lead."

"What about the governor?" Holt asked. "He'd have the power to do all that. Access, relations, money. It fits."

"Pfft," I reacted, "he's too old."

"To kill someone?" Holt asked, his eyebrows raised high and crinkling his forehead in a display of skepticism.

"Tell me, if you are twenty-something-years-old, and you're going to rape a teenager with someone, would you do it with a fifty-two-year-old man?"

"What? Jeez, Baxter... ew," he reacted. "Thanks for putting that visual in my mind."

"He's sixty-three now, he was fifty-two at the time of the rape. A well-known public official, having been governor for a few years already."

"Yeah, you're right," Holt replied, "and Maddie would've recognized him. She was thrilled her sister was marrying him. If he'd been the rapist, she wouldn't've been that happy about it; she would've remembered him."

"Right... Then who? Who would a man like Hayden go drinking and drugging and raping a young girl with?"

"A good buddy, a longtime friend, someone he trusted implicitly," Holt replied. "That's not something you do with a guy you just met."

Holt pulled near the police line surrounding the new crime scene and cut the engine.

"Then there has to be a trail," I muttered, "someone out there must remember this third man."

I went over some options in my mind, and none worked. I could go ask everyone who'd been around Pelucha eleven years ago, but risked fueling the harassment lawsuit his attorneys were probably busy filing at that very moment. I could ask his ex-wife, but something told me she valued the unhindered stream of cash coming from her former husband more than she cared about helping us find a killer. I could poke around the judge's friends and coworkers, and risk alienating relations between the criminal district and LVMPD to a degree for which not even firing me would quench DC Wallace's rage.

Thankfully, I had other ways I could get what I needed. I had an idea, not a brilliant one, only something that could work. Maybe.

"What are you saying?" Holt asked, frowning, holding the door for me.

"I'm saying, can you please cover for me? I need a few hours," I said, smiling innocently. I was about to break a personal rule, because this was, technically, during business hours, and I was about to engage in some extracurricular activities, but I didn't care. Maddie's killer was still out there, and I was willing to bet my life his name wasn't Raymond McKinley. I also couldn't risk being caught working the case again, unless I walked in the precinct with the killer in handcuffs. Otherwise, Wallace wouldn't think twice before firing me on the spot. It was funny how all the lawful options available to me led to only one possible outcome, my termination with prejudice for any number of police code violations, mainly insubordination.

"Sure, where should I drop you off?" he offered, like the perfect gentleman he was.

"No worries, I'll take a cab," I replied, and he accepted unexpectedly quickly, so quickly it made me a little anxious.

I had no way of knowing that, as soon as my cab turned the corner and took the on-ramp to I-15 south heading to my place, Holt asked Nieblas to cover for him and peeled off in a hurry to catch up with Las Vegas Yellow Cab #2532.

47

Disguise

I believe I've said it before; I'm a much better thief than I am a hacker. My skills are limited to mostly figuring out the thought processes in people's minds when they set their passwords, and even that skill is about to become irrelevant, as more and more people use password management tools that offer highly complex, unique passwords for every access point login. However, password managers don't yet manage the initial computer login password, the one we all customize and rarely ever change, at least not for our personal devices. That's where the pet's name, the wife's birthday, or our favorite sport comes into play. That's where I excel. One look at who you are, at what you post online, at what you like the world to know about you, and I have a decent chance to crack that initial login password. Once I'm logged into your device, your own password management tool will work for me just as well as it does for you.

I have some other technical skills I picked up along the way, but they're not top notch either, I'm afraid. For example, to gain remote, unrestricted access to all of his honor's personal files, I actually had to physically break inside his house and plant a Trojan, a piece of malware on his laptop to make it happen. And that sucked. It was broad daylight; I had no idea if the judge went home after the questioning, or if he decided to resume his normal schedule. I had no clue whether his wife or kids decided to stay home for the day, being that it was the Friday before Thanksgiving week, or if his housekeeper had chosen that day to vacuum all their carpets. I just hoped the house was empty, and his honor back to work, eager to dismiss the rumors that he'd been busted for something or other. I was sure that whoever was helping him had already made it all go away.

I spent a little time rapping my fingers against the kitchen counter, thinking what persona had the most chances to get away with what I had to do, or to survive if caught in the act. I opted for athletic gear, although impersonating a youthful, energetic jogger was a stretch from what I was physically able to do. I wasn't even able to walk without a limp yet; running, even for a short distance, could prove a serious challenge.

I put on black, compressive tights, cropped a few inches above the ankle.

The fabric was going to keep my muscles warm in the brisk November chill. A long-sleeved, tight sweater and a down vest completed the attire, all in dark gray colors. Then I let my hair unfurl from my typical bun and tied it up in a loose ponytail, then put on a white baseball cap and shades. The final touch, a pair of tethered earbuds hooked to my iPhone, so that anyone interested could see I was listening to music, oblivious to anything else.

I checked the mirror and smiled. A stranger smiled back at me, unrecognizable, anonymous. I searched the stranger's eyes in the mirror and didn't see any fear, reserve, or shred of a doubt. Only determination, a hint of excitement, the anticipation of the adrenaline high when I'd finally collar that third man, Madeline Munroe's killer.

I was ready.

48

Stakeout

Holt kept his distance from the cab, staying well behind and letting a few cars slide in between. He didn't believe Baxter would turn around and look, but he didn't want to risk it either. The traffic wasn't heavy, and he fell even farther behind when he realized the cab was taking Baxter home. If she was tired or needed a break, why didn't she say so? She had every right to be exhausted, after the past few days and nights.

He pulled over on the street intersecting Baxter's, close enough to the corner to see her, and watched from a distance, as she paid the cabbie, then entered her home. He almost started the engine, but decided to give it a few minutes. He didn't understand what he was hoping to find out, or why he was staking out the partner who'd only the day before had risked her job and her freedom to help him keep his. If anyone deserved to be trusted, that was Baxter. And still, there was something keeping him pinned in his car, his eyes riveted on Baxter's front door, curious, suspicious, unwilling to let it go.

More than forty minutes later, he was about to give up and leave, convinced Baxter must've passed out on the sofa, fast asleep. When she came out of the house, he almost missed her; she was unrecognizable, in both attire and apparent intent.

"You got to be kidding me," he mumbled, watching Baxter's slim figure dressed in fashionable athletics as she closed and locked the front door. "The woman feels like running? They haven't even removed her stitches yet, for Pete's sake."

But she didn't start jogging; instead, she climbed behind the wheel of her white Toyota and drove away, passing so closely by his SUV that he was convinced she'd spotted him, even if he'd let himself slide lower into his seat, barely visible above the wheel.

She drove away after doing a California roll at the stop sign at the end of the street, and Holt waited a few moments before starting his pursuit. Where the hell was she going?

A few minutes later, he thought he had the answer. Baxter drove straight to the Regional Justice Center, where Judge Hayden had his offices. Was she going to challenge the judge again? That sounded like a terrible idea, although now it was starting to make sense why she'd left him behind at the new crime scene; she probably didn't want to bring him down with her.

He stayed at a reasonable distance behind her and trailed her as she entered the parking structure slowly. She bypassed several open parking spots without changing speed. Judging by the way she drove, she was looking for something other than parking. For what?

Baxter's taillights flickered red when she touched her brakes for a moment; he saw her giving an Audi A6 a good, long stare. Then she moved off, taking the exit route and driving faster. There was no need to pull the license plate on that Audi; he'd seen the same car the night before, parked in a driveway next to a trash can he'd taken two bags of garbage from. The car belonged to Judge Hayden, and, apparently, Baxter wasn't there to speak with him. She was there to make sure the judge was at his place of business, for a reason he'd uncover soon enough.

She drove out of the parking structure rolling through yet another stop sign, then went for the nearest interstate ramp, the one at Bonneville. Holt drove two cars behind her the entire way, and frowned when she took the exit leading to Hayden's neighborhood.

"What the hell?" he muttered, slowing down abruptly when she took the off-ramp. No other cars took that exit, and he risked landing right behind her. He waited on the ramp until the lights turned green and she turned the corner. Then he resumed following her from an increasing distance, shaking his head in disbelief and muttering curses under his breath. She parked on the adjacent street, in front of a convenience store, and started a light jog, with visible difficulty, toward the judge's house. What the hell was she doing on Hayden's street, in plain daylight?

Holt waited until she was far enough out of sight before he got out of his car and approached the corner, staying hidden behind a lush, neatly trimmed hedge surrounding the corner property. He almost lost her; he barely caught a glimpse of her bouncing ponytail as she entered the Hayden's backyard like she lived there, without a hint of hesitation.

"No, no, no… jeez, woman, what the hell are you doing?" he grumbled, but took position to watch the traffic and see if Hayden returned home. There were no other cars in the Hayden driveway, but the house had a three-car garage and any number of people could've been home.

He waited impatiently, counting the seconds, watching the traffic, waiting for Baxter to finish whatever she'd gone there to do. Breaking and entering? He would've never pegged Baxter for that, not ever, not even after yesterday's incredible display of audacity, dexterity, and finesse. So much for his cop instinct. Apparently, all his instincts weren't worth a bucket of rain-soaked manure when it came to this woman.

A minivan slowed next to him, signaling right, and the driver, a middle-aged woman, gave him a long stare before turning onto the street. That woman could mean trouble, if she was one of those busybodies who called the cops for the tiniest reason, like a strange man lurking about where he didn't belong. He watched her drive down the cul-de-sac, feeling his heart thumping harder against his chest with every yard she advanced. Then the woman signaled briefly and turned into Hayden's driveway.

"Oh, fuck…" he said, considering his options in a frenzy of erratic thoughts. He could run over there and keep the woman busy under some pretext until Baxter had a chance to walk away unseen. He could call Baxter and give her the heads-up. He could stay put to be the first at the scene when the woman's 911 call would be dispatched, although Homicide rarely took dispatched calls involving breaking and entering.

He started running toward the house, not sure what he'd do once he got there, but he wasn't fast enough. The woman quickly unloaded two kids from the minivan and unlocked the front door. The three of them entered the house, and the door closed behind them. A second later, Baxter exited the backyard in a light jog step, making him stop in his tracks and turn his back to her, as if studying the property across the street.

"Smooth," he said to himself, admiring how composed and sure of herself his partner was. He crouched behind a parked car pretending to tie a shoelace, waiting to be called out by Baxter, but no such thing happened. She probably avoided looking at him, so she wouldn't be recognized if cops were called to the scene and recorded witness statements. Still, one of these days he should give her a talking to regarding her apparent inability to perceive her surroundings. Considering what she'd just done, she needed to pay more attention if she wanted to stay out of prison.

From his crouched position, he watched her run lightly, calmly, with an almost permanent wince of pain written on her face. He grinned, realizing she was good at breaking and entering, so good she must've done it before. His grin instantly disappeared when he asked himself whether he cared that she was breaking the law, and realized he didn't, not really, not with what was at stake. If she'd broken into the judge's house, she must've had a solid reason, and she'd soon share that with him. He knew Baxter was out to get Maddie's killer, but what kind of cop did that make him, watching a felony being perpetrated and standing down, unwilling to uphold the law? For how many people would he do that?

Not for many. Until last week, not for anyone.

"Damn it, Baxter," he whispered, "you drive me fucking crazy."

She approached the street corner and didn't stop; she made her way to the car and drove off, leaving Holt running quickly to catch up before she disappeared onto one of the many streets in the posh residential neighborhood.

He drove behind her from a careful distance, wondering what she found in Hayden's house, or if she felt the risk she'd taken had been justified.

"I better act surprised when she tells me," Holt said to himself with a light chuckle, "or else it will be hell to pay."

He followed her all the way back to her house, then waited for another thirty minutes or so, curious to see if she was going anywhere else. Instead of Baxter leaving again, his phone rang. He smiled, reading her name on the car's display.

"Hey," she said, sounding a little out of breath, "why don't you get us some coffee and come pick me up?"

"On my way," he replied, then drove off to run the errand, with only one question in mind.

Should I call her on it?

49

Suspicion

"Whew, that was close," I said to myself for maybe the fifteenth time since I'd left Judge Hayden's property. I managed to make a clean getaway, although I'd done none of the typical homework I do before one of these illicit incursions. Normally, I think things through after I collect some information, such as schedules for the entire family, whether there's a dog on premise, a maid, or video surveillance inside the house. For someone like the judge, neither of those scenarios were inconceivable.

I'd had zero time to do any of that, and I had to shoot from the hip, but what if anyone saw me? What if someone out there was looking for the jogger who'd entered his honor's backyard? I took a deep breath, calming my stretched nerves. Ha! Good luck finding me... an anonymous figure with a ball cap and dark lens sunglasses that covered half my face.

I was sure I left everything just the way I found it at the Hayden's residence. All I did was plug a thumb drive into his laptop and fire it up. The Trojan malware on that thumb drive was auto executable, requiring no keystrokes to start running and installing itself in the background of the laptop's file structure. The rest I was able to do remotely, from the safety and privacy of my own home. And Hayden had made that quite easy for me.

Normal people keep their photos in a file folder named simply, "Photos," or sometimes, "Pics." Hayden was no exception, although I couldn't think of him as normal people. Someone who pins down a teenage girl to be raped by his buddy doesn't deserve the adjective normal. Nevertheless, his photos were all archived in one aptly named folder, by year, making it very easy for me to browse his collection remotely and find what I'd been looking for. And, bollocks, did I find what I was looking for...

Bloody hell... How will Holt take what I'd just discovered? Will he still give me the coincidence spiel? Or will his eyes open, just as mine did, and have the same aha moment I had? Mine was followed by a long and detailed curse, because I never saw that coming.

The doorbell rang, and I limped over to open it. The jogging routine that morning had worsened my pain and the throbbing, dull-yet-burning sensation in my calf was almost permanent. Nothing an icepack and an over-the-counter pain killer wouldn't fix though.

I let Holt in, a bit worried to notice how he scrutinized me, how he checked me out head to toe, as if he knew something I didn't. He looked at me like a cop sizing up a suspect, not like a partner concerned for my health, or a lover wanting for more. I frowned and invited him to take a seat at the dining room table, and he obeyed without a word. He actually hadn't said a single word since he arrived.

I needed one more minute, to run that one photo that changed everything through a piece of software that rummaged the entire internet for places or websites where it could've been found through browsing or research.

"Give me one minute, all right?" I asked, and he nodded, then offered me one of the coffee cups he'd brought, and a warm croissant. I didn't like seeing him so quiet; in the few days I'd known him, that usually spelled out trouble. Holt was silent when he was suspicious, chasing his own theories in his mind without thinking of sharing. I hated that; it made me feel paranoid.

I shrugged off my concern and ran the search for the photo I'd found, but the software returned no matches. That particular photo had never been posted online, never shared on social media, hence there was no way I could justify having gained access to it through any legal means. Nevertheless, I had to show it to Holt; like an idiot, I started by saying the one thing I should've never said, not to a headstrong cop like him.

"Please don't ask me how I got these… Let's just say I dug them up online."

He stared at me for a long moment, then nodded, still silent. *Bollocks… he'll never let this one go.*

I turned the laptop toward him, so he could see the screen, and I walked him through what he was seeing.

"These few photos go back to eleven years ago," I said, displaying them one by one, "and were taken around the time Maddie was assaulted. You see Hayden with Pelucha; we've already established they knew each other, but we didn't have a clear understanding of *how well* they knew each other. Apparently, well enough," I said, displaying another photo showing Pelucha and Hayden playing beer pong, then drinking shots together in what appeared to be some kind of contest, based on how many empty shot glasses were lined up in front of them on a tacky bar counter.

"Okay, I get it, they were tight," Holt finally said something, while a deep furrow started developing on his brow.

"Then look at this," I said, displaying the one photo I needed him to see. It showed three men, waist deep in a hotel pool, leaning against the edge, drinking, laughing. Pelucha was in the middle, facing the camera, while Hayden and a third man were flanking him, turned sideways and engaged in lively chatter. By the shape of the décor, the colors of the wall behind them, and the white cabana in the background, it looked like the Royal Hall hotel pool, maybe taken on the day Maddie was assaulted. They all wore dark sunglasses and held umbrella drinks in their hands. Hayden wore a straw hat just like Maddie had described in her diary.

Holt squinted, leaning closer to the screen. I zoomed in for a closer view. "This is our third man," I announced, the one we've been looking for.

"Who is he?" Holt asked, his frown depend by frustration. "Do you recognize him?"

"Don't tell me you don't," I blurted, but his expression remained one of confusion. "I know it's not that obvious at first because it's a profile photo of him, but okay," I continued, "add eleven years, take away a lot of hair, and add at least twenty-five pounds."

"Oh, fuck me," he reacted, "it's Wallace!"

"Deputy Chief Wallace himself," I replied, and as I said those words, all my excitement disappeared, leaving behind weariness and bitter disgust. A man who was mandated to protect people, to uphold the law, to defend innocent girls like Maddie, was a rapist and a killer. It made me sick.

"It fits," I continued, feeling so drained I could barely speak. "His seniority level grants him access to make record changes in AFIS. He knows police procedure well enough to get away with murder in the middle of a crowded hotel. He worked with Hayden to string us along into chasing that Raymond McKinley, while covering his own tracks."

"I can't believe it," Holt said, rubbing his jaw with tense fingers. "Wallace is a self-serving, ambitious schmuck, but he's not a killer. Not a rapist."

"He chose both of us to work this case, thinking he could scare us into submission. We both have, um, issues on our records. He wasn't in the office that day, the day Maddie was killed; we had to wait for him to arrive, remember that? And he controlled all the interactions we had, under the pretense of playing it safe from a political perspective."

"Yeah, but he approved the subpoena for the family financials—"

"Because it led us away from him," I replied calmly. "Under the right circumstances, if Maddie had met with Emilio Macias, the man sent by her mother to scare her, we would've collared that man for murder."

"Wallace spoke with the family in our place, but got us the information we wanted," Holt insisted, running his hand over his scrunched face.

"He kept us away from the family, away from anyone who could've shared information about Maddie's rape. He *controlled* the information we received."

"I still can't fucking believe it," Holt said, then started pacing the room like a caged animal.

"Think about it, he knew everything we were doing, because he read our reports. When we brought in Hayden for questioning, he was there, controlling the situation. No wonder Hayden froze when Wallace entered the room to 'observe,'" I added, making air quotes with my fingers. "Hayden couldn't spill his name with him in the room."

"Unbelievable," he said quietly, then stopped in front of the window and absentmindedly looked outside.

"One more thing, Holt," I said, feeling a surge of anger lighting my blood on fire. "He knew we were going to Maddie's apartment again to look for evidence, the day I was shot; we told him when we spoke with him on the phone that morning. He had no idea what we'd find at her place and was cornered. He delayed us with TwoCent's arrest, to give himself enough time to send Camacho," I added, then swallowed with difficulty, feeling my throat parched dry. "Wallace ordered us killed, Holt. He might try it again."

"Because we wouldn't give up," Holt said, just as quietly as before. "I just don't understand why, that's all. Why do all this? He had a career ahead of him. Why jeopardize that for... Maddie?"

I thought for a while before answering. The reason was incomprehensible for someone highly rational like Holt or me, but it made sense for Wallace.

"It wasn't about Maddie. She was just... there, a beautiful Las Vegas girl at the wrong place and the wrong time," I replied, feeling a wave of sadness for the poor girl who'd done nothing to deserve what happened to her. "Wallace sought acceptance and approval, access to the ranks of those of power and wealth; he still does. That's the Wallace we all know so well. Pelucha's net worth is almost a billion dollars, and a judge can make a cop's career skyrocket," I said, and with each word, it made more sense to me. "Maybe Maddie was right in her diary, and this was Wallace's rite of acceptance, of initiation in the closely knit group of three."

"I bet Pelucha was thrilled to have a career cop rape someone in front of witnesses. That was his get out of jail free card, for years to come. What was his rank eleven years ago?" Holt asked.

It took me a while to dig that up. "He was a lieutenant eleven years ago. A year later, he made captain, one of the youngest in the history of LVMPD. And Hayden was an ADA."

He scoffed. "Not bad for Pelucha. They were all young, hungry, career-oriented. This was meant to be a lifelong relationship, a partnership."

"Only Maddie's sister got engaged to the governor, and Wallace freaked out. He was afraid that Maddie would reopen the issue, and that the governor would listen to what she had to say. Wallace had no way of knowing how much Maddie still remembered."

"Uh-huh," he muttered. "But Wallace would've known better than to leave fingerprints at the scene of a murder. I never understood why someone so organized made such a rookie mistake. If he'd worn gloves, this would've been the perfect murder."

"Cops never really stop searching for the killer in such cases. Wallace left prints behind because he knew those prints led to McKinley, and that meant he was off the hook indefinitely."

He groaned and shook his head, then turned toward me and looked at me with a concerned look in his eyes. "You can't show this photo to anyone, can you?"

"No, I can't," I replied, sustaining his gaze without blinking.

"We need solid evidence, and a court-admissible paper trail to lead us to that evidence. But first, I just want to be one hundred percent sure."

I chuckled softly. "You still have doubts?"

"I'd like to have some solid evidence, that's all. I've known Wallace for years, I worked with him... I thought I knew him enough to trust that he's a good cop. An ambitious son of a bitch and a political wannabe? Sure, no doubt. But a killer and a rapist? No way..."

I let him process everything, knowing it was a shock to him as it had been to me, and I had a good thirty minutes to think things through and make sure I wasn't looking at circumstance and coincidence. He was right to want solid evidence before letting himself be persuaded; that's what made my partner a damn good cop.

"Fingerprints usually solve dilemmas like this one," he said after a while, "but if what you're saying is true, he's altered those by replacing Raymond McKinley's ten-card with his. I wonder whose fingerprints the system returns if we search for Wallace by name."

"We'll probably never know," I replied. "If I were in his shoes, I'd use someone as innocent as possible and deceased for a while, like an old lady from rural Kentucky dead fifty years ago, then delete her original record from AFIS altogether."

His crooked grin reappeared. "You're a devious woman, Baxter; I better keep that in mind."

I smiled back, relieved to see the tension in the air was dissipating. "We might never know who altered Wallace's ten-card in the system, but we should at least try to find out. Let me ask a favor from a friend."

His eyebrows shot up, but I smiled reassuringly and dialed a number from my phone's memory.

"Anne? It's me, again. You still have your federal credentials?"

50

Party

Anne met us at the Flamingo Starbucks, after moderately protesting having to leave her office. I hinted privacy was critical for our conversation, and her protests subsided immediately. Then she took her black, grande java with cream from my hands and stared at the photo I'd displayed on my laptop screen for a long while, her hand stuck in midair, holding the coffee cup only an inch away from her lips.

"What the fuck," she whispered, shaking her head as if to send away remnants of a nightmare. "This can't be."

"You mean, it shouldn't be," I replied in a subdued tone of voice. "I agree. It shouldn't."

"We need to find out for certain," Holt said. "We need proof."

"Damn right you do," she blurted, in a rarely seen display of aggravation. Whenever she was disturbed or shaken by something, her vocabulary reverted back to the slang of her military past, without any transition.

"Now you understand," I said, "why I asked you to find out who made changes to Raymond McKinley's ten-card in AFIS, and go from there. Maybe there's a link between that person and Wallace, or maybe it was Wallace himself, leaving a trail in the system. You're our only chance; we can't take this to anyone else."

"I looked at AFIS in detail," Anne said, her eyes still riveted on the photo of the three men in the Royal Hall Hotel pool. "The IP and time codes associated with critical changes in AFIS, such as ten-card uploads, deletions, changes, and new record creations are available only to a system administrator."

"Oh," I reacted, unable to swallow my disappointment.

"Fortunately, I used to date someone who's now in charge of the local bureau's systems," she added, with a hint of a smile. "The IP that made the change was associated with LVMPD, but he can't pinpoint it more precisely than that."

"How about a user name we could trace?"

"Back then, local precincts had only one AFIS administration user name allocated per division to share among senior officers, and many read-only credentials, for all cops to use. The person who altered Raymond McKinley's AFIS record used that divisional login to make the change. My friend was able to confirm the change that was made was a replacement of the existing ten-card with a new one."

I shook my head, defeated.

"It's not nearly enough," I replied. "We have nothing."

"Far from it," Holt intervened. "Now we know it's a cop, one of ours, who we need to trace."

"We also know," Anne continued, "that the ten-card in question was replaced eleven years ago, on August 27, on the same date that Wallace's own record in AFIS was altered."

"Immediately after Maddie's rape," I added. "Now we're sure they're related."

"We're not that sure, as in irrefutable evidence sure," Anne tempered my zeal. "We need DNA, fingerprints. You don't want this mess to blow up in your faces."

"Do you think a judge, other than Hayden, of course, would grant us a warrant for Wallace's DNA?" Holt asked, although he had to know the answer.

I shook my head again, and my frown deepened. "No, I don't believe that can happen. Everyone will walk on eggshells with this. We need a different approach."

I could easily think of several ways to get my gloved hands on Wallace's DNA, but I needed more than that; I needed a clean, above-the-water approach to obtain it without breaking the law, and that was only half of my problem. I'd found out about Wallace by breaking and entering into Hayden's house and hacking into his computer. Those were details I preferred not to mention while taking the stand. But how else could I justify suspecting Wallace? A unique trail left in AFIS would've been so nice. Unfortunately, all we had was a lead that took us to an entire precinct with hundreds of potential suspects. No judge would issue DNA warrants for everyone in the building.

"I have an idea," Anne said, "that you might not really like."

"What does it involve?" Holt asked, seeming genuinely concerned and trying to hide it behind a tentative smile.

"You two will be masters of ceremony at someone's birthday party today."

"Whose?" I asked, while Holt's eyebrows shot up and his grin vanished.

"I don't know yet," Anne replied, while dialing a number on her cell. "But it better be someone's birthday."

Holt and I looked at each other for a moment, both of us equally confused, waiting for Anne to end her call.

"We're in luck," she said, as soon as she hung up her call. "You know little Louise, the tiny blonde in HR? She's turning twenty-six today."

"And?" Holt asked, frowning.

"And you'll get her an awesome cake and soft drinks for the entire building.

Make sure they come in large bottles, not individual cans," Anne replied, then turned toward me. "You'll personally invite the entire building to attend, say, at 3:00 PM, and make sure Wallace attends too."

"Ah, I see," I replied with a wide, excited grin, starting to see where she was going with her unusual strategy. "What if he doesn't fall for it?"

"You're going to say what he needs to hear to believe you've dropped this case. He'll feel relieved and willing to participate, to negate his own conscience."

"Meaning?" Holt asked, still frowning.

"He knows what he's done, and he's afraid others can see it too," I replied. "It's typical human behavior. As soon as he learns he's off the hook, he'll be willing to socialize with us, as if to prove he never meant us any harm. That will work, at least in theory. If he still resists, I'll find a way to up the ante."

He tilted his head a little, as if to convey his amazement, and glanced at me with squinted eyes. He probably wondered if I twisted his brain the same way.

A few hours later, one of the big conference rooms was hosting an impromptu birthday party, and guests were starting to arrive. Louise was overwhelmed to the point of tears and told everyone what a fantastic surprise it was, when no one really had their birthdays celebrated at the office like this.

Through some miracle that would probably remain unexplained, Holt had talked Nieblas and Croker into serving people with drinks. He'd probably told them he suspected a dirty cop, because they religiously wrote people's initials on the red solo cups before filling them with a drink of their choice. A large bin, fitted with a new, heavy duty garbage bag stood by the door, and a sign pasted on the wall above it read, "Please recycle."

I walked by the conference room to make sure everything was in place, and saw that Assistant Sheriff Dunn was already there, chatting with a flushed, almost hysterical Louise. I didn't stop; I continued walking toward Wallace's office and forced a breath of air into my lungs and a smile on my lips before knocking on his doorjamb.

"Come in," he said, without looking up from his paperwork.

"Sir," I replied, and remained standing.

"Something you need, Baxter?"

"A couple of things," I replied, then cleared my throat discreetly. "I wanted to let you know that if you need to review the Munroe case file, it's been archived with the status 'looking for main suspect.'"

He looked at me intently for a brief moment. "Okay, good. What else?"

"It's Louise's birthday, and you're invited," I said, continuing to smile. "I'm here on behalf of the entire team to extend this invitation." He didn't say anything, just continued to look at me with a scrutinizing gaze. "There's cake," I added, hoping he had a sweet tooth.

"Baxter, I'm busy," he replied, sounding unconvinced.

"Everyone is, sir," I replied candidly, looking at him with the full wattage of my charming hazel irises. "Even AS Dunn is there, and I heard that Sheriff McGoldrick was going to come down in a few minutes."

"All right," he said, standing and arranging his necktie. Then he frowned a little and asked, sounding a little irritated, "Who is this Louise, anyway? Why the big hubbub?"

I pressed my lips together for a fraction of a second, feigning hesitation. "I can't be sure, but rumor has it she's related to the vice president, sir."

"The VP of what?" he asked impatiently, walking toward the conference room with large strides, while I could barely keep up.

"Of the United States, sir," I replied in a low voice.

He froze in his tracks. "Are you sure?"

"No, sir, I'm not," I replied, struggling to keep a straight face. "It's just an unconfirmed rumor for now."

"You need to tell me these things ahead of time, Baxter. I didn't get anything for that poor girl's birthday."

"Noted, sir," I replied, unable to stop thinking of where he was going, if I was right about him. Not that many birthday parties in jail for him to worry about attending without the proper gift offering.

When we arrived at the conference room, I was relieved to see Holt had replaced Nieblas at the improvised drinks counter. He nodded a greeting at Wallace, then quickly wrote the letters DCW with a Sharpie on a fresh cup plucked from the stack. Then he filled it with Pepsi, per Wallace's preference, and the deputy chief thanked him before taking a few thirsty gulps.

I breathed, a long sigh of relief. I knew I was right about Wallace; I felt it in my gut, every time I looked into his cold eyes. Soon we'd have proof, backed by the irrefutable evidence of DNA.

51

Las Vegas Girl

About 7:30AM, Holt pulled in at the curb in front of the Wallace residence. I gave the house a look and whistled between my gritted teeth. Whatever career strategy the DC had employed, it had worked nicely for him. He lived on the southern side of the same Spanish Trail Country Club, across the fields from Mrs. Munroe, in a million-dollar house. I could close my eyes and visualize a huge kitchen done in marble and stainless steel, incredible views of green, and sunlight that filled every corner of the mansion through immense windows. Nice standard of living; too bad it belonged to a murderer.

"Are you ready to do this, partner?" Holt asked.

"Bloody hell, yeah," I replied, feeling the excitement coursing through my veins in anticipation of bringing Maddie's killer to justice.

Holt rang the bell, and Wallace opened the door with a menacing frown on his face.

"What do you need?" he asked in a low tone of voice.

"Wanna do the honors?" Holt asked me, with a mischievous grin. I nodded and turned to Wallace.

"Mark Wallace, you're under arrest for the murder of Madeline Munroe. You have the right to remain silent," I said, unable to contain my slightly sarcastic grin. "You have the—"

"Are you fucking crazy, Baxter?" Wallace said, propping his hands on his hips and stepping outside on the porch. "Is this your idea of a joke?" His frown deepened, and he thrust his chin forward in an aggressive stance.

"We traced the change that was made to the Raymond McKinley AFIS record," Holt said. "Yeah, I know we disobeyed a direct order, but it doesn't matter anymore. McKinley's AFIS record was altered by someone at LVMPD."

"And? What's that got to do with me?"

I took two steps forward, until I was in his face. "And then we invited you to a party," I whispered close to his ear, continuing to smile. "You left your DNA and fingerprints on the Pepsi cup. It took the ME half the night, but she thanks you for your contribution."

Without notice, he grabbed me by my throat and slammed me against the wall. "When I'm done with you, Baxter, you'll be begging for a rent-a-cop job to walk the malls. No one in this city will hire you again, you hear me?"

He pulled his gun and shoved the barrel at my temple, then snaked his arm around my throat and pulled me against his chest. I saw Holt aiming his service Glock at Wallace's head, and I managed to nod twice, hoping he'd fire that weapon and rid the world of the bloody wanker already.

"Drop it," Holt said quietly. "Drop it now, and you get to live. You know how this game ends, Wallace."

He didn't budge, but he was panting from the effort, from fear. "I don't care. At least I take one of you with me."

"Suit yourself," Holt said, after looking into my eyes with a reassuring plea. Then he corrected his stance and stretched his arms, in a textbook posture for precision shooting.

I felt the barrel of the gun tremble in Wallace's hand, and the pressure against my temple decreased. He lowered the weapon but still brandished it in the air, unsure of what to do.

"This is all a misunderstanding," he babbled, "and I can overlook your insubordination. When you find McKinley, you'll understand."

"Drop that weapon to the ground," Holt ordered, and Wallace obeyed reluctantly, as if someone had hypnotized him and he was moving against his will.

I kicked the gun toward Holt, then I turned and hit Wallace hard below his belt with a thrust of my knee. "This is for Maddie, motherfucker," I said, watching him gasp and bend over, grabbing his abdomen. Then I punched him in the jaw with all my strength. "And this is for pulling your gun on cops."

He let himself be handcuffed without resisting anymore, keeping his eyes riveted on something behind me, somewhere on the street. Curious, I tightened his cuffs and turned to see what had caught his attention.

Another unmarked SUV had pulled in at the curb next to ours, and Sheriff McGoldrick stood next to it with a steeled expression on his face. His gaze burned through Wallace until the now former DC lowered his head, defeated.

I escorted Wallace to the curb, and Holt took over from me.

"Read this perp his rights again," I said, "we don't want to screw this up."

"Thanks for cleaning up my house, Detectives," McGoldrick said, then climbed in his vehicle and took off before we could say anything.

Yeah, that was one way to put it... We still had work to do though. Next, we were going to pay Mrs. Munroe a visit and acquaint her with the justice system and the inner workings of detention centers. Not for the first time, I asked myself what she'd choose to wear for jail.

After booking her for conspiracy, we had to pay a visit to Judge Hayden later today, not before discussing it with the ADA and figuring out his charges. Obstruction, for sure. The rest, it's Gully's job, and I knew he'd make us proud.

We had a long day lined up ahead of us, but I wouldn't have it any other way. I sat on the cold, marble steps in front of Wallace's house and breathed in the brisk morning air, savoring it. Across the street, Holt was loading Wallace in the back of a patrol car, and I let my mind wander as I was watching him.

My first thought went to Maddie and the life she'd lived. Not unlike me, she was a Las Vegas girl leading a double existence, hiding in the shadows what she needed to do to stay sane, to feel she was winning at the game called life. No matter how many years Wallace would spend in prison, Maddie's life had been wasted, compromised, and the harm done to her would never be reverted. Nothing I do will bring her back, but her killer will be brought to justice, and that's as good as it can get for a cop.

A flash of anger coursing through my veins reminded me of Dr. Beville and his bloody notebook. Maybe in one of our future sessions he could explain to me why defeat made me so damn angry, and why a solved case felt like a defeat to me. Maybe because Pelucha walked free.

The law held nothing for him, but now he had me to worry about. You see, I couldn't care less about the statute of limitations on Maddie's rape. Pelucha had been the one to instigate and facilitate that assault. If it weren't for him, she'd still be alive today. That was enough to make him my next mission, and there's nothing worse than pissing off a cop. No amount of money and no horde of lawyers will keep him safe from me, when his time comes. From now on, I'll be onto him like fleas on a stray, watching him, waiting for him to make the tiniest mistake, and then I'll reel him in hard and make him pay. It was only a matter of time, but not even that could bring Maddie back.

I'd grown to know Maddie, and to like her as if I'd known her when she was alive, as if she were my friend. A girl in search of her lost identity, of discovering her new self.

Not unlike me.

My name is Laura Baxter, and I'm a homicide detective. That much I know.

I was born and raised in London; I still recall beating the drizzled, foggy streets of my hometown as a young copper. I still remember the day I met a young American pilot whose wallet had been stolen and who, in turn, stole my heart. I'll never forget London, and I'll never forget Andrew.

But the memories of London slowly fade away, obscured by the myriad colorful lights of my new hometown, burned into oblivion by the scorching desert heat. At times, when it's cold outside and drizzle coats the asphalt with a new shine, I feel I could extend my arm and reach my past. But then the bright desert sun shines high the next morning, chasing all my shadows away and leaving behind the bluest sky I've ever seen.

I looked at Holt, and his loaded gaze met mine from across the street. I smiled, then I bit my lower lip in a silent invitation and chuckled when I saw him loosen his tie with an urgent gesture. Then I veered my eyes to the side and lowered them under batting eyelashes, shamelessly flirting. Maybe later, after we finish our rounds and all the perps are locked up, the two of us could grab a nice dinner. And then... we'll see. Who knows where the night might take us.

I'm no longer lost between two worlds. I know who I am, and this fascinating city is my home.

My name is Laura Baxter, and I'm an American who sometimes swears like a Brit.

By day, I'm a Las Vegas cop. By night, all bets are off.

I don't play by the rules.

~~ The End ~~

Read on for an excerpt from

Casino Girl

In Vegas, secrets can kill.

.

~~~~~~~~

Thank You!

A big, heartfelt thank you for choosing to read my book. If you enjoyed it, please take a moment to leave me a four or five-star review; I would be very grateful. It doesn't need to be more than a couple of words, and it makes a huge difference. This is your link: http://bit.ly/LVGReview.

Join my mailing list for latest news, sale events, and new releases. Log on to www.WolfeNovels.com to sign up, or email me at LW@WolfeNovels.com.

Did you enjoy Baxter and Holt? Would you like to see them again in another Las Vegas crime story? Your thoughts and feedback are very valuable to me. Please contact me directly through one of the channels listed below. Email works best: LW@WolfeNovels.com.

Connect with Me

Email: LW@WolfeNovels.com
Twitter: @WolfeNovels
Facebook: https://www.facebook.com/wolfenovels
LinkedIn: https://www.linkedin.com/in/wolfenovels
Web: www.WolfeNovels.com

Books by Leslie Wolfe

BAXTER & HOLT SERIES

Las Vegas Girl
Casino Girl
Las Vegas Crime

TESS WINNETT SERIES

Dawn Girl
The Watson Girl
Glimpse of Death
Taker of Lives

SELF-STANDING NOVELS

Stories Untold

ALEX HOFFMANN SERIES

Executive
Devil's Move
The Backup Asset
The Ghost Pattern
Operation Sunset

For the complete list of Leslie Wolfe's novels, visit:
Wolfenovels.com/order

Preview: *Casino Girl*

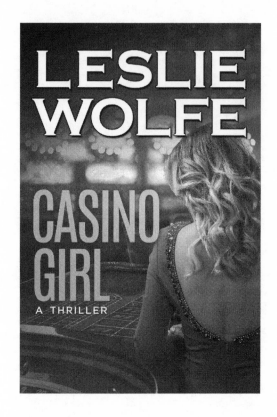

1

ODDS

They're called quasi-strippers.

They don't really bare it all, like real strippers do behind the darkened glass doors of specialty adult clubs, but they aren't exactly fully dressed either while they perform.

Crystal preferred the term exotic dancer. Five nights a week she took the small stage at the center of the high-limit blackjack tables, in the glamorous Scala Casino. Five nights a week she danced and smiled and undulated her perfect body to the rhythm of sultry songs, carefully chosen to lure the gamblers' attention away from the cards and the ever-diminishing stacks of their chips. In the background, nothing is more Vegas than the Scala Casino floor, filled with a million noises, dazzling lights, and excess adrenaline. Nothing is more alive.

That's where she belonged, among the glitter and the gold, the glitzy and the rich.

She wore strappy lingerie with black and gold lace accents on beige silk, designed to trick the mind's eye into believing she was naked. Black, knee-high stiletto boots completed her attire, her black, garter-belt straps attached to them, sexy and kinky and fun. The appreciative looks she basked in that night told her she'd chosen her ensemble well. It was going to be a profitable evening.

The familiar music seemed a bit too loud, making her wince, a little dizzy. She grabbed the pole tighter, aware she was dancing out of rhythm, but knowing the customers were too far gone to notice. It was almost four in the morning, and by that time, most of them were pleasantly inebriated, high on their own excitement and maybe more, living the Vegas dream.

The only danger was that asshole, Farley, a fat, lewd pig who liked to scream at the girls, giving them a hard time for everything they did, right or wrong regardless. Two minutes of being late or changing clothes mid-shift and she'd get pulled inside the pit manager's office for another scolding session.

But she held her head up during those moments, aware they were going to pass and even more aware they were meant to intimidate her into offering sexual favors in return for a privileged work atmosphere.

Oh, hell, no.

Not ever. Not even if the prick turned blue in the face from too much screaming, or his waiting-to-happen stroke knocked him dead right before her eyes.

But even Stan Farley was looking away that moment, focused on a newly arrived high roller who'd taken a seat at one of the blackjack tables with a view of the stage. She didn't know that one, but judging by the way Farley fawned over him, he must've been someone important.

Someone rich.

Someone who didn't care that the odds at his blackjack table were stacked higher against him, just because the table came with a view of full inviting cleavage and tight little buns.

Hers.

She felt beads of sweat bursting at the roots of her hair and forced some stale air into her lungs. Maybe the air conditioning was off, or something. The cigar smoke made it almost unbreathable, but it was an acceptable tradeoff for being allowed to work the high roller pit, not some fifty-cents-minimum roulette floor, where the tips were always Washingtons, never a Franklin and rarely a Lincoln, and not a whole lot of them to count at the end of a shift anyway.

No, she'd been lucky, and her luck had started to play in her favor about a month after she'd been hired. For that she probably had Devine to thank.

Her sweaty palms made it difficult for her to get a good grip on the shiny, chrome pole, but she managed a back hook spin and landed facing Devine. Her best friend danced some 30 feet away, on a small, elevated stage set among four, high-limit, roulette tables.

She waited until she could make eye contact with Devine and waved discreetly at her best friend. Just seeing her smile back made her feel less lonely, less vulnerable. Maybe she was going to be okay. Maybe things would work out after all.

Without realizing, she put her palm on her belly in a soft, caressing gesture, aimed to comfort the tiny sparkle of life growing inside her. She wasn't showing a baby bump yet, but soon that would change, and with it, her entire life as she knew it.

She skipped out of rhythm again, but soon snapped out of her trance, motivated by Farley's mean glare. She focused on her customers for a while and, within a few minutes of smiling provocatively and wiggling her rear, a crisp fifty-dollar bill landed under the thin strap of her thong, delivered by long, hairy fingers that reached lower and lingered longer than was necessary.

Sometimes she was happy the payout was 6:5 instead of 3:2 on a blackjack at the tables facing her; those jerks deserved to pay.

But she smiled at the man who'd delivered the tip and mocked a reverence without letting go of the pole. Then she let herself fall into a back bend and frowned when she saw Farley was approaching.

"What the hell is wrong with you, huh?" he snapped, after grabbing her arm and pulling her close. The music was loud, and no one could hear his words; not that anyone would care if they did. "Could you be bothered to do your job tonight? A deaf penguin has more rhythm than you."

"I'm working it, Stan, what the hell? I haven't taken a break in two hours."

"The hell you are, bitch. You see those bozos? If they're looking at their cards instead of your ass, you ain't earning your keep."

He let go of her arm and disappeared before she could say anything. He was a two-faced creep; with her and the other girls he showed his real charm. For all the patrons and the rest of the Scala staff, he was a perfect gentleman, always dressed in an impeccable suit and starched, white shirts, pleasantly smiling and accommodating.

She knew better than to let him get under her skin.

But her head was spinning, and she held on tight to the pole, not as part of her routine, but for much-needed balance. The music changed, and she welcomed the new beat, one of her favorites. She knew the playlist by heart; the casino had a limited supply of premixed tracks, but the customers didn't seem to care.

Cheers erupted at the table in front of her, and one of the players lifted his arms in the air, beaming. The croupier pushed an impressive pile of chips in front of the man, and she quickly flashed her megawatt smile and made lingering eye contact. He didn't disappoint; he picked one of the chips and sent it flying her way. She caught it gracefully, then placed it on the floor, next to the pole. Her barely-there panties weren't made to hold casino chips.

When she looked up, she startled.

It was him. It was Paul, and he was furious, by the angle of his eyebrows, by the deep ridges flanking his mouth.

He stood right there, next to her stage, glaring at her with a loaded gaze filled with such hatred that her breath caught. He beckoned her to come closer without making a single gesture. She approached him hesitantly and crouched to bring their eyes on the same level, aware not even Farley would dare say a word. She shot a quick glance toward Devine's stage, but she was gone, nowhere in sight.

His eyes drilled into hers, close enough she could see his dilated pupils. Without a word, he shoved a purple and white chip deep inside her bra, then grabbed the thin strap, pulling her closer to him. He said something, keeping his voice low and menacing. She couldn't make out his words but didn't dare to ask. She wanted to explain herself, wanted him to understand her motives, but she couldn't find her words.

She didn't want his money, and she didn't deserve his anger.

When he finally let go of her strap and pushed her away, she almost fell. Her knees were shaking, and she felt the urge to sit for a moment, to catch her breath. She grabbed the pole tightly and did a clumsy back slide against the shiny surface, landing hard on her butt, then folded her legs to the side. She let her head hang low, and her long, wavy hair covered her face, hiding the fear in her eyes until it subsided a little.

Then she wrapped her hands around the pole again, planning to stand and do a pirouette, but her arms and legs felt numb, listless. She tried to breathe, but air refused to enter her lungs. Frantic, she looked around, searching for someone, anyone, who could help. Only one man was looking at her, but her desperate and silent plea was misunderstood.

The man licked his lips, arranged his crotch with a quick gesture, then looked away at another dancer.

She gasped for air a couple of times, then the bright lights of the casino seemed to dim, inviting darkness to engulf her view of the lively floor. Silence came, heavy, palpable. Against it, not even her own heart beats could be heard.

Defeated, she let go. Her body landed on the stage floor with a loud thump that no one heard. Unnoticed, a white and purple casino chip fell out of her top and rolled onto the floor, stopping under a table.

For a long moment, Farley thought the immobile pose was part of Crystal's routine, some new dance move that she was trying. Customers really enjoyed seeing girls crawling on the stage; it made the viewers feel powerful, superior, in control. By the time Farley realized he'd been wrong, she was already gone. His chubby fingers felt for a pulse and found nothing.

Now he'd have to call the cops and close the pit. His worst nightmare.

~~~End Preview~~~

Like *Casino Girl?*

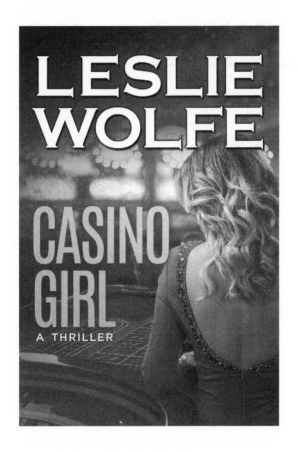

Read it now!

About the Author

Leslie Wolfe is a bestselling author whose novels break the mold of traditional thrillers. She creates unforgettable, brilliant, strong women heroes who deliver fast-paced, satisfying suspense, backed up by extensive background research in technology and psychology.

Leslie released the first novel, *Executive*, in October 2011. It was very well received, including inquiries from Hollywood. Since then, Leslie published numerous novels and enjoyed growing success and recognition in the marketplace. Among Leslie's most notable works, *The Watson Girl* (2017) was recognized for offering a unique insight into the mind of a serial killer and a rarely seen first person account of his actions, in a dramatic and intense procedural thriller.

A complete list of Leslie's titles is available at https://wolfenovels.com/order.

Leslie enjoys engaging with readers every day and would love to hear from you.

Become an insider: gain early access to previews of Leslie's new novels.

- **Email: LW@WolfeNovels.com**
- Follow Leslie on Twitter: @WolfeNovels
- Like Leslie's Facebook page: https://www.facebook.com/wolfenovels
- Connect on LinkedIn: https://www.linkedin.com/in/wolfenovels
- Visit Leslie's website for the latest news: www.WolfeNovels.com

Contents

88787791R00129

Made in the USA
San Bernardino, CA
15 September 2018